A Page
Out of Life

**Center Point
Large Print**

**This Large Print Book carries the
Seal of Approval of N.A.V.H.**

A Page Out of Life

✂

Kathleen Reid

CENTER POINT PUBLISHING
THORNDIKE, MAINE

This Center Point Large Print edition
is published in the year 2008 by
arrangement with The Berkley Publishing Group,
a member of Penguin Group (USA).

Copyright © 2008 by Kathleen Reid.

All rights reserved.

The text of this Large Print edition is unabridged. In other
aspects, this book may vary from the original edition.
Printed in the United States of America.
Set in 16-point Times New Roman type.

ISBN: 978-1-60285-290-7

Library of Congress Cataloging-in-Publication Data

Reid, Kathleen.
  A page out of life / Kathleen Reid.
    p. cm.
  ISBN 978-1-60285-290-7 (library binding : alk. paper)
  1. Scrapbooks—Fiction. 2. Female friendship—Fiction. 3. Large type books. I. Title.
  PS3618.E536P34 2008b
  813'.6--dc22
  2008020684

A Page Out of Life

CHAPTER 1

Ashley

"Darling, I'll just get right to the point. You've got to pull yourself together. That T-shirt you're wearing has stains all over it. Those sweatpants look like something from the Salvation Army. And your hair, it's completely unkempt. I don't know how you walk around like that."

Ashley gaped at her mother in dismay, unable to respond. She glanced down and immediately noticed a glob of applesauce—left over from her youngest daughter Sally's breakfast—stuck to her shirt, but she refused to budge.

Her mother, Marrie, was as fashionably dressed as always, even on a visit to the grandchildren. Her impeccably groomed frame was adorned with low-rise black jeans, a peasant blouse that made her look curvier than a sixty-something woman had a right to, and chic bronze four-inch heels that belonged on the feet of a twenty-year-old. *It isn't fair,* Ashley thought for the millionth time, *to have a former model for a mother.* Even worse to have one who actually still had a career. Marrie crossed a slim leg and continued on. "I'm just trying to be helpful, dear. What does Steve say about all of this?"

"He doesn't say anything about it, Mother," Ashley

said tersely. "And as for being helpful, give me a break! You don't have a helpful bone in your body."

"Really, dear, that's completely untrue! All I'm saying is that you're an absolutely beautiful young mother, but . . ."

"I'm fat, right? Is that what you're trying to say?" said Ashley, feeling the heat rise in her cheeks.

Marrie opened her mouth to speak, but suddenly closed her full red lips. "It's more like you don't care about yourself," she implored.

"You're just embarrassed about the way I look. All you've ever cared about is your public image. Spare me the 'I'm in touch with my daughter's feelings' routine. Do you have any idea how hard it is to raise four children, Mother? Unlike you, I take care of my kids. I do *everything* for them. I don't have time for myself." Ashley's voice rose, loud enough to set Sally crying.

"Then make time," Marrie insisted, maintaining her composure. "I'll even help hire you a nanny . . . and maybe a housecleaner?"

"Listen, I'm a good mother!" Ashley said, picking up her daughter to dry Sally's tears. "Do you hear me? My children are the most important thing in the world to me. Not how I look or how my house looks! I know you find it impossible to understand, but I want my kids to just have a normal family life."

"You're missing the point completely," Marrie insisted. "And I refuse to continue this conversation while you're acting irrational. I'm going upstairs to pack."

"You do that," Ashley snapped. "Your plane back to New York leaves in two hours. I'll put Sally in the car and we'll head out in fifteen minutes."

Ashley was so angry that she had trouble clearing the dirty dishes off the table. After loading the dishwasher and changing Sally's diaper, she sat for a moment trying hard to regain her self-possession and dismiss her mother's digs about her messy home and appearance. A few minutes later, Ashley felt guilty watching her mother lug two gigantic suitcases full of designer clothes and shoes down the stairs, all the while maintaining her balance in those bronze heels. It was a feat a professional tightrope walker would have envied. When Marrie arrived at the bottom on the stairs, Ashley took over and carried the bags herself the rest of the way to the SUV. Yet on the way to the airport she also made sure to play some Barney tunes—not just to entertain her daughter, but knowing it would drive Marrie crazy.

They didn't speak until Ashley pulled up to the sidewalk check-in.

"Oh, I almost forgot to tell you," her mother said cheerfully, clearly deciding to ignore their earlier argument. "I'm off to Paris for an ad campaign. I may meet up with your father while I'm there. It's for that Vie perfume that you love. I'll send you some."

"How lovely," Ashley muttered. "I can't wait." She watched as a porter eyed Marrie's world-famous figure exiting the car and immediately brought over a cart to retrieve her bags.

"One more thing," said Marrie, leaning back to face her. "There's this great shampoo called Amour on Rue St. Honoré. It'll work wonders on those split ends of yours, too. I'll include that in the package. *Au revoir!*" she said happily, as she shut the door.

Ashley dutifully waved good-bye and drove off, once again fuming inside. Just like her mother to think that beauty products were the key to solving any and all problems.

The phone was ringing as Ashley returned home, and she raced to answer it. It was her husband, Steve, wanting to know if she could get a babysitter for a client dinner the following week.

"Seven o'clock sounds good. I think I can get one of the other kids on the street," replied Ashley, fumbling through a pile to find her desk calendar. "Though Tucker never gets his work done when that cute sitter comes over."

"He's got good taste. Hey, why don't you go out and get yourself something nice to wear?" he suggested.

"What's that supposed to mean?" Ashley said. "I don't have nice clothes?"

"I thought you'd enjoy it, that's all. You used to love to go shopping."

I hate looking at my backside in the three-way

mirror, she thought as she adjusted Sally's sleeping form to make her more comfortable. "Sure, thanks," she replied hurriedly. "I'll figure something out. I've gotta run and get Sally. I can hear her crying," she lied. Hanging up the phone, Ashley again felt especially frumpy in her drawstring sweatpants, oversized shirt, and sneakers.

Passing by the living room on her way upstairs, she wondered what people thought when they observed the dowdy room. There were various pieces of furniture that didn't go together: from her grandmother, she had inherited a camelback sofa that needed a fabric update, two brown side tables, and several lamps, none of which really matched. Plastic bins of children's toys lined the fireplace. A few blocks and a rag doll littered the floor. The worn blue silk curtains had been left by the previous owners; the kids played hide-and-seek behind them.

A large cardboard box filled with fabric samples had been sitting in one corner of the room for months. The box was flanked by back issues of *House Beautiful*; her mother's annual Christmas present was a subscription renewal, a not-so-subtle reminder that she considered Ashley's decorating uninspired. Of course, Marrie wanted Ashley's home to look picture perfect, as if no one actually lived there. Each month, when the magazine arrived, Ashley would promise herself that she'd improve things when she had time.

Suddenly, Ashley felt embarrassed by her inability to transform herself or her house into something special. There was a time when she'd considered herself incredibly organized and chic, but her pres-ent surroundings seemed as scattered as she now felt. *You've got to pull yourself together,* she thought miserably as her mother's words echoed inside her mind.

Ashley put Sally down in her crib for a morning nap, then headed to her bedroom. The idea of a sexy black dress dominated her thoughts. She imagined three faceless white dummies wearing various black dresses, calling to her like sirens from the storefront windows of Saks Fifth Avenue. But Saks might as well have been located on another planet. The possibility of getting there from Belloix, Alabama, was remote. After all, not too many babysitters, including her own mother, could take on four kids for more than a couple of hours. At thirteen, Tucker was too young to handle all of his younger siblings. Perhaps he could have watched seven-year-old Janie and three-year-old Sally, but there wasn't a chance that his ten-year-old brother Cameron was going to listen to him.

She'd bought a dress in Paris years ago, and she knew she'd saved it somewhere. Trying to recall its location, she realized that her drawers were largely filled with what she called her suburban housewife attire. She headed to her closet, where her party clothes were put away at the far end. After several minutes of digging, she found the dress way in the back. Ashley ran her hands over the expensive fabric; she hadn't bought anything like it in fifteen years. It was sleek, with narrow straps and a tight-fitting bodice, beautifully made for a size four frame.

Ashley looked at herself in the full-length mirror, focusing on her sandy brown hair, high cheek-bones, and long neck. At least her neck and shoulders still looked okay, she thought. She stared at the body that had given birth to four children. It seemed strange to run her hands over so much flesh. She wanted to shout that this woman in the mirror was an impostor. There must be some mistake.

"Oh, Ashley," she said to her reflection. "What happened?" Feeling self-pity start to consume her, she took a deep breath, trying to be positive about herself and the life she had made. It was hard always feeling inadequate compared to her completely glamorous mother. Ashley couldn't help herself; she was a woman with an ego. Her rational mind told her that this vanity-induced depression was absurd in the scheme of things in life. After all, every woman had moments of self-doubt about her appearance; it was a universal phenomenon that was embedded in the XX chromosome at conception.

She decided to phone a friend.

"Megan," said Ashley. "Do you have a minute?"

"Sure," Megan said. "What's up? Everything okay?"

"Not really. I'm having a fashion crisis," said Ashley. "Steve wants me to go to some client dinner next week. You know how long it's been since I've eaten at a fancy restaurant? Anyway, I just pulled out a pre-kids black dress and I can't even get one of my thighs in it!"

"What were you thinking? You're not single, semistarving, and twentysomething anymore. Your life has changed. Don't worry about it. That dress is probably out of date anyway."

"It's so beautiful," gushed Ashley. "It would be nice to feel sexy again."

"You don't want too much sex appeal, honey. Four kids is enough. I'd say you should tie a paper sack around your body!"

Ashley laughed, relaxing a little. "You've got a point. Will you go shopping with me tomorrow? There's got to be some middle ground." She fiddled with the string of her sweatpants. "For one night, I'd like to feel like something other than a large napkin."

"I understand, Cinderella. I can squeeze in an hour tomorrow morning around ten. Would that help?"

"That's perfect. Thanks for your support. I'll see you tomorrow."

Ashley sat morosely on the edge of the bed, wondering how she could drop twenty pounds in a week. Several drastic diets entered her thoughts as she envisioned living on chicken broth and lettuce for the next seven days.

Just as she was about to erupt into an inner tirade, she caught sight of a picture of herself and Steve taken at a friend's apartment in New York; they were probably headed out to some fabulous dinner, on a weeknight, no less. They used to have so much fun, she remembered, studying the photo of her dark-haired husband. The dimple on his right cheek made him look mischievous. She studied their expensive, stain-free clothing, admiring his brown suede jacket and stone-colored pants. Gazing wistfully at his handsome face with its high forehead, straight nose, and full lips, she remembered what he'd been like then.

Ashley looked at her own outfit in the snapshot: skinny white pants, tailored beige jacket, pearl necklace, high heels, and coordinating caramel-colored handbag. Her brown hair had expensive blond highlights and was angled perfectly at her shoulders. Back then, as the public relations manager for Anna St. Clair, a major fashion house in New York, she had been a constant advertisement for the fashionable woman. Staring at her pointy heels in the photo, Ashley suddenly laughed aloud, recalling the one time Steve had come with her to Bergdorf's.

It had been a sunny Saturday in spring. She'd needed to pick up a pair of pink high-heeled sandals for a work function the following Monday. Certainly Steve hadn't been thrilled at the prospect, but he'd insisted that he wouldn't mind if she had a look.

The air in the store smelled like lavender and musk oil. A tall, black-clad store model with slicked-back hair was standing at the top of the stairs, spritzing guests who came up the escalator. Hordes of shoppers all seemed to be searching for the ultimate springtime pump. The shoe displays looked like rows of pastel candy, enticing buyers to let go of black and embrace color. A second after Ashley spotted the right shoe, it was snapped up by a woman with short-cropped brown hair and an angular face.

Ashley flagged down a sales associate and asked about the shoe sample the woman was holding. Moments later, the associate returned to inform her that it was the last pair in her size. Moreover, she explained, she had just done a check earlier and she couldn't locate them in another store. That style had recently been featured in one of the latest fashion magazines, and it seemed there had been a run on them.

"Come on, Ashley," said Steve. "You can't just give up. I thought this was the female version of the caveman experience. Go fight for it."

"What?" Ashley exclaimed. "I can't just go up to her and demand she give me the shoes. That's rude."

"This is New York. You shouldn't take no for an answer." He walked over to observe the woman trying on the pink shoes.

Ashley watched as the woman noticed the young man looking at her.

"I like those shoes," he said as he studied her feet in the mirror.

"I do think they're nice looking," the woman said.

Steve folded his arms. "You don't think they're too pink, do you?"

She looked at her feet. "No, I really like them."

"I do, too," he said.

She laughed. "Not for you, I hope. Pink isn't your color."

"Not mine. Hers. I'll win big points with my girlfriend if I can get her these shoes. It seems you've got the last pair in her size." He winked at her.

The woman considered his request, then smiled. "Ah, spring is in the air." Her features softened. "Here, kid. I can't let pink shoes stand in the way of young love. I hope she's worth it."

"Absolutely. And might I say that you'd look just as lovely in that green pair over there."

She handed him the box. "You'd better get lost before I change my mind. This is my first good deed in a month."

Steve grabbed the shoes and brought them over to where Ashley stood.

"I can't believe you just did that! You're amazing," she whispered excitedly, as she quickly slipped into one of the sandals to check the fit. "They're perfect."

"I think that wraps up this Prince Charming's work for the day," he said with another wink.

She threw her arms around him and kissed him.

✂ ✂ ✂

Snapping back to reality, Ashley went about her day, straightening up the house, driving the kids to after-school activities, and making a quick detour to get Sally some new sneakers. By three o'clock, the house was overtaken by the chaos of her children. Fortunately, at least Cameron was an easygoing and independent ten-year-old who preferred the quiet of his room to the zoolike atmosphere created by his siblings.

"Mom," said Janie, bursting into the room, "you promised to help me with my spelling words!" Ashley inwardly cursed the teacher who gave second-graders weekly spelling tests.

"Janie, honey, I'll be right with you," said Ashley patiently as the sound of a horn blared in the back driveway.

"Mom!" exclaimed Janie impatiently. "I need help!"

"Just hold on, little monkey," said Ashley. "Tucker just got home and I need to make a schedule change with Mrs. Rivers."

Ashley picked up a doll from the floor and nearly tripped over a pair of shoes. She noticed dark fingerprints on the wall by the door and quickly grabbed a wet dishtowel from the sink to wipe them clean. Her house was messy, not dirty, she told herself. The kids would just have to help more.

A car bearing her eldest son, Tucker, was in the

driveway and she headed outside to greet him. He seemed to have grown a foot in the last year. Having reached five foot seven at only thirteen years old, he not only was taller than she was but also seemed destined to reach well over six feet given the size of his shoes. She gave him a quick hug, knowing that he didn't want her to lavish too much affection on him in front of his peers.

Once the car was backing down the gravel driveway, Ashley caught Tucker's solemn expression. "Everything okay?" she asked.

He shook his head and stared at his feet. "I got a bad grade on my math test."

"Do you want to talk about it?"

"Nope."

Janie reappeared wearing a ballet tutu. "Mama, look at me!" she shouted as she began twirling in the driveway.

"Janie Gates, dance yourself right back upstairs and get started on your spelling." Ashley watched as Janie lifted her tutu and ran off, giggling. "Tucker, get yourself something to eat while I take Sally upstairs. I'd better help Janie or else we're going to be subjected to another costume change."

"Tell her not to put on the dog outfit and start licking me again," he said. "I'm not in the mood. Mr. Waters put a note at the top of the test for you." His chestnut bangs flopped over his right eye.

"I'll take a look in a minute," she said, scooping up her baby girl.

On her way back down the stairs, a photograph in a dusty plastic frame caught her eye. She smiled at the picture of her own gangly form at fifteen. Snatching it up, she continued downstairs to have a talk with Tucker. He was seated at the kitchen counter staring morosely into a bowl of ice cream.

"Hey, there," she said, sitting beside him. "It can't be that bad."

"Yes, it is. Take a look at this." He handed her the test with red pen marks all over it.

Ashley read the note on the top of the test, indicating that Mr. Waters wanted to speak with her directly about Tucker's performance in school. *It's only seventh grade,* she thought, annoyed, wondering what academic challenges high school would bring. "I'll talk with Mr. Waters about where to go from here. You may need a tutor to get you through this unit. Don't beat yourself up about it. We'll figure it out."

"At least Ronny Walker told me he'd play me in tennis sometime."

"What? Do you think you're ready to play the Alabama state champion?"

"My coach thinks the only way to learn how to win is to learn how to lose. He wants to see if I can win some games."

"Well, you've got a great serve; if you work on your net game, you may have a chance of winning some points." Ashley pulled out the dusty picture. "I wanted to show you this. I'd forgotten all about it."

Tucker stared at the photograph of the skinny girl holding a large silver trophy. "Who's that?" he asked, taking a bite of his ice cream.

"Me," replied Ashley. "I was fifteen when I won the state singles championships in Connecticut."

"Why didn't you ever show me this before? You never said you were that good. You always say you played tennis a lot, won some things, and that's all." His excitement seemed to make him forget his math grade. "I don't think I've ever even seen you play!"

"I haven't made the time," she said. She remembered how much she had once enjoyed the competition. "I was actually pretty good at one point."

Tucker stood up. "Pretty good? You were state champion. That's totally awesome! I can't believe you never told me."

"I'm sorry. I guess I didn't think anybody would care. It was a long time ago." Ashley grabbed a paper towel from the plastic holder near the sink and began wiping the counter.

"I care. Why don't you ever go out and hit with me?"

"You'd be much better off playing kids your own age. I mean, it's not that I don't want to, but I'm not sure my forehand is going to have any power. I'm not even positive I could get the ball over the net anymore."

"Come on, Mom. Be serious. I'd really like it if you'd go with me sometime."

"Ask your dad."

"He's always working," said Tucker quietly. "He never wants to do anything but play golf with his friends on the weekends."

Tucker's disappointment mirrored her own; Steve was always busy these days. He rarely found time for his family, let alone their marriage; the intimacy was all but gone. Their conversation consisted of discussions of household problems and quick updates on the kids.

She looked down at the way her belly extended over her pants. She had put on more weight recently, maybe ten or fifteen pounds. None of her clothes fit; that irritated her. For the past year, she'd been promising herself that she'd go to the gym, but it never seemed to happen. She was always on the run, eating food off the kids' plates when it suited her. It occurred to her that she needed a reason to get back in shape.

Ashley sucked in her stomach and stood up straight. "Okay, I'll do it."

"All right!" exclaimed Tucker, smiling. "When?"

"Um," said Ashley. "Saturday morning? I'll talk with your dad about watching the other kids."

"You're going to what?" Steve laughed, removing his tie, then stripping down to his boxer shorts. He got into bed and reached for the television's remote control.

"I thought I'd go over to the tennis club and hit

some balls with Tucker for an hour on Saturday morning," she repeated.

"You're kidding, right?" He surfed through several channels, settling on a reality show that featured women in evening gowns competing for a single male. "You won't last ten minutes on the court."

Ashley was stung by the insult. "What's that supposed to mean?" she shot back. "I was pretty good once. I could help him."

Steve laughed harder. "Honey," he said. "Have you looked in the mirror lately? You're not very fit." He looked at her condescendingly. Then he rolled over and turned his attention to the television set. Suddenly she felt like a huge sausage encased in sweatpants and a sloppy T-shirt.

Ashley felt herself burning with shame, but refused to let Steve see her cry. Grabbing her book, she mumbled something about not being tired and headed downstairs to the kitchen. The shiny refrigerator beckoned her, offering satisfaction via her favorite ice cream bars. Ashley opened the freezer door, peering inside, a blast of cold air hitting her in the face. Undeterred, she reached for the silver-coated square inside the box, resolving to eat just one. Several packages of frozen vegetables fell out onto the floor. *So much for my organizational skills,* she thought, stacking them back together and installing them in the side door. She promised herself that she would put her freezer in order this week.

The ice cream bar tasted great, a soothing balm to her troubled mind. It was an easy fix and she knew it, but it was working. It actually made her feel better, she rationalized, opening the freezer door again to get another bar. This time she ate it a bit more slowly, savoring each bite, really allowing the chocolate coating to tickle her senses. *I didn't eat much today,* she thought, remembering that she had just picked at the leftovers on the kids' plates for her dinner. No wonder she was still really hungry.

Before she knew it, she had consumed four bars and felt sick with self-loathing. It hadn't taken long. She peered at the sticky wrappers and wondered what she had hoped to accomplish with this binge. Even at that moment, she realized it was a temporary salve to bigger problems that she couldn't seem to solve on her own. She needed to figure out how to meet some of her own needs; all of this giving to her family at the expense of herself was draining her.

The silver wrappers decorated the counter. Ashley used to pride herself on her self-discipline; once, it had been an integral part of her personality. But no answers were forthcoming from her exhausted mind on how to redirect her energy. She imagined a jury of twelve impressive, neatly manicured mothers staring at her with disgust. Ashley wondered why she couldn't seem to do this suburban housewife thing well enough. Nothing was as it should have been: her house, her figure, her marriage. She felt utterly alone and embarrassed by her inability to figure a way out of the rut she was in. She was so tired that she felt she would drop. Her eyes filled with tears and she sat down on a stool, put her head down on the counter, and soon fell asleep.

The next sound she heard was Steve's voice. "What's going on, Ashley?" he demanded. "The kids are going to be late for school."

He was standing above her, dressed in a suit and tie, clean and smelling of citrus-scented aftershave.

"What does it look like, Steve?" she asked, jerking awake. "I've had a great night's sleep. Why don't you do something to help with the kids?"

"I've got a breakfast meeting at seven. Unlike you, I have to go to work."

"You think I don't work?" she snapped. "I take care of the kids, do the laundry, run errands, and clean the house. I can't do it anymore. I'm exhausted. I can't do everything." She watched him glance over at the ice cream wrappers.

"Then hire a housekeeper," he replied. "We can afford it." He straightened his tie and looked at her as if he found her loathsome. "I've gotta go," he said.

Ashley picked up the wrappers and walked into the bathroom to splash water on her face. The person who stared back at her seemed a caricature of her former self. Her hair was matted to one side of her face; her hand had left an imprint on her cheek. The T-shirt had a piece of chocolate stuck on it.

She couldn't bear to look down at her stomach, which had once been concave. With quick strokes, she tried to neaten up her hair, tuck in her T-shirt, and put a smile on her face for the children; then she ran upstairs to get them ready for school.

The boys walked to school. After Janie was picked up by her carpool, Ashley drove Sally to a three-day-a-week preschool program at the local church. The house would be quiet for the next three hours. Ashley showered and then sat down to make some notes on what needed to be accomplished this week. Something had to change; she had to get her act together. For the first time in years, she took a moment to think of what she wanted to do for herself. Her mind went blank.

Just then, her friend Megan honked for her outside. If it weren't for Megan, Ashley would be completely starved for female friendship. With short, wavy hair, freckles, and a ready smile, Megan was one of those people who could flow through life, unfazed by any bumps that came her way. Ashley would always think of Megan as the friend with the Band-Aids. They had met on the preschool playground years ago when Tucker and Megan's son, Mike, had collided on the monkey bars. Megan was quick to respond, remaining completely calm while both boys wailed in dismay. Ashley remembered how Megan had pulled out several Band-Aids from her jeans pocket, offering each boy a choice between a Batman or a Spider-Man print.

Their injuries were immediately forgotten as the boys contemplated the merits of each superhero.

Ashley ran out to the car. After the first few minutes of conversation, Megan asked, "Ashley, are you okay?"

"Not really," she replied. She heard her voice quiver. "I just need to get out of the house and do something different. I used to be so together, way back when. Now, it's like each day, I'm just surviving. I don't know." She knew she was babbling.

"Look, retail therapy is always a good thing. We'll have fun looking at dresses at Blair's. You know what, I just had a great idea."

"I could use one right now."

"After we go shopping, I want you to come with me to meet my scrapbooking friends. I know I've talked about them before, but I'm sure you've forgotten. Anyway, they're such a great group of women. We get together on Tuesdays to work on our scrapbooks," Megan explained. "Next year, Sally will be in preschool five mornings a week, which will give you a bit more time. Maybe you should start thinking about doing something new."

"You're right. I feel so lost. It's like I don't recognize myself anymore. Am I making sense?"

"Yes, you're making perfect sense. Sounds like a case of kid burnout. Maybe you should start by taking more time for yourself just to have fun."

"*Fun* is definitely not in my vocabulary anymore. I need a housekeeper, a handyman, a decorator, and a live-in nanny to get my life together. Unfortunately, a staff is not in my budget right now."

"I hear you. But you're never going to manage everything perfectly with four kids, so give that up. I'm just talking about taking a small block of time for a hobby. You don't have to come to every meeting; we're a very laid-back group. I really think you'd enjoy scrapbooking. The books are a way to preserve your family history. You'd be amazed at some of the old photos that some group members have found. It's really cool; you can even design your own pages any way you want. We're kind of like artists of memories."

"I'm not really good at the arts-and-crafts thing," said Ashley, recalling the myriad school projects her kids had made out of egg cartons, milk containers, and cereal boxes. "You should have seen what happened last time I helped Cameron with his history presentation. We decorated this poster together, and Dolley Madison came out looking more like James."

"Come on, Ashley. I know how creative you really are. Do you take any time away from the kids to do things you enjoy?"

Ashley thought for a minute. "Is that a trick question?"

"See what I mean?" said Megan firmly. "We're having a lunch meeting today at noon at Tara West's house. You can see some of our books, which are amazing. You know that this has been my passion for years. You've got to come with me. What do you think?"

"What about Sally? I have to pick her up at preschool at noon."

"How about asking Linda Murphy to take Sally for a few hours? Isn't her daughter in the same class? You can ask her a favor for today and have her little girl over later in the week. She's so nice; I'm sure she won't mind." Megan rattled off Linda's phone number.

"Okay," said Ashley, summoning up her courage. "I hope she can do it on such short notice."

"It's worth a try," said Megan. "And if Linda doesn't work out, we'll come up with another idea."

"Thanks," said Ashley gratefully.

CHAPTER 2

Ashley

Though she tried to suppress the feeling, Ashley was irritated at the thought of having lunch with a group of women she didn't know. Her free time was precious and her house, as usual, was a mess. Ashley wished she had driven herself, and tried not to feel like a prisoner in Megan's car. But Megan's enthusiasm, and of course her own lack of transportation, prevented her from returning home to tend to her chores. And after all, Megan *had* just helped her select a great-looking black dress that made her look ten pounds thinner.

Peering over at her friend's outfit of pale pink top and chocolate-brown pants, she realized that while Megan always seemed so put together, it was in a way that didn't feel intimidating. Maybe that's why Ashley had agreed to come today. They didn't see enough of each other these days, but as usual, Megan was always there for her as if those lapses in time didn't exist.

"Wait till you see Tara's house," said Megan. "It's absolutely gorgeous." She popped a breath mint into her mouth. "Want one?" she asked.

"No, thanks," said Ashley. *Great, seeing another woman's beautifully decorated home will certainly make me feel much better about my own junk-filled abode,* she thought sarcastically.

Megan parked her car in front of a charming pumpkin-colored stucco house with a curved front archway. Terra-cotta pots filled with colorful zinnias decorated the walkway. Ashley thought of the empty pots and dead plants littering her own backyard. She was already counting the minutes until this event was over.

When Megan pushed open the front door, Ashley looked around, noting contemporary paintings, antique marble tables, and cream-colored silk draperies.

Megan whispered, "Tara doesn't have children."

"Thanks," said Ashley. "That's good to know. I was feeling a bit overwhelmed. This place looks like something out of a magazine." Following Megan's lead, she put her purse on a whitewashed carved French table in the front hall. Ashley paused to check her appearance in the large vertical gold mirror and noticed her dilated pupils. She immediately checked her clothes for stains, discreetly wiping a spot off her white blouse. She tried to tuck in her shirt, but that only made her belly look bigger. Hunting for Megan to make up an excuse to leave, she found that her friend had already gone into the other room. There was nothing she could do but summon up her courage and follow the sound of animated conversation.

As she stood in the doorway, Ashley scanned the dining room for Megan, wondering what to do next. She saw several women gathering around a lively woman with cropped white hair and horn-rimmed glasses. Edging closer, Ashley noticed the woman's trim figure, pressed linen slacks, and white blazer. Her black flats were stylish and expensive. Ashley was grateful that she had at least managed to stuff her own puffy feet into a pair of black open-toe sandals. She watched as the woman pulled out a large black-and-white photograph from a caramel-colored leather tote bag.

"I just picked up this picture from the restorer yesterday. They did a marvelous job," said the woman, pointing to several creases. "This is my grandmother Victoria Randolph Griffiths—she was raised to lead a life of leisure in the South, but it didn't work out that way. Her first husband was William Charles Morrison, a tobacco heir. She always said that he was the love of her life. Anyway, he was killed during the First World War, and apparently Victoria was never the same after that. Happily, he left her a rather large fortune so she could travel wherever she pleased.

"Years later, at the ripe old age of twenty-six, she met my grandfather Frederick von Shwepke at a gaming table in a Paris château. He was a German aristocrat who was completely taken with her brash American charm. They soon married and had two girls. I think they had a happy ten years before the Nazis came to claim his castle as their own. They fled Germany in the middle of the night and returned to America, but things were never right afterward. Frederick became depressed and started drinking heavily." She looked up, studied her audience, then squared her shoulders. "Really, I hate to bore everyone with this!"

"Absolutely not," said one woman, adjusting the belt of a brown-and-white lattice-print wrap dress. "You've got to finish the story. Then what happened?"

Ashley observed the attractive woman in the figure-flattering dress and was relieved to see that she didn't have perfectly manicured nails. *These women will probably think I'm a total slob,* she told herself, gingerly picking up a chilled bottle of water from a cooler beneath the table.

"Thinking he had lost everything, my grandfather couldn't adjust to life in America. After all, they were living on her money, and it bothered him. He shot himself one afternoon while my grandmother was at a lawn party drinking mint juleps with her friends. Most women would have fallen apart. Not Victoria. She came home, dealt with the police investigators, had the staff clean up the blood stains on the carpet, and made sure supper was on the table that night as scheduled. Victoria was certainly not someone who let a little thing like her husband's suicide interfere with her daily routine."

Ashley was completely transported, thinking her problems were trivial in comparison.

"Anyway, she raised her children by herself. Let me correct that. She had a full staff who attended to them while she entertained, did her charity work, and gambled at night. Her late-night soirées were notorious. Once the children were grown and safely married off, she went off to Italy to live and study art. Rumor had it that she was involved with the great sculptor Bandolini. She died peacefully in his studio one winter night. Apparently, Bandolini was so upset by her untimely death that he kept her corpse there almost thirty-six hours while he sculpted her likeness."

"Bandolini? I'm not sure I've studied him. I'll look him up next time I'm researching in the library," said the woman in the wrap dress thoughtfully, smoothing back a strand of her shoulder-length brown hair.

"I don't want to know! If he didn't exist, I'd hate to ruin our family folklore with the truth." The lady with the white hair winked. She held up the photograph again. "Don't you think I look like her, especially around the eyes?" She carefully placed the old photograph back in the bag.

"That was wonderful, Annie," said Megan.

Ashley wondered what other stories might be uncovered by looking at family photographs. The woman in the wrap dress approached her with a smile.

"Hello, I'm Tara. You must be Megan's friend."

"Oh yes, I'm Ashley, thanks for having me," said Ashley, shaking her hand. She hoped Tara didn't notice her clammy palms. "I guess I got caught up in the story."

"That's what I love about seeing everyone's old photographs. There's always a story. It's fascinating."

"How interesting," said Ashley politely. "Your house is amazing. I was just admiring the zebra skin on those chairs."

"My father went hunting in Africa and sent them to me. Anyway, I didn't know what to do with them at first, so they just sat around for months. Finally I decided to reupholster those two chairs. They're kind of hairy, don't you think?"

"Yes, but they look great. I didn't think anyone was actually supposed to sit on them." Ashley sucked in her stomach and took a sip of water.

Tara laughed. "You're right. Why is it women have such a keen understanding of other women's homes? My last boyfriend couldn't understand that these chairs were no longer available for regular use. It drove him crazy."

"It could be worse," offered Ashley. "You could be like me and have four wild kids running around who think the house is their own private jungle."

"Oh, four kids! You're so lucky."

Ashley answered Tara's questions about the names and ages of each of her children, pleasantly surprised by her interest. "My three-year-old, Sally, seems to want to be an artist. I guess she sees her bedroom walls as a blank canvas. Last week, she drew clowns all over them."

"She sounds like fun; I'd love to meet her," said Tara.

"You may regret those words," Ashley cautioned with a laugh. "Anyway, I must say that woman's story commanded my attention."

"That's Annie Griffin. She's the wife of our senator. She's always got a good tale to tell. But she's not the only one. Let me introduce you to Margy." She gestured toward a woman with strawberry-blond hair pulled haphazardly into a low ponytail, funky gold hoop earrings, and stacked colored rings on several of her fingers. She wore a blue-

and-green print blouse, jeans, and black flats. Ashley thought that Margy seemed like the most approachable of the women.

Ashley was certain she wasn't going to remember everyone's names, but she noticed that the woman Tara had pointed out as Margy carried an oversized blue tote bag with bamboo handles. Remembering a trick she used to use in business, she tried to think of catchphrases about the woman that began with the letter M: marvelous smile, messy ponytail, and magnificent handbag. It was corny but it worked for her.

"That bag's terrific," sighed Ashley, looking at Margy's tote.

"Oh, thanks," said Margy. "I made it."

"Wow! That's amazing. Unfortunately, I need something waterproof and kidproof with an automatic filing cabinet inside."

"There's always vinyl," said Margy.

"That's the story of my life. I've already considered the possibility of covering my furniture in it. Seriously, you're so talented."

"Thanks," said Margy. She dug into her purse, shuffling through her personal belongings. Several buttons fell out of her bag, and she quickly stuffed them back inside. "But really I'm just an accessories addict. I collect buttons, ribbon, fabric, feathers— you name it. Making handbags is simply a way for me to deal with my compulsive collecting personality." She seemed to be ogling Tara's arrangement of glass vases filled with colored marbles.

"I've got thousands of plastic doll pieces that you could use," suggested Ashley, drawn to Margy's creativity.

"I could do a Barbie-themed bag," said Margy gamely.

"You're welcome to come over to my house and take any game, toy, or doll accessory you want." Ashley actually hoped that Margy *would* come over to her house, knowing instinctively that she wouldn't judge her kid-cluttered environment.

"I just may take you up on that!" said Margy.

A tall, elegant woman with chin-length, jet-black hair joined them. Her smooth olive skin didn't appear to have a single flaw, Ashley noticed, except for a distinctive brown mole centered on her right cheek. The woman's hot pink beaded tunic top was paired with jeans.

"This is one of my favorite people in the world," said Tara. "Tina is an expert on Indian art. She's helped the museum nearly double its collection."

"That was before I had girls in middle school! Now, I'm not sure I'd call myself an expert at anything," said Tina with a wave of her long fingers.

"How old are your girls?" Ashley inquired, admiring her swanlike gesture.

"They're thirteen and fourteen. Let me tell you, it's not easy having teenage girls. The phone seems to ring constantly." She rolled her eyes.

"My thirteen-year-old son likes playing sports

more than the phone. I've also got two girls, but at seven and three, I've got a few good years left before the phone officially becomes headache material. So, how is it that you have an English accent?" asked Ashley.

"You think so? That's wonderful. I grew up in India, but my family moved to London when I was about twelve. To complicate things further, I ended up going to college in the States. My parents are simply horrified that I've become so 'American-ized,' as they say."

"Tina's kids love McDonald's!" added Tara.

"So do mine," said Ashley. "Isn't that just awful?"

"Yes, but it certainly saves time some nights."

"You're so right," agreed Ashley.

"Let's get started," said Tara. She pointed to the neatly displayed box lunches on the table. "I've got turkey sandwiches, chicken salad, and a vegetarian option."

As Ashley reached for a sandwich, Megan came over to stand beside her. "Are you doing okay?"

"Yes, I'm having fun. Who's the woman with the short blond hair?" Ashley whispered. She admired the woman's pixie haircut, high cheekbones, and wide smile. Observing the woman's simple white blouse, star-shaped belt buckle, and skinny jeans, Ashley tried again not to think about her own lack of style.

"Oh, that's Catherine Davidson. We call her the supply guru. Seriously, she works part-time out of her house selling everything and anything that has to do with scrapbooking. You should see her guest room. It looks like a store."

Tara ushered the group into the living room, telling everyone to make themselves comfortable and take a seat.

How ironic, Ashley thought as she eyed the expensive furnishings. The room wasn't exactly designed to accommodate spills. Ashley took a seat next to Megan by the fireplace; she gingerly took out the boxed lunch, consisting of a turkey sandwich on thick sourdough bread, orzo salad with sun-dried tomatoes, and fresh-cut melon, all pulled together in green plastic wrap tied with a ribbon. *I'll just eat half the sandwich,* she told herself, wondering if her stomach was hanging over the front of her pants.

Tina came to sit beside Ashley. "I must tell you all that Ganesha has returned to the Belloix Museum. He's been on exhibit in California for the past year."

"Who's Ganesha?" asked Ashley, hoping she didn't sound completely ignorant. She hadn't been to the museum in years.

"He's the god of good fortune, worshipped by many in India. He has an elephant head on a human body." Tina shifted in her seat, then crossed her legs.

"I don't think I've seen him. Why does he have an elephant's head?" Ashley realized how much she had allowed her natural curiosity to slide. In the last few years, her most penetrating questions were more like, "What do you want for dinner?"

"There is a wonderful Hindu story about Ganesha," Tina began, clearly delighted to have a chance to tell it. "Long ago, Parvati, the goddess of the earth, needed someone to protect her. She used dust and water to make a child, whom she named Ganesha. She asked little Ganesha to stand outside her door to keep unwelcome people out. When the god Shiva came to visit Ganesha, Ganesha refused to let him see Parvati." Tina turned to Ashley to explain. Clearly, everyone else in the room knew who Shiva was. "Shiva is the god with all the arms and legs. In Eastern culture, artists showed the superpowers of the gods by adding limbs."

"Ah," said Ashley, trying not to blush. "Please, go on."

"As the story goes, Shiva became enraged and lopped off Ganesha's head. When Parvati found out what had happened, she was angry and demanded that Shiva do something to fix little Ganesha. Shiva made amends by offering to replace Ganesha's head with the first thing he saw. As it happened, the first thing he saw was an elephant, which was how Ganesha got his elephant's head. Shiva then made Ganesha 'Remover of All Obstacles,' the one to help people get what they want in life."

Ashley was delighted by Tina's story. "Wow! I need to bring my kids to the museum to see this . . .

What is it exactly?" Ashley wanted to joke that she needed a Ganesha around her house to help her clean up, but worried that Tina might not find her remark funny. After all, she wanted to make a good first impression.

"A sculpture," said Tina patiently. "It's made out of stone. They'd love it. I'm at the museum all the time. Next time you go, ask for me. If I have time, I can show you some of the collection."

"Really?" said Ashley, putting down her sandwich. "That would be great! I mean, I would love to get them learning about art and culture."

"I'd be happy to help," said Tina.

"I'm so glad Ashley could join us today," said Tara once the conversation had quieted down. "When Megan phoned this morning to say she might bring her friend, I thought that we should have a few scrapbooks for her to see, just for fun. I immediately called Margy and asked her to bring one of her spectacular books about her daughter, Erin."

"Oh, I love Margy's books," cried Megan, adjusting her pink top. "They're so clever." She smiled at Ashley.

"I nearly forgot it as I raced out the door today. But here it is," Margy said nervously; several clumps of strawberry hair had fallen loose from her ponytail and carelessly hung forward. Reaching for another tote bag, this one in animal print, she removed a large bound scrapbook to show Ashley.

41

The book had a dazzling front cover festooned with fabric, ribbons, and printed paper. Erin's name was spelled out in pink silk; a layer of plaid ribbon edged cach of the letters. Three rainbow-colored stars surrounding her name were outlined in gold. A green and pink striped ribbon formed a border that framed the cover page. Margy had used textured zebra-print fabric on the binding for contrast.

"This is unbelievable! It looks like a work of art," said Ashley, placing the album carefully on her lap. "Do all the covers look this good?"

Megan slid over to sit next to her. "Margy's books are exceptional, so we wanted you to see hers first, just to give you some ideas. There are lots of ways to make your scrapbook creative and good looking without designing your own covers."

Margy looked at Ashley apologetically. "I'm a designer, so this is what I do. I mean, I have loads of extra fabric and supplies at my house. I love working on my pages, because it fuels ideas for my handbags. Did you notice the animal print on the binding? When I mixed it with the pink plaid for Erin's cover, I suddenly thought I could use that idea for the lining of my next handbag. It was an accessory moment," she said playfully, leaning forward in her chair.

"Your story reminds me of when I worked for Anna St. Clair in New York," she said, feeling her heart pound. Ashley was acutely aware of having the others' attention focused on her. "I used to love going down to her studio to watch her. She would mix the most unusual textures and fabrics. I've really lost sight of how much I enjoyed being part of the creative process—even though I was on the public relations side, I learned so much." Ashley looked down at her hands to combat her nervousness. *Don't judge me by the way I look now,* she thought.

"I forgot that you worked for Anna St. Clair!" said Megan excitedly. "I should have brought you here ages ago!"

"That's amazing," said Margy. "You must be so talented. Those jobs were hard won."

"I don't know about that," said Ashley modestly, leaving out the important fact that her successful supermodel mother had helped her get the job. No one here knew her parents, which was something of a relief. It had been years since she had talked about her career in New York; it felt as if it had been a lifetime ago. "But I enjoyed my job a lot. I've been so busy with the kids that I'm not sure if I have any brain cells left to be creative anymore."

"Sure you do, honey. One step at a time. It's tough being a young mother," said a woman with frosted blond hair. "I'm Libby, by the way. How old is your youngest?"

"Three," said Ashley, responding to the warmth in the woman's blue eyes. Something about Libby's comfortable blue linen dress and sandals gave Ashley the feeling that she was accustomed to being around children.

"Before you know it, she's going to be graduating from high school. It goes so fast. I promise you." Libby gave her a reassuring smile, then pushed her glasses back on her nose.

"Okay, back to fabric talk," said Margy. "I have loads of new scraps for anyone who might be interested."

"Margy, could you please bring some to next week's meeting at my house?" said Catherine, the supply guru, looking down at her notepad as if she were running the meeting. "Where's Tara's book?"

"Are you sure? I mean, poor Ashley may not want to experience my obsession with Monet firsthand. She may never come back again!"

Ashley smiled. "Of course I want to see what you've done. But if I keep looking at Margy's creative pages, I may develop a scrapbook phobia. This really is fantastic!"

"Once you see other examples, you'll realize that everyone has a different style," said Libby. "I think my books focus more on the actual photographs because that's my interest. Tara's scrapbooks have a more clean-lined, modern style. What about yours, Annie?"

"I'd call my books 'crafty with a twist,' " said Annie. Her red polished nails caught the light as she placed her glass of soda on a side table. "I do a lot of rule breaking because I like trying new techniques."

"Talk about no time—Annie is the master organizer! She even brings her materials on the campaign trail," said Libby, sitting up in her chair and pointing to Annie. Ashley could tell they were close friends.

"The truth is I don't sleep well in strange hotels on the road. Scrapbooking gives me something productive to do late at night."

"How can you possibly bring supplies on the road?" asked Ashley.

"I don't take too many, just enough to fit in a handbag-sized case. I bring some scissors and double-stick tape, and my favorite decorations go into Baggies. When I'm busy being creative, it takes my mind off a race."

"And Tom's lengthy speeches on education reform," said Libby, finishing Annie's sentence for her. Both women laughed like schoolgirls sharing a private joke.

"Go on and get your book, Tara," said Megan, glancing at her watch.

A few minutes later, Tara returned to the living room carrying a small book with a green leather cover. "And now for a trip to Paris," she announced. She handed Ashley the book. "I'd like you to see how I used overlays on some of these pages. They look great and they're a wonderful way to keep your pages clean and simple." She added, "You'll notice that I didn't make my own cover on this project. You can do as much or as little as time allows. I think the leather looks elegant."

Megan leaned over Ashley's shoulder. "One of the things I like about Tara's pages is her use of color. See how the overlay is purplish blue? It picks up the water lilies in this photograph."

"Generally, I try to only use three colors throughout a book so that it looks unified," offered Tara. "As you can see here, I selected yellow, purple, and celery green for my accents and pages. This book is a little more flowery than most of mine because of the subject matter. But I did have fun making cutouts of my version of the water lily and anchoring them on these pages."

"This book makes me feel like I'm in Paris," said Ashley. "I've only been to Europe once on business, when I visited Milan during Fashion Week." She turned to the next page. "These photographs are so perfect. Wait, this one looks like a Japanese tree. That can't be right."

"Actually, you're correct. That was really observant of you. I used the Japanese print in the background to show how much Monet was influenced by Asian art. There's another page that shows sections of the lilies in l'Orangerie. I wanted to capture how Monet showed the light throughout one given day. I didn't have the right camera at the time, so I used the lighter and darker background papers to give the right effect. It actually worked pretty well."

"I see what you did. How interesting," said Ashley, looking around at the other women. "I like the fact that this book is only fifteen pages long and yet you accomplished so much. Thanks for sharing it with me."

Catherine, the one scratching down notes on a spiral pad, promised that she would bring some new ideas to the next meeting. Ashley watched her intently, trying to come up with three C phrases to remember her: cat eyes, craft supply queen, cool white clothes. It was the best she could do, she thought.

"Anyone here babysit?" asked Ashley, scanning the group.

Libby raised her hand. "I'd be delighted to help you. I can't get enough of children now that I'm retired and mine are grown."

"Are you serious?" said Ashley, looking askance at Libby.

"She means it," added Tara, neatly placing her book on a mahogany end table. "She'll have your kids playing educational games in no time! She's such a gifted teacher."

"I'd really love it," said Libby. "I'll give you my number before we leave. Feel free to call on me anytime."

Ashley was astounded by Libby's generous offer. Later, as the group gathered their things, Ashley went in search of Tara. She found her in the kitchen.

"Thanks again, Tara. I've had such a nice time today. I really didn't know what to expect when I came. I'll definitely come again," she said sincerely.

"I'm so glad," said Tara kindly. "Maybe we could get together for lunch sometime?" she added. "There's a new sandwich place that just opened."

Ashley tried not to look too surprised by the invitation. "I know the place you're talking about. It's got that cute black-and-white striped awning in the front. That would be fun to try out. I'll see if I can get a sitter for Sally."

"Why don't you just bring her?" said Tara. Her eyes seemed to light up at the mention of Sally's name. "I don't get to see children much these days. It would be a treat for me."

"Are you sure?" said Ashley.

"Positive," said Tara.

"I'll call you tomorrow and we can set up a time," said Ashley, trying to sound like lunch with a female friend was a regular occurrence.

"That would be perfect," said Tara. "I'll look forward to it."

"Me, too," said Ashley. "Bye."

Once outside, Ashley spotted Megan's monstrous SUV and hurried to get into the car. "I didn't think I'd want to get involved in scrapbooking," she said honestly, buckling her seat belt. "But after today, I definitely want to come back. What an interesting bunch of women. I was captivated by Annie's stories about her grandmother. I guess I haven't put much thought into my ancestors."

"You know, that's what I love about these women. Someone always has a story to tell. Or sometimes even a family scandal. You never know what's going to happen next."

"I'm definitely intrigued," said Ashley.

CHAPTER 3

Tara

She maneuvered her black hardtop convertible into the restaurant's drive-thru lane. The car's tan interior still smelled new, and the wood-paneled console was in pristine condition. A vent blasted cold air in her face as she shifted channels, trying to find some music to wake her up. A song by U2 caught her attention and she turned up the volume, her shoulders moving in time to the pulsating beat. She didn't slow down at the intercom but instead continued forward, the car jerking a bit as she put a little too much pressure on the gas pedal.

The attendant used a two-handed grip to hold out her supersized soda. In a series of fluid motions, she halted the car, rolled down the window, turned down the music, and grabbed her usual breakfast.

"Good morning, Miss Tara," said Ronnie, a curly-haired teenager with braces. "You really drink this whole thing, huh?"

"Sure do," she laughed, taking her first sip of morning caffeine. The cold liquid soothed her dry mouth.

"Why are you always in such a rush? Those dead people you're studying aren't going anywhere." He leaned forward toward the open glass window. His rectangular name tag glinted in the morning light.

"They're famous artists," corrected Tara, downing another swig of the drink. "And I can't get my degree without them."

"Whatever. When are you going to marry me?" he said with a mischievous grin.

"We'll talk about it when you graduate from college."

"High school," he shot back.

"See you tomorrow," she said as she drove away.

She took a few more sips of the ice-laden soda, savoring the caffeine fix. Her head was full of ideas for the next chapter of her dissertation. She wanted to show how Calder and Miró's work paralleled each other even when they were living on different continents. She mulled over several pieces of their work to compare.

According to her schedule, she had nearly three hours to do library research this morning. As she sipped her drink, Tara thought about how much she had enjoyed meeting Megan's friend Ashley yesterday. She couldn't imagine having one child; this woman had four. *She's so lucky,* Tara thought, wondering if fate was ever going to help her find the right guy. Right now, a stable relationship seemed an impossibility. Fortunately, she had her passions to keep her going: art, travel, yoga, and scrapbooking.

With her usual discipline, Tara determined exactly what she wanted to accomplish this morning. The reference librarian had found a rare video-taped interview that Miró gave before his death. It was only twenty minutes long, but Tara was spellbound by his words. When he said, "For me, an object is alive," Tara felt goose bumps on her arms. *That's what made him such a genius,* she thought. Tara watched the tape six times, rewound it to listen to specific sections, and then decided to return home to eat some lunch and record her reactions on her computer. Checking her watch, she realized that five hours had passed. Two hours longer than she'd intended.

From her cell phone in the car, Tara called her regular lunch place and ordered up their special so it would be ready when she got there. With her favorite chicken salad sandwich in hand, she returned home to study her notes and quickly eat at the kitchen counter.

Once she finished, Tara freshened up a bit before sitting back down at her desk for the rest of the afternoon. She combed her thick brown hair into place. Her last boyfriend, Carl, had always liked it when she wore her hair down. It had been over a month since they had spoken. She wondered if she should try to patch things up.

Suddenly a vision of Carl leaving a restaurant

with flatware in his pockets came to mind. She quickly dismissed the notion of calling him. Although she admired the fact that he was brilliant and spoke five languages, she didn't condone stealing, no matter what his idealistic excuse had been. Still, she had to admit to herself that she was tired of being alone.

She couldn't help conjuring up an image of her thesis advisor, Peter Bergen, and his brooding features. She liked the way he furrowed his brow when he was deep in thought; she could almost hear the strains of Bach that he played in his otherwise quiet office. A slow smile spread across her face as she remembered the time she had looked up from her notes to find him staring at her. When their eyes met, she was certain that her flaming red cheeks had betrayed her. She had quickly averted her gaze, focusing instead on the brown pencil holder on top of his desk.

He's married, Tara told herself firmly. It didn't matter what that smile meant. Peter had recently completed an award-winning biography on Miró; their mutual passion for this remarkable artist was the basis for her attraction. Her fascination with him was simply because she adored the depth and breadth of his knowledge. Despite her rationalizations, she felt like a schoolgirl in the throes of her first crush. *This is completely stupid.*

Sometimes, it amazed her that she'd actually gone back to school after years in a demanding investment banking job on Wall Street. The stress had been overwhelming, and she had grown weary of sixteen-hour days and the drama of the stock market. Though she'd made a small fortune, she'd had no time for anything. The move to Belloix, however drastic, had allowed her to change her entire lifestyle for the better. *Green grass is a good thing,* she thought with a laugh. *So is having time for friends and family.*

Stepping over to the full-length mirror, she assessed her outfit. She looked good, she thought. A large oval blue moonstone ring decorated her right index finger; it was a gift from her father. It suited her but, more important, he had brought it from India. That meant that he had thought of her despite being a continent away. Tara took one last look in the mirror. She liked seeing herself meticulously groomed.

The house was quiet, the silence familiar, Tara thought. When it was quiet around lunchtime, she often thought about her mother. She had always done such a great job, taking good care of her when she was growing up. Never once did she complain about her husband's demanding job, referring to him proudly as an "international journalist with pressing demands." If filling her daughter's world with enough love for two parents wasn't enough, she was a wonderful cook, a ruthless board game player, and an all-around caring person. When she wasn't taking care of their home, Candice had taken on charity projects such as helping out at the local battered women's shelter, raising money to stop child abuse, and heading up outreach programs for the elderly at their church. It was still hard to believe that this once stay-at-home mom had transformed into a nonprofit powerhouse these days.

As for her father, every one of his intermittent arrivals at their home in Washington, D.C., was like a holiday. Her mother seemed to come alive again during those visits. It was like experiencing a glorious heat wave after months of frost. Tara saw him as a mythic figure who came into their life to bring warmth and joy. They would all go to the movies, or spend an afternoon at the zoo, or go out for a fancy dinner.

Tara recalled the time her father had taken her and her mother on a trip to New York to celebrate her tenth birthday. It was a Friday morning. She got dressed for school, made her bed, and headed downstairs for breakfast. To her surprise, her parents were waiting for her by the front door with several suitcases. They plunged into an off-key rendition of "Happy Birthday." At first, she thought that they were playing some sort of joke on her. Fortunately, her father's enthusiasm for the unexpected took over, and he soon convinced her that they really were off on their first family adventure. They rode in a limousine to the airport, where a private plane was waiting.

They stayed at the Plaza Hotel, dined at La Tulipe and Elio's, and then they went to see the Broadway show *A Chorus Line*. Her father had arranged to have her picture taken with several of the show's stars after the performance.

The whirlwind of a weekend in New York ended, like most of his visits, just as quickly as it came. Tara always knew when he was about to leave because he presented her with a special gift such as a doll, a necklace, or sometimes even a book.

Books were her salvation. She was a voracious reader, even at a young age; she devoured Mark Twain's *Huckleberry Finn*, Jane Austen's *Pride and Prejudice*, and even books on history and art. It was not unusual for her to stay up all night reading, only to start a new book in the early hours of the morning. One night, when she was about thirteen years old, her father came into her room to find her engrossed in a book about Egypt.

"Tara, darling, what are you doing up so late?" he said, coming to sit on the edge of her bed. He smelled of cigar smoke, aftershave, and liquor.

"Reading," she replied, as if there were no better reason on earth to go without sleep. She flipped open a page to show him. "Isn't it interesting how the figures in this wall relief all look the same except for the pharaoh?"

Her father stared at her, his crystal blue eyes assessing her. He seemed surprised by her comment and inordinately pleased. "Yes, it is," he replied. "It wasn't until Roman times that artists started to depict people as individuals. I know of a fantastic book written by a friend of mine that will show you Roman portraiture."

"I'd like to see it sometime," she said cautiously.

"I'll remember to do that," he said, kissing her on the forehead. "You've got a fine mind, my girl. I'm delighted to see you doing so well in school."

"Thank you, Father," she said demurely.

A month later, the book on Roman portraiture arrived in a worn yellow envelope bearing a German postmark. On the front cover was a photograph of a marble bust of a large-nosed, aristocratic-looking man. With great care, Tara studied each page of the book. She was delighted to have finally found a way to capture her father's attention. Once she finished, she wrote him a long, detailed letter on how much she enjoyed the book, highlighting specific pieces of art that intrigued her.

Soon after that, he sent her another book on Joan Miró, whom he had just met in France. Her letter must have pleased him, she thought. The exchange sparked a new beginning in their relationship; he started sending her books from all over the world. In response, she wrote him long, colorful letters discussing both the intellectual merit of each book and her personal viewpoint on its subject. She and her father became pen pals of sorts. Tara finally felt validated.

The first few times that her father wrote to her,

her mother asked, "Did your father include a note for me?" When Tara searched the package and found nothing, she concluded that her father was probably going to correspond with her mother separately.

When she was sixteen, she was old enough to realize that her father's life as an international journalist suited him. He thrived on pursuing a story for a specific period of time before boredom could set in. Then he was ready to move forward to the next adventure, wherever it took place. He didn't like to be in one location for more than a month or two at a time. After that, he was ready to cover a fresh subject. Eventually, Tara came to accept that his visits would always be short and intense.

She looked over a photograph taken after the show that weekend in New York. It would always remind her of what it felt like to have a wonderful family experience. Why hadn't she taken more photographs on that trip?

The doorbell rang.

When she opened the door, she greeted Larry, the "postman with a personality," who always took the time to hand-deliver her mail.

"Afternoon, Tara," he said, his round cheeks forming a smile.

"Hi, Larry," she said, taking the bound package of materials. "Gosh, what a load!"

"I know," he said. "Check out these muscles." He lifted his skinny arms for effect.

"Amazing," Tara replied, shutting the door with a smile before he could engage her in further conversation. Flipping through the pile, she noticed a London postmark.

A letter from her father was always an unexpected treat; his correspondence was often filled with his views on current events or interesting information about a dignitary he had recently met. His last letter had indicated that he was heading to the English countryside to interview a member of the royal family who wanted to highlight his achievements in a documentary. She imagined the estate's lavish furnishings, paintings by the masters, and crystal chandeliers. Perhaps this letter was a continuation and would tell her about some unusual aspect of this aristocrat's daily life.

Her father had a gift for making celebrities seem more approachable in his stories by focusing on everyday activities that defined their character. When she was little, he had given her a copy of the book *What Did George Washington Eat for Breakfast?* This book, he explained, was his particular favorite because he felt it would help her understand what he did for a living. Even now, Tara remembered little details of Washington's life—how as a boy he had ruined his teeth by cracking walnuts in his mouth, and how when he lived at Mount Vernon, he rose at dawn and ate three "Indian hoecakes" along with tea at seven a.m. Ashley had asked her father what a hoecake was.

He had laughed and called it a glorified pancake made out of cornmeal.

Tara ripped open the envelope and pulled out a letter in her father's familiar scrawl. At the top of the page, the name *Lee* seemed to jump out and slap her in the face.

Dearest Lee,

I've been thinking about you and wondering how you're doing. I know you're angry with me, but you've got to realize that my travel schedule has always been extremely demanding. Some weeks I've woken up in a strange hotel room only to wonder what city I'm visiting. Please try to understand that my inability to focus on our relationship has no bearing on my feelings for you.

Having just returned from a week's worth of meetings with members of Parliament and various Labor Party leaders, I'm excited about the positive changes in domestic policy that are soon to take place. It's going to be very interesting to see when these reforms are announced, especially if they occur when it's time to elect the next prime minister. Right now, all things considered, I predict it's going to be a very close race. I'm going to wait and see which of these leaders follows through on their proposed legislation before I publicly endorse a candidate.

So here's my good news. The network has asked me to anchor a prime-time news and entertainment program featuring A-list celebrities, business leaders, and my friends on Capitol Hill. There's going to be a lot of hype about it in the coming weeks, so I wanted you to hear it from me first.

Hopefully, you'll reconsider your decision and I'll hear from you soon.

I miss you.

Kent

Confused by the salutation, Tara read the contents again, wondering why he was upset that Lee refused to have any contact with him. Why did he need to focus on their relationship? Some instinct told her that Lee was a woman; she just knew it. In the last paragraph, he also mentioned that he would be the host of a new television program that would receive much media attention. He had signed it simply, *Kent.*

How strange, thought Tara. Who was Lee? Clearly, the tone of the letter was more pleading than businesslike, so Tara suspected that the woman was not a colleague. Had her father been having an affair?

The letter seemed to sizzle in her hands. Tara began to pace back and forth in her living room, trying to calm her racing heart. He must have mistakenly put her address on this note. He was getting older, she thought; his seventieth birthday was less than a year away.

If her father was having a relationship with another woman, her mother would be devastated. After all, she had spent the last forty years waiting for him to come home. He seemed to come and go as if *they* were having an affair, not a marriage. While this way of living appeared to suit him, Tara had always sensed that her mother wanted more, but was afraid to demand it for fear of losing him. Despite their often strained relationship, she knew her mother would never dream of looking at another man.

She stared at the offending name at the top of the page. The letter was dated five days earlier. When she read his words again, it did seem as if he and "Lee" had had a falling out of sorts. That didn't seem so bad for her mother. Given his choice of words, however, it appeared that he wanted them to go back to their previous relationship, whatever that meant.

Tara sat down and tried to think rationally. She was paralyzed with indecision. It wasn't as if she could tell anyone, and she certainly couldn't phone her mother and ask her for help.

There were two things that she could do. The easiest path would be to dispose of the letter and pretend it had never arrived. She mulled over whether she would be able to forget what she had just read, but it seemed unlikely. Something wasn't right, and it was going to nag at her until she figured it out.

The most direct option would be to go to her father when he was back in Washington and tell him about his mistake. Tara felt a few beads of sweat forming on her brow at the prospect of confronting her father. But how else could she find out who Lee was?

CHAPTER 4

Libby

Gardening was her own private therapy; it forced her to stay in the present and focus on specific tasks that would enhance the beauty of her garden. She squinted hard, willing her eyes to see the details: the tiny yellow pods inside a tulip, the curling shape of a daffodil, the variations of color in each flower's petals. Reluctantly, she reached for the insufferable glasses that hung on a rainbow-colored cord around her neck. Despite the fact that they allowed her to behold the vibrant details of her red tulips and yellow daffodils her new bifocals were irritating, she decided.

Looking down at the soil under her polished finger-nails, she affirmed that there was something really satisfying about working with one's bare hands.

She loved being outdoors, feeling the warm sun on her back. She took out a clump of dandelions and then smoothed dirt over the hole. The earth felt cool to her touch.

At least my nose still works, she thought, breathing in the smell of hyacinth, which always signaled the beginning of spring. She grabbed her pruning scissors to cut several thick, white stems; she would put the blossoms on her bedside table. Then the weeding consumed her again. She removed another growth of ugly green sprouts from her burgeoning flower bed.

A large straw hat shielded her face from the afternoon sun. She had changed into baggy trousers, one of Ed's old shirts, and sneakers. She smiled, knowing that her former students would have adored the red flower on the back of her hat and, of course, Mrs. Marshall's dirty hands. She laughed aloud at how much she still enjoyed getting messy. The brown dirt looked good against her pale white skin.

Pausing for a moment to admire her handiwork, she surveyed her garden with a critical eye; it was pretty, she concluded, but it still needed a few more years to reach the abundant state that she sought to achieve. The sunroom's French doors opened up onto a rear terrace surrounded by four large oval plant beds soon to be filled with bright reds and yellows. A white picket fence separated the garden area from the neatly manicured back lawn.

They had installed a pond near the terrace's sitting area, filling it with big, fat goldfish that delighted her grandchildren. With the flick of a switch, a fountain embedded in the rocks sent water rippling down to the surface. The peaceful whirring sound of the water quieted her mind while she worked.

Ever since she had retired from teaching five years ago, Libby had indulged in gardening to improve the house's beauty, in cooking to make Ed happy, in yoga to nurture her spiritual self, and in scrapbooking to keep track of her family's activities. Next she planned to take a photography class so that she could generate more photos for her scrapbooks. She was lucky; they had saved enough money to allow her the freedom to do the things she enjoyed. She just wished Ed would slow down and savor life too, but he didn't want to give up his position as chief financial officer for an international insurance company.

Sweat trickled down between her shoulder blades. She paused to wipe her brow. After crouching for so long, she had to stretch for a moment. Judging by the angle of the sun, she calculated that she'd probably worked for more than two hours. Her lower back felt stiff. That was the usual indication that she'd done enough for one day. *Perhaps it's time to take a break,* she thought, wishing she could sustain another hour of work in order to start mulching. Remembering her hyacinth plants, she lifted them up by their stems, being careful not to disengage any of the tiny flowers. She inhaled deeply, enjoying their sublime aroma.

She removed her shoes and hat and then headed into her bright yellow sunroom to wash her hands in the bar area's sink. This was her favorite room in the house. Often, she curled up here with a good book or just enjoyed the view out onto her garden. The room was filled with things that she loved. Photographs of her three children and four grandchildren dominated the bookcases. Her eldest daughter, Caroline, was pictured first as a young ballerina, then in a Dalmatian costume, as a serious-minded college graduate, and as an elegant bride. Libby was so proud of the compassionate young woman they had raised. Caroline had married her high school sweetheart, Johnny Travers; there was a photo of the smiling couple posed by a one-story home they had built on a church mission trip.

She chose not to display any photographs from the year Caroline was in a car accident. It made Libby shiver just to think about how close they had come to losing her. When Caroline was seventeen, her friend Jennifer had been driving them home from a late play rehearsal when she'd hit a patch of ice. The car smashed into a tree, killing Jennifer. By some miracle, Caroline survived, sustaining injuries to her right leg and breaking her right foot. Libby recalled the months of painful medical procedures and subsequent physical therapy. Several operations helped repair Caroline's physical injuries, but the grief of losing her best friend was immeasurable.

Libby couldn't remember exactly how or when they'd come up with the idea of a scrapbook celebrating Jennifer's life. All she knew was that the project had revitalized both of them. For weeks, she'd sat by Caroline's bed, cutting and pasting pictures, talking about their memories. They also contacted Jennifer's other friends and asked each of them to make a special memory page to include in the book. Once Caroline was well, she gave the book to Jennifer's parents. Making that scrapbook was difficult, yet healing for mother and daughter. It also led to their shared passion for creating visual representations that captured life's most precious moments.

These days, Caroline and Johnny, an attorney, lived just minutes away with their two little girls. Sarah, Libby's eldest grandchild, was now nine years old and a steady, responsible child who loved to paint, play soccer, and write short stories. Often, Sarah helped Libby plant bulbs in the garden. A hot pink beaded frame held a picture of Sarah's seven-year-old sister Alexandra, wearing the flowered pinafore dress that Libby had given her and proudly displaying her violin.

Libby's middle child, Pamela, had been an accomplished gymnast and skater as a child, with an assortment of eye-catching leotards. She had performed in competitions all over the country before marrying Carl Roberts, a commercial photographer.

There was a gorgeous recent photograph of them at the beach with their daughters, eight-year-old Margaret and five-year-old Casey; the children were standing covered with sand, in front of a dinosaur sculpture.

Libby's photographs of her youngest, Robby, always made her smile. In one of them, he was dressed as an Indian for Colonial Day at his school. A photo of him wearing an orange wig caught her eye; he must have been off to cheer for his college football team. He was a charmer, she thought, gazing at his dark, curly locks and muscular frame. The phone used to ring nonstop with girls asking him out; the calls were still coming and they drove her and Ed crazy when he visited. Last time, she threatened to throw his cell phone away if he didn't turn it off during meals.

As her eyes swept the room, she took in the ceramic art made by her grandchildren, the abstract landscape painting over the white mantel, and the terra-cotta pots filled with fresh flowers. On weekday nights, she and Ed liked to eat dinner in here and then climb onto the overstuffed blue sofa and watch a television program. A large tufted ottoman doubled as a coffee table and requisite footrest.

Libby checked the time, thinking she needed to pick up a few things at the market before Ed came home. She wanted to try to make some spinach frittatas that she had heard were really good. He would certainly grumble at such healthful fare, making some comment such as "Looks good, Lib. But where's the meat?" She'd have to bribe him with a great bottle of wine and something sweet for dessert.

She walked to the kitchen to check her phone messages. The all-white room, with its high-tech stainless steel appliances, was spotless. Bright, colorful ceramic dishes adorned the tops of the cabinets, and an oversized purple orchid decorated the counter. She hoped her daffodils would be everywhere soon. Remembering Ashley, Libby thought it might be nice to bring her a bunch of flowers once they bloomed up. She recalled all too well what it was like to be a young mother. It was hard to believe that her baby was in his midthirties and still a bachelor.

Five messages were waiting for her. Two were from Ed. The third call was from her hair salon, reminding her of an appointment the next day. A fourth message was from a friend asking her to lunch. The fifth voice was that of her son, indicating that it was really important that she call him at home immediately. That seemed odd, given the time of his call. She phoned him back, hoping that she had been mistaken about the distress in his voice.

"Hey, kiddo, I just got your message. How are you?" she asked cautiously, idly toying with a pencil on her desk.

"Not good, Mom. I've got some bad news."

Libby's heart thudded in her chest. "Are you okay?" she said breathlessly.

"My company's gone belly-up and I've just lost my job," he said. His voice was flat. "My stock is now worthless."

Libby exhaled, relieved that his problem wasn't health related. "I don't understand. What happened? Whenever we asked about the company, you were always so optimistic."

"It's a long story. Too long for this phone call. It's been going on for months. I thought we could beat it, but the telecommunications industry has taken a nosedive and we've lost all investor confidence. It doesn't help that our CEO is being investigated."

"Robby, I know things look bleak right now, but you're a smart guy. You were at the top of your class in college and business school. You'll bounce back."

"It's not that easy, Mom. I'll be labeled a failure in the business world. Plus, I've got expenses, debts. My net worth is gone." His voice cracked.

"I know you're upset, but this situation is only temporary," she said hopefully, not knowing what else to say to comfort him. "I promise you we'll map out a plan and figure it out." She recalled offering him a brownie while she helped him through school problems. She wished this burden could be lightened as easily.

"I feel like such an idiot," he said. "I should have seen it coming."

"Son, you're not omnipotent, so stop blaming yourself. How about if I drive to Atlanta and we can have lunch tomorrow, maybe sort some things through?"

"No," he said forcefully. "I can handle it."

"Think about it. I really want to come anyway. You know your poor retired mother is always looking for something to do."

"Really, Mom, I'm okay. I just needed a shoulder to lean on."

"You know how much your father and I love you. You're a successful, intelligent man and we're so proud of you. I won't push, but just say the word and I'll be there." Libby had a feeling in the pit of her stomach that he was worse off than he sounded.

"Thanks. Bye," he said, abruptly hanging up the phone.

Knowing Robby wasn't accustomed to failure of any kind, she pondered what to do. He didn't seem to be taking things very well. She didn't want him to think she didn't believe in him. After all, she was his mother. She and Ed would need to hash it out; perhaps they could come up with something. Adult children's problems seemed so complex. How was she to help him without hurting his pride?

That night, after Ed had finished his meal and was enjoying a glass of red wine, she broke the news. She didn't want him to overreact to Robby's situation because she was trying to keep his stress levels under control; his high blood pressure worried her. Still, she hadn't expected his quiet acceptance of his son's problems, as if nothing were wrong at all.

"Lib, what are we supposed to do? Robby's a grown man. He's almost thirty-six years old, for God's sake. We raised him right. He'll figure it out."

"Ed," she said, "he may be thirty-six, but he'll always be my baby."

"You should stop coddling him," he chided her. "He's got a good head on his shoulders. He'll come to us when he's ready."

Libby didn't push the subject any further. She strongly disagreed; she had heard the anguish in her son's voice and knew how much his company's sudden financial crisis had affected him. But now was not the time to debate the topic. There was a reason children had two parents—she was the overprotective mother and Ed was the logical, pragmatic father. Somehow, she trusted, the two styles balanced each other out.

Libby made an elaborate presentation of her homemade chocolate mousse, which they heartily devoured. They turned to a safer topic: planning a family trip to their beach house. Libby enjoyed nothing more than being at the ocean with her grandchildren. The red wine dulled her anxiety while she and Ed talked, but she still ruminated on how to help Robby.

That evening, she got a call from the principal at

Radford Elementary, asking if she would be willing to substitute teach for a second-grade class the following day. Thinking Robby might call, she almost said no, but she figured that she could phone him on her break. In any event, classes ended at two-thirty, so she could still make the drive to Atlanta in the afternoon if necessary. Although only about sixty miles separated them, Libby was frustrated by her inability to get to Robby's house as quickly as she would have liked.

That night, Libby tossed and turned, worried about her son. She almost woke Ed, but decided to wait and call Robby in the morning. She and Robby were both early risers, so she felt comfortable about phoning him around six thirty. There was no answer, so she left a message.

School turned out to be a welcome diversion. There was nothing like the sound of a second-grade chorus saying, "Good morning, Mrs. Marshall," to start her day off right. She plunged into the daily routine, starting with math and then moving on to reading. When the lunch break came at eleven o'clock, she called Robby. Again there was no answer. She left a second message.

The day wore on. Libby diligently helped the children make ceremonial masks out of paper bags; they were part of their study on Africa. She read them a story called *The Jade Stone*, about a master carver named Chan Lo who was summoned by the Chinese emperor to carve a dragon out of a magnificent piece of jade. The trouble was that the carver wanted the jade to tell him what it wanted to be. The story reminded her of Robby, who as a child had always had a deep love of the English language and was a wonderful writer. But instead of becoming a novelist or a professor as Libby had hoped, he'd followed a high-intensity career path to make a lot of money.

At two fifteen, she helped the children pack up their cursive homework in order to head home. It felt so good to be back in a classroom again. She had loved every minute of her teaching career; she wondered if she had made a mistake in retiring.

On her way home from school, she happened to catch the hourly news. There was a report on the recent collapse of Robby's company, the telecommunications giant Amvale, due to fraudulent accounting practices. Apparently, all of senior management was under fire and the stock had just plummeted by ninety-eight percent.

Oh my God, she thought, her hand shaking as she turned up the dial. Robby was not dishonest; he would never be involved in unethical business practices. Libby punched her speed dial to Ed's office.

"I just heard a report on the radio about Amvale. The company held a press conference this morning and admitted to overstating its profits," she said. "I think Robby's in over his head. He needs a lawyer."

"I know, Lib. I tried to reach you earlier and left two messages. You were right. This is a big mess. I didn't realize . . ."

"What can we do?"

"I'll call Adam Chandler and see what he has to say. I'm hoping Robby was unaware of what was happening. It could complicate things."

"And if he knew—what then?"

"Lib, let's take this one step at a time. Have you spoken with him today?"

"No. I've left several messages."

"Me, too. I tried to reach him at his office this morning, but his secretary said he wasn't there."

"Something's wrong, Ed. I've got a bad feeling about this situation. I think I'll run by the house, pack an overnight bag, and head to Robby's place."

"What if he's not there? He hasn't returned our calls."

"Where else would he be? I just spoke with him yesterday. I'm worried about him. I'm going to go anyway and if he's not there, I can stay at a hotel."

"Well . . ." He paused a moment. "Actually, I do think you should go. It's worse than I thought, for a company like Amvale to admit publicly that they've been cooking their books. Maybe I didn't want to realize it. . . ."

"Ed, if I get on the highway by three thirty, I'll be at his house around five depending on the traffic. Should we call Caroline and Pamela?"

"We can do that later on. Call me when you get

there. I've got two meetings this afternoon that I need to attend. After that, I'll see where we are. Okay?"

"Call me on my cell phone and tell me what the attorney says."

"Certainly. We'll work it out and find some sort of solution. Try not to worry too much, Lib."

Libby couldn't control her watery eyes. "Thanks," she said quietly.

It was one of the things she loved about Ed; he took charge in difficult situations. She was certain that he would have an excellent lawyer standing by if Robby hadn't found one already. He would remain logical and practical no matter what happened; she could always count on him.

Libby left a message on Robby's machine that she was on her way. Her hands tightened on the steering wheel as she imagined all sorts of unpleasant scenarios. She wondered about the girl he had been seeing. Her name was Duney or Dunnie or something like that; one night, while they were alone eating dinner, Ed had mistakenly referred to her as "Dummy," and it had sent them into peals of laughter. The girl was tall, blond, and pretty, what they used to call "arm candy." There didn't seem to be much of a future there; Libby was certain that she'd be gone at the first sign of trouble.

Her thoughts turned to Robby's last visit home at Christmastime. He'd appeared uneasy. The signs of stress must have been there, but in the excitement of their family reunion, she had failed to see them. And she was still a bit irritated with him after the way he had behaved on Christmas Day.

She took pride in the fact that her home always looked so beautiful around the holidays. She began decorating on the first of December, cutting magnolia leaves from the garden and arranging the branches in urns to be set on the living room mantel. Large pots of paper whites added their perfume to every room. She usually worked on the downstairs rooms before she and Ed put up the tree together that Saturday. She adored pulling out their decorations, filling each room with things like Caroline's white ceramic snow angel, the drawings of Santa that Pamela had made in second grade, gold balls and ribbon woven into branches of evergreen, the beautiful terra-cotta crèche they had found in France, large stuffed bears with Santa hats, nutcracker figures, candy-striped candlesticks, and pots and pots of poinsettia plants.

She had wanted everything to be perfect for their annual Christmas Eve dinner. Weeks of preparation went into planning, shopping, and cooking. The menu didn't vary much from year to year. She enjoyed making everyone's favorite dishes: roast beef, turkey, potatoes au gratin, and creamed spinach. The little girls were happy as long as they could have chocolate cake for dessert. This year, Pamela and Carl had called a few days earlier and said that they would be coming in for Christmas Eve dinner and the next morning's celebration.

That night, the girls put out cookies for Santa, sprinkled a package of "reindeer dust" (their teachers' term for reindeer food) on the front lawn, munched on too many sweets, and sang for the family. As they all gathered around a fire in the living room, Sarah read "The Night Before Christmas." Afterward, Casey and Margaret stood up and sang a beautiful version of "Silent Night;" their sweet little-girl voices nearly bringing everyone in the room to tears of joy, except Robby, who looked like he wasn't even listening. Libby watched him that night, wondering why he seemed so preoccupied; he was drinking more than usual. He didn't seem interested in the celebration and slipped out several times to take calls on his cell phone before eventually leaving to meet up with his friends. She thought that perhaps he was feeling acutely conscious of his single status.

On Christmas morning, the grandchildren took turns trying to wake up Uncle Robby, but it was impossible; he had been out late the night before and no amount of cajoling was going to make him get out of bed. Finally, he yelled at the girls, telling them to get out. Poor Sarah was really upset, and Caroline had spent a good while drying her tears. Libby and Ed were furious that he had chosen a family holiday to go drinking with his friends; it just wasn't like him.

He finally emerged from his room around three o'clock that afternoon, after his sisters and their families had gone back to their own homes. It took all of Libby's self-control not to snap at him for his bad behavior to his nieces. She busied herself wiping the kitchen counters and removing the leftovers from the refrigerator. She set a place at the breakfast table for him.

"Long night, huh?" she remarked, handing him a cup of steaming coffee.

"I'm in the doghouse, aren't I?" He looked up sheepishly. His large brown eyes and handsome face always disarmed her.

"You got it. I told the little girls that you had the flu. Your sisters were not convinced. Pamela was so mad that she wanted to dump a pitcher of cold water on your head. You're lucky your father stopped her."

"Ouch," he said. He pointed to his cup. "This is great coffee, Mom."

She looked at him sternly. "You know I can't tell you how to live your life, but your father and I would have appreciated it if you had made an appearance this morning."

"Sorry, Mom. I've got some things on my mind. Work's been so stressful that I guess I just needed to cut loose for a night with my old friends. Will you forgive me?" He got up and came around the table to give her a peck on the cheek. She softened.

"Whew! Honey, you smell like a distillery!" She eyed him warily. "Want some aspirin?"

78

"Sure," he said. "I think a shower would help, too."

"And a shave," she replied, rubbing his cheek.

To his credit, Robby was his old self that night at dinner. He regaled them with stories about his recent trip to St. Bart's, naming all of the celebrities he had met while staying on a friend's private yacht. It sounded as if Robby had grown accustomed to socializing with the world's rich and famous. Certainly, Libby knew how charming he could be, so it came as no surprise that he had gained access to such exclusive circles. He could make people laugh in any situation; he could talk about something as mundane as a trip to the grocery store and make it sound like an adventure.

The rest of the evening included the exchange of gifts and a light supper by the fire. Ed and Robby played a game of backgammon. Next morning, Robby headed out early after a quick breakfast. Once the house was empty, Libby kept busy.

Now in the car heading to Atlanta, Libby unconsciously pressed the accelerator harder. By her calculations, she had another hour left if she hit no traffic. She flipped on some music to try to keep her mind from wandering. Gradually, she began to feel a little less anxious. After all, Robby was too levelheaded to get mixed up with unscrupulous businesspeople. If he had known there was a problem, Libby was sure he would have resigned or alerted the authorities.

She looked down at the beautiful gold bracelet she wore; it had been a Christmas gift from Robby and was no doubt expensive. He had given Ed a new set of golf clubs. His selections had been really extravagant. It was clear that he was accustomed to spending money these days. After all, he drove an expensive German convertible that his nieces liked to call his "James Bond car." He was always impeccably groomed. His shirts were custom made, as were his suits. Libby remembered talking with him one day at the office when his tailor was there measuring him. She remembered thinking that a personal tailor who made office calls was a pretty lavish expense. She hadn't said anything at the time because she believed that it was none of her business.

When she turned the corner to the fancy neighborhood where Robby lived, the stately Georgian homes and the plethora of BMWs made her agitated all over again. She hoped that Robby had managed to save some of his assets. If he had, in fact, lost all his personal wealth, then he was in for a rude awakening.

Turning her car into the winding driveway, she noticed a nondescript blue sedan parked there. A young man wearing a suit got out of the car and seemed to be inspecting her. When she saw his serious expression, Libby was seized with anxiety. She prayed that Robby was all right. She immediately pulled her car to a halt.

"Hello," she said nervously. "I'm Libby Marshall, Robby's mother. Who are you?" she asked, trying to keep her voice calm.

"I'm Agent Tom Hudgins, ma'am."

Libby felt light-headed for a moment. She'd never had much contact with law enforcement officials. "I just came to see my son. Is everything all right?"

"Why don't you come with me," he suggested.

CHAPTER 5

Ashley

After the luncheon at Tara's house, Ashley was motivated to check out the small room off the kitchen to see if it could be used as a possible workstation. When she surveyed their assortment of household junk, she was overwhelmed by the amount of clutter. There were stacks of boxes, odd chairs, an old table, mismatched lamps, and peeling grayish paint on the walls. This area had seemed too small for everyday use, so she had shoved storage items in here and simply closed the door on the mess.

Looking at the two windows on either side of the room, she realized that the long, outdated curtains could be what made the space look so dark and dreary. Climbing over boxes, she moved one of the panels aside to reveal a nice view of the back lawn. Deciding that this neglected space had possibilities, she grabbed a chair to stand on and yanked down the offending fabric. Suddenly filled with enthusiasm, she envisioned a desk area with bookshelves, perhaps a small sofa for reading, and a side chair. It was time to stake her claim, she thought.

She really didn't have any personal space in the house. She craved a bit of peace and quiet each day, or, more accurately, a place to retreat and get organized. If she was ever going to have time to do anything besides taking care of the children, she would need to have her household in better order. Scrapbooking intrigued her, and she had really liked the women she met yesterday, especially Tara. But the thought of having any one of those women visit her home in its current state made her cringe. Perhaps this room was a place to start.

"Hi, Mom. What are you doing in here?" asked Tucker, eyeing her curiously.

"I was thinking of clearing it out to make this my new office. Do you think maybe you could help me lift some of these boxes?"

"Sure, I'll help you."

"Thanks. Is your homework done?"

"Yes, I finished everything except one sheet that's not due for another few days. Don't you think it's a little late to be starting this now?" He pointed to the clock. "When's Dad coming home?"

"He's got a meeting tonight. He won't be in until later on." She took down several pictures and placed them in a stack on the floor. "I don't know why I save everything. These things are just plain ugly." She laughed as she pointed to a painting of some large sunflowers.

"You're in such a good mood. I mean, you've been smiling all afternoon."

"Really?" she replied. "Is that so unusual?" She watched his expression and said, "Wait, don't answer that."

They worked in relative silence, moving boxes out to the garage. In just a little over two hours, Ashley was amazed at what she had accomplished.

"This is a really great space," she said with excitement, her head filling with ideas. "I could paint the room pale blue, have some carpeting installed, and maybe even add some lighting. We can put in shelves up here so I can get the piles off my desk." She saw him yawn. His eyes glazed over. "Okay, I see you've had enough. Let's get you to bed. You've been a terrific help."

"Does that mean you're still going to play tennis with me on Saturday?"

Ashley thought of Steve's remark about her fitness level and felt herself shrink inwardly. She was worried that she would be winded too quickly. "I might not be too good at first, okay?" she asked.

"So you'll do it?"

"Yes, I'm going to try. I've just got to start, right?

I'll buy some new tennis stuff tomorrow and check to see if the tennis club will lend me a racquet. Anyway, I say we go for it."

"All right, Mom!" he said, giving her a high five.

Feeling energized, she sat down on the floor to go through a box of old photographs. Each one that she pulled out was like a small treasure. She started separating them into piles, one for each of her children. There were huge gaps in time between the events recorded in the snapshots. She sorted them out, surprised by how much the kids had changed, and how quickly. *I really haven't been paying enough attention,* she thought, rubbing her aching back as the hours passed.

She pulled out a fairly recent photograph of her parents that looked like an advertisement for an upscale clothing company. Her father wore a navy blazer and a crisp white shirt. His slightly gray hair, horn-rimmed glasses, and high forehead gave him an intellectual air. Her mother was immaculately groomed, as always. She looked dignified in her blue silk dress and high heels. Her thick blond hair brushed her shoulders, making her look years younger. When she visited, many people thought she was Ashley's older sister.

As she continued to gaze at the photograph, it was hard not to become emotional. Certainly the two of them made a handsome couple, but as parents they had been dismal failures. They weren't bad people, she allowed, it was just that neither one of them was cut out to be a parent. Her mother believed that looking good was a way of life. It was exhausting to listen to her drone on about the merits of plastic surgery, hair dye, and skin care products.

Since Sally's birth, her mother had been highly critical of Ashley's appearance. She was still furious over their quarrel the other day. Her comments had hurt Ashley deeply, and she'd decided not to speak to her for a long while. Though she might not look her best anymore, she was proud of her happy kids. She deserved more respect, she thought. She worked hard, trying to sustain a normal family life without support from her parents or her emotionally unavailable husband. Some days, it seemed impossible.

As for her self-absorbed father, she was tired of listening to his excuses as to why he couldn't be present at important family events. His career always came first. Ashley was certain that if she ever quizzed him on what each of his grandchildren was doing, he wouldn't be able to respond.

She was sick of both of them. The last time they visited together, it had made her so uncomfortable that she felt physically ill for two days beforehand. She worried about everything: what meals to serve, whether one of her children would spill something on her mother's expensive silk clothes, how her parents would handle it if the boys started to rough-house. As for her father, he spoke to Tucker and Cameron as if they were forty years old, and with the assumption that they understood politics and world affairs. One time, she had asked him to go shoot hoops with the boys. He had looked completely horrified.

Ashley looked at their picture one last time and then put it back in the box. Perhaps she would add photographs of her parents to the children's scrapbooks later.

Standing up to stretch, she was tired, but it felt good to see a slight degree of order around her. Steve still wasn't home; she wondered if she should worry, but then figured that he was probably talking about a business deal and had lost track of time. As she crawled into bed that night, Ashley pondered the luncheon, thinking about Tara. Though their lives were completely different, she'd felt a connection to Tara, and was looking forward to their lunch date.

On Saturday morning, Ashley ate a healthy breakfast of yogurt and granola to give her more energy. Thanks to his midnight arrival home, Steve practically drained his coffee cup in a matter of minutes. When he sat down at the breakfast table, he glared at Sally when she squealed in delight over something Janie had said. He gave Ashley a strange look during the meal, but refrained from comment. It was almost a letdown that he hadn't made a snide remark. Ashley had spent a block of time planning her defense for this round; she wasn't going to allow him to make her feel bad again.

After breakfast, Steve announced that he would be playing golf with his friends all day. That came as no surprise. She wondered if he ever considered asking her or the kids to do something with him on a weekend; for her part, she refused to initiate anything or even point out the fact that they rarely had fun together anymore. She got up from the table without another word.

Once in her bedroom, she pulled the tags off a white Lycra sleeveless top and a tennis skirt; she had known without even trying it on that her old workout gear from years ago would no longer fit properly. Her new sneakers could easily be used for cross-training, Ashley thought. Steve would most definitely give her a heated lecture on unnecessary spending when the credit card bills arrived. She could hear her own voice two weeks from now when she justified the expense, explaining that the tennis club had a strict dress code. At least, she thought, the code required that players wear half white as opposed to all white. The black skirt would minimize her rear end, or so she hoped. Ashley prayed that she would look presentable.

Checking her appearance in the mirror, Ashley tried not to be too hard on herself. Her eyes went right to her thighs and thick arms. She might not have the nerve to appear in public in such scanty attire. She'd spent the last few years hiding her body in sweatpants and now she felt like an overweight turtle without a shell. *Breathe,* she told herself. *I can do this,* she thought, putting on a black zip-up jacket and pulling her hair back in a ponytail.

Ashley held her breath as she walked into the kitchen to stand before her family in workout clothes. If anyone made a joke, she swore she'd run upstairs and immediately jump into her bed for the rest of the day.

"You look great, Mom," said Tucker. "Let's go."

Ashley was so overcome with relief that she was on the verge of tears. She refrained from sending her husband a challenging stare. "Thanks, kid," she said. "Now I want to see my star athlete show me what he's capable of."

"Mama," called Janie. "When are you going to be home? I want to be with you, too."

"Me, too," whined Sally, running over to grab her legs.

"I'll handle this," announced Cameron, bending down to pick up Sally. He began singing Sally's favorite song when she refused to move. Ashley was so proud of Cameron's sudden leadership that she was practically speechless.

"Maybe we don't even need a babysitter around here!" Ashley remarked proudly, reaching over to give her second son a loving pat on the head.

"Good, that'll save me some money," remarked Steve, missing the point as usual.

Moments later, the babysitter arrived to take over. Ashley gave Sally a big kiss and bribed her with a promise of a late-afternoon ice cream cone for good behavior. She thanked Cameron for his help and promised to spend some time with Janie later. Refusing to even look at Steve, she headed out the door.

"Have fun. Let me know how she does," added Steve as he waved them off.

Ashley wasn't sure what he meant by that comment. She decided not to say anything. She kept telling herself that helping her son was more important than her vanity.

Ten minutes later, they arrived at the bustling tennis courts. Adjoining the courts was a shop and snack bar with a lounge area. Several tables overlooked four indoor courts. Ashley debated how she was going to feel in front of the spectators in the window. A group of young children were seated at one table playing a game of Monopoly; she assumed their parents were hitting in front of them. Loud popping noises blasted from a television anchored just below the ceiling. Ashley looked up at it, recognizing one of Sally's favorite cartoon programs.

Four sweaty women with racquets in hand stood in a circle by the snack bar, chatting and drinking water. One young woman in a flattering tennis dress with a racer back waved to her. Ashley recognized her face but couldn't place her.

"Ashley," she called. "What are you doing here?"

Ashley wanted to disappear. Was the woman implying that she looked too fat and out of shape for the tennis court? Perhaps she was being too sensitive. She reluctantly waved back to her. "Hi," she said weakly. Turning to Tucker, she asked, "Don't we need balls?"

"I'll get some new ones."

The woman walked over to where she stood. "Hi, Ashley. Remember me? I'm Kate Gibbons. Our daughters are in the same class."

"Oh yes, Kate," Ashley replied, trying to assume a confident tone. "Nice to see you again. Did you have a good match?"

"It was fun," she replied. "Especially since we won."

Ashley gave her a smile even though she had long forgotten what it felt like to win or lose at anything. As Kate walked away, Ashley turned her attention to borrowing a new high-tech metal racquet from the tennis shop. Given the number of choices, she asked the assistant to select one for her because she hadn't played in so long. Afterward, they headed out to Court B, where she could begin her public humiliation.

She played with her grip, twirling and moving the steel in her hands. This racquet was a far cry from the old wooden racquets that she had used as a kid.

"Let's go," she said.

It took a moment to adjust to the lighting, the smell, and the feel of the courts. Several of her first shots bounced up too high. The borrowed racquet and new outfit felt strange. After struggling for the first ten minutes, she went back to the baseline to hit some ground strokes. Suddenly, she felt a jolt of familiarity. She drew her racquet back, released her swing, and hit a powerful right hook into the corner at Tucker's baseline. She didn't know which of them looked more shocked.

"Mom!" he cried. "Great shot!"

His compliment spurred her on as she moved about the court. All too quickly, her breath came in short gasps and she began to sweat furiously. Loath to let Tucker down, she moved up to the net and worked on her volleys. Her play was erratic after so many years, but something was happening. In the last twenty minutes, she hadn't thought of anything but whacking that yellow ball. It was cathartic.

Suddenly, she pictured Steve laughing at her. In one swift motion, she heard the pop of the ball as it connected, sending Tucker flying to the left to get it.

"Nice angle," he said.

She was able to hold her own for another ten minutes before signaling to him that she needed water. Tucker didn't say one word about the sweat pouring from her body or her heavy breathing. She wondered how he would feel if his peers were watching; they would surely make fun of her. Mercifully, he didn't even comment on how she was moving a bit funny. Stretching before attempting a sport she hadn't played in fifteen years would have been a smarter way to begin.

"You could be really good again if you started practicing. Look at what you just did."

"You think so?" she replied.

"I mean it. You've got a wicked forehand," Tucker said.

"I actually felt pretty good out there," she said. Mostly, she wished she were in better shape. "But this isn't about me, right? Let me see you practice your serve."

The next hour flew by as they played. Reluctantly, Ashley finally left the court with her son. Tucker asked if they could do it again the following weekend, and she agreed. This would make his siblings jealous, she brooded. She would have to figure out how to get some private time with each of them. The kids needed more from her because Steve seemed to be completely absorbed these days in his career and his golf game; she would have to address the situation soon.

After lunch, Ashley decided to put the kids to work. She made a trip to the paint store, where she purchased several rollers and equipment to paint "Mommy's new office." She picked a shade of aqua, hoping that would help make the room bright and cheerful.

Sally was beside herself with joy. "I get to paint, Mama!" she said, clapping her hands.

"Only where I say," warned Ashley. "We're not going to start right away. First, I need Tucker and Cameron to help me move the tables and lamps into the garage. Janie, you can be in charge of the masking tape so we don't get paint all over the baseboards."

She rounded everyone up. "Okay, team, we're not going to finish today, but maybe we can get one of the walls painted with the new color."

The kids jumped into the painting project with zeal. They taped the baseboards of the small room, put an old sheet on the floor, and began to scrape the old paint off the windowsills. Several hours passed as they worked diligently. Ashley was so pleased with her kids.

When a third of the wall had been painted, Ashley announced it was time to assess the color. They all gathered around, shouting their approval. For the next hour, things ran fairly smoothly until Janie and Cameron started fighting about who was doing a better job. Paint splattered from their rollers and Ashley had to call a halt to the project. Still, the half-painted wall showed promise. Ashley helped the children clean up in the downstairs sink and sent them off to relax. She shut the door, hoping to eventually surprise Steve when the project was complete.

CHAPTER 6

Tara

Around three a.m., Tara awoke feeling as if someone had poured a gallon of coffee into her system. Her heart was racing as she contemplated how to approach her father. Flipping the switch on her bedside lamp, she flinched as her eyes adjusted to the light. She cursed the letter that hinted at a secret. If only her father had included the infamous Lee's last name, she thought, staring morosely out of her bedroom window. She imagined herself in the role of a private investigator, checking out what this particular female might possess in looks or intellect that would attract the consummate adventure seeker Kent West. Her father had always seemed distant; the letter was a poignant reminder of how little she really knew him.

Tara got up to retrieve her tote bag full of her latest research. She decided to use her time constructively by reading and collecting ideas for the next chapter. At least that way her meeting this morning with Peter would be more productive.

Their twice-weekly meetings in his office were becoming increasingly uncomfortable as she struggled to remain distanced from her feelings. Few men had ever challenged her intellect. Just last week, the soothing baritone of Peter's voice had wrapped a spell around her as he described Miró's move from Paris right before the outbreak of World War II. She could almost see Miró's color paper blocks wrapped in a canvas as he and his family fled from the German invasion. Although it was a breezy Tuesday afternoon, Tara had felt hot, almost breathless as she listened to him tell the story. A lively discussion followed as they debated what had brought Miró to the height of his brilliance during wartime.

Once in Peter's tiny space, she didn't hear the chatter of the students outside, or the bells, or the notes of a symphony humming in the background. Even the squeaking of his worn leather chair didn't intrude. Somehow, her thesis meetings had become more exciting than a Saturday-night date. Even as she drifted off to sleep, she was soothed by recalling the sound of Peter's voice.

An ice-cold gulp of caffeine helped clear her head the next morning. Diet soda was the greatest invention on the planet, she decided. She peered at her reflection in the driver-side mirror. Her new black shirt was certainly not a sign that she was trying to impress anyone, right?

She watched Peter as he jotted down notes on a yellow legal pad. While standing in the doorway, she was able to get a good view of his clean-lined profile offset by the scraggly long hair covering the top of his collared shirt. His hand rested on his chin as he stared out the window. The image of Rodin's *The Thinker* popped into her mind. She remained still, unwilling to interrupt. Suddenly, he must have sensed her presence because he shifted his gaze and smiled warmly at her.

"Good morning, Tara," he said. "You caught me," he added, standing up to greet her.

"Caught you?" she said, stepping into the office. With its tall dark bookcases, masses of books, and soft music, it reminded her of a cocoon. Several framed posters of Miró's work lined the walls.

"I was completely uninspired until you walked in," he said, his gaze roaming over her. "I've been trying to come up with a witty opening remark for a talk I'm giving next week. I'm afraid I'm not very creative until I see you."

Tara silently took pleasure in the compliment. She playfully waved her plastic cup in the air, then placed it in her usual spot on the front edge of his desk. "I've told you that diet soda works wonders. You should try it."

"Are you trying to corrupt me?" he said with a wicked grin.

"Of course not," she replied. "I can certainly see the merits of that awful-tasting protein drink you swear by." She put down her bag and reached for her notebook filled with questions.

Suddenly, he grabbed her drink and took a sip. "Not bad," he said, sitting back down. "I had a dream about you last night. You were sitting on the sand beside me looking out at the water. I can still see your hair blowing in the wind. It was lovely."

Tara hid her surprise by fumbling around in her tote bag. She reached for a pen before meeting his gaze. Sighing heavily, she rummaged through her bag again.

"You seem distracted this morning. Is everything okay?" asked Peter.

"Fine," she answered quickly, wishing she could tell him that he was part of her problem.

"You're not very convincing," he said softly.

"Well," she said, "I'm having a bit of a family issue that concerns my parents. That's all." When he didn't say anything, she added, "It's hard, you know."

"I understand," he said. "I'm a good listener if you need me."

Tara wanted desperately to talk with him about the letter, but it didn't feel right. Who was she to discuss her fear that her father was having an affair, she scolded herself, when she secretly wished for a relationship with the man seated across from her? *How ironic,* she thought. "Thanks for your help. I need to speak directly with my father about some things. He'll be in Washington, D.C., next week so I'll probably go there."

"Funny you should mention D.C." His intense brown eyes watched her. "I'm also traveling there next week to give a talk on my book at the National Gallery."

"I don't think I've heard you speak since that night at the Belloix Museum of Fine Arts."

He laughed. "That was years ago. I must not be as interesting a speaker as I thought I was."

Tara noticed the boyish sparkle in his eyes. "Oh no," she said nervously. "You know I didn't mean it that way."

"Perhaps you'll need to come listen to my talk to convince me of your sincerity." He leaned forward in his seat, his stare all-consuming.

"Perhaps," she said boldly, meeting his gaze. "Who knows? Maybe I'll learn something new."

"Experience is life's ultimate teacher," he said.

"How profound," said Tara. "Can I quote you on that?"

"Sure," he said with a grin. "I told you that you inspire me. I can use that line somewhere in my talk." He jotted down his quote on a piece of paper and underlined it. "It's good to know that I have such a brilliant and beautiful student. Now," he said. "Let's discuss form and movement. Shall we? What were your latest questions?"

For the next hour, they talked about various pieces of art as Tara asked him for explanations on certain fine points of her analysis. As she stood up to leave, she thanked him for his time, suddenly feeling a bit shy and awkward. Her cheeks were burning. "Good luck with your talk," she said.

"I'm looking forward to it. A change of scenery is always good. Belloix can sometimes feel too small. Sometimes it's nice to be in a larger city where one can feel anonymous."

"Right," she agreed. Tara busied herself with putting away a pen. He was so near that she could almost smell his clean male skin.

He reached over and brushed a strand of her hair back into place. She thought she might faint. As soon as she shut the door to his office, Tara froze for an instant. Confusion was foreign to her analytical mind. She made her way down the long hallway filled with several abstract paintings done by graduate students. When she turned the corner, she collided with a dark-haired kid who nearly knocked her down.

"Hey, watch where you're going," he snapped, rushing off.

Tara was too dazed to reply. She really shouldn't see him in Washington, she told herself. She should just make up some excuse and forget the subtle invitation. Her attraction to him was interfering with her work, she concluded. He was unavailable, and anyway, a relationship would make her life much too complicated.

I don't trust myself right now, she decided. Too overwrought to head to the library for a day of research, she headed for her car. She wondered which of her friends would be home this morning. Advice from someone older and wiser would be most welcome. The idea of talking with Libby occurred to her, but she quickly discarded her as a confidante; she was nervous about revealing something this intimate to her. She was closer to Megan, and a good dose of guilt from a happily married friend with kids would stop her from entertaining ideas about a relationship with Peter.

Moments later, she'd phoned Megan and promptly invited herself over for a late-morning cup of coffee. *That's just what I need,* Tara thought, *another jolt of caffeine to jangle my nerves even more.*

Tara couldn't contain her shock. Megan's new pink-and-green flowered wallpaper assaulted her senses; she felt as if she were inside a dollhouse.

"What do you think?" Megan asked, handing her a cup of coffee.

"It's . . ." Tara paused. "Happy looking," Tara concluded with a smile. "Like you." Tara admired Megan's slim form in low-rise blue jeans and a simple turquoise beaded top. Her wavy locks were pushed back behind her ears, making her look like a teen mother.

"I can tell you hate it." Megan laughed amiably. "And no, I won't hold it against you. My opinionated seventh-grader has let me know that it's way too pink; fortunately, Hannah agrees with me and I think it's fun. This kitchen was so dark and dreary before. I guess I went for the other extreme."

"It's colorful," Tara said. "And you're wrong. I

don't hate it." Color was indeed a form of self-expression, she thought. "So, things are well?" she asked politely.

"We're all doing well, but the kids have already started looking forward to summer vacation. Phil and I are finally planning a getaway weekend two months from now. Can you believe it takes that long to line up a sitter and pick a date? What a novelty—time alone with my husband. Anyway, the kids are doing great in school. But I know you're not here to talk about Mike and Hannah."

"I always love coming to visit," said Tara, taking another sip of her coffee.

"Idle conversation is not your specialty. You've definitely got something on your mind, so spill it. Besides, if you tap that table any harder, you're going to wear a hole in it."

"Oh," said Tara, quickly placing her hands in her lap. "Okay, I'm trying to decide whether to go away for a few days with Peter Bergen."

"I was hoping you'd meet someone else and get over your crush on him," said Megan. "Well, I must say, he's pretty sexy. I haven't read his book, but his picture on the jacket is hot."

"Megan!" Tara exclaimed. "Stop it! You're supposed to be talking me out of this." She stared out at the swing set in the backyard. "Maybe it's just intellectual lust, but I can't seem to disconnect. He's so much more sophisticated and interesting than anyone I've ever met."

"So it's a meeting of the minds? Sorry, honey, there's also pure sex appeal and he's got it."

"I can see I came to the right person," muttered Tara, placing her face in her hands. "You're a real help."

"Aha! I knew it. You want me to give you the whole lecture on love and the sanctity of marriage."

"Yes, that's what you're supposed to be doing. I'm really crazy about this guy. I'm thinking of going to D.C., where he's speaking, so that we can spend some time together. I really want to go, but part of me thinks I'm a fool for falling for someone who's unavailable. I'm so confused."

"Honey, it's your decision, not mine. I do know there are a lot of great guys out there who are single, but of course that doesn't solve your problem."

"I've never felt this way about anyone. He's funny, charming, and passionate about his work."

"Fun and commitment are two different things. Are you really going to be happy playing second to his wife? You can't just forget she exists."

"He once told me that he and Rosalyn didn't speak the same language. I don't mean to sound flippant, but I sense he's not happy in his marriage. It's weird. It's kind of like I've always known him. We think the same way. I can't describe it any better than that."

"No one says anything has to happen if you go. You might find him utterly boring outside the lecture hall."

"Don't you think that's a little unrealistic? He's very attractive."

"All right," said Megan, holding up her arms in mock surrender. "I don't know what to tell you. That's your choice. Sex is only one part of a relationship." She thought for a moment. "But I do know you've never been one to act on impulse, so there must be something there for you to consider sleeping with your mentor."

"All my life, I've been logical and practical. But now, it's like I can't control these feelings anymore. I want to go and see where this leads."

"Then go," said Megan. "But realize that you could be setting yourself up for a very precarious future. Can you handle that?"

"Maybe I need a little chaos in my life," said Tara. She looked at her friend. "Thanks for not judging me."

"I don't want you to think that I approve, because I don't," Megan stated firmly. "You don't need to settle."

"I'll take things slow. Who knows? You could be right and I could find him uninspiring."

"I hope so," said Megan, "for your sake."

Once she returned home, Tara called her father's personal assistant, Roberta Langstrom, who knew more about her father's whereabouts than she did. Tara rolled her eyes heavenward at the oddity of having to make an appointment to see her own father. In a businesslike voice, she told Roberta that she planned to be in town next Friday and wanted to schedule a time to get together. "Tell him that it's important," she added.

"I'll see what I can do, but I can't promise anything," said Roberta in her stuffy British accent.

"How kind of you," responded Tara dryly, trying to keep the sarcasm from her voice.

Misinterpreting her statement, Roberta warmed. "Don't worry, Tara. I'll help figure something out. Maybe I can have you come to the station to squeeze in a coffee or something."

Tara reined in her temper. She was tired of standing in line just to have a tiny part of her father's busy life. It occurred to her that she could just stop trying to have a relationship with him. She wondered why she continued to make an effort. What difference did the letter make anyway? After all, it wasn't her problem. "Thanks," said Tara, quickly hanging up before she said something that she would regret.

Tara debated calling her mother, feeling the first stirrings of guilt about Peter creep into her consciousness. She decided to wait until she knew what was happening with her father. Normal communication was not possible with her parents; it was always a scheduling challenge. To think there were people out there who could phone home whenever they needed some emotional support. Tara couldn't imagine such a luxury.

Before she could change her mind, she phoned

Peter to tell him that she would be in D.C. the following weekend. He was delighted to hear that she was coming and suggested they grab a cup of coffee soon.

She threw herself into her work for the next few days. A friend called and asked her to a small dinner party but Tara refused, waiting to hear from Peter. To mitigate her anxiety, Tara cleaned her closets and walked five miles. She organized her pictures and began working on a few scrapbook pages that she would never share with the group. This album contained pictures of her old boyfriends. *This is sort of embarrassing,* Tara thought, flipping through the pages.

I certainly don't date just one type of guy, she concluded, looking at a picture of her old boyfriend, Michael, standing in front of the Duomo in Florence. They'd met at an art opening and instantly hit it off. Aside from being an accomplished violinist, he was Italian and very good looking. Although he was on the road four to five months a year, he spent the rest of his time living in his family's home in Florence. She could have dealt with the fact that he was thirty-eight years old and still had his mother ironing his pants; however, his widowed mother and twentysomething sister expected to go everywhere with them. Tara decided that there wasn't room for four people in their relationship.

But she'd enjoyed a wonderful visit to Florence. Adhering a red gerber daisy on the upper right hand side of a cream-colored page, she then placed a black studded button in the daisy's center. She used a circle cutting tool on the picture of Michael. To add a mat, Tara used the same tool on plain navy blue paper. She was pleased with the effect and decided to just label this page *Florence*.

A nagging little voice in the back of her mind told her that she was a fool to keep waiting for the phone to ring. She painstakingly forced herself to write two new pages of her chapter. The work seemed tedious since her mind was otherwise occupied with thoughts of Peter. No matter how many times she told herself that she was being ridiculous, she just couldn't help herself. So when his e-mail arrived, Tara was overjoyed. The words *I miss you* seemed to bounce off the computer screen and erase any misgivings she'd had about meeting him in D.C.

The phone rang Sunday afternoon. Hoping it was Peter, Tara raced to answer, and was surprised to hear Megan instead.

"Hey, Tara," she said. "Glad I caught you. I don't know if you've been listening to the news but they've been featuring all of these stories about Amvale. Have you heard anything?"

"No, I've been writing, and not really paying much attention. What's going on?"

"I think Libby's son is in trouble," she said.

CHAPTER 7

Libby

The moment felt suspended in time: the smell of honeysuckle in the air, the sound of Agent Hudgins's lace-up shoes as they hit the pavement, and the sunlight attacking her poor vision. Libby's eyes watered. Sweat trickled down her back. She told herself to remain calm.

The walk from her car to the front door felt unbearably long. She slowed her steps to keep her trembling limbs steady. Her son was in serious trouble; the police visit told her that Robby was more involved in the scandal than she had originally suspected. She had observed his expensive lifestyle over the last few years. It'd bothered her that he had become so interested in material possessions—sports cars, fancy suits, and first-class accommodations. She thought that she had raised him right. *What happened?* she wondered sadly.

Making her way through the marble front hallway, Libby observed Robby's prized bronze of a Greek helmet, his sleek chenille sofa, and the modern-art portrait of a man made from thousands of pieces of white paper. Following the sound of voices to the back library, she walked into the room to find her son seated in a leather chair. He was wearing handcuffs. Libby thought she might faint.

"Mom," said Robby. Surprise invaded his guarded expression, and then his mouth formed a thin line.

Libby was unable to move. "What's going on?" she demanded nervously. Her gaze moved back to the gleaming steel chains in disbelief. She suddenly thought back to a time when Robby was little and his friends used to play cops and robbers. How she wished he would jump up and yell, "Just kidding!" Mentally shaking herself, she swallowed hard.

"Mom," repeated Robby, shifting his gaze downward. He seemed to be staring at his own hands. "What are you doing here?" he asked, looking up again to face her.

"I came because I was worried about you," she said. She turned to Agent Hudgins. "I don't understand!" she cried. "Why is my son handcuffed? He's not a criminal! Remove them at once!" She felt her own panic rising.

"We can't do that, ma'am," said a wiry-looking man in a sport shirt and tailored pants who'd been in the room with Robby when she entered. "I know you're upset right now."

"Upset!" she exclaimed. "Outraged is more like it! This can't be happening. Why are you doing this to him?"

Agent Hudgins held his ground. "Mrs. Marshall, your son is being investigated for accounting and securities fraud. We're going to take him down to the station to question him further."

"Oh my God," said Libby. "Robby, there's got to be some mistake. I'm sure of it. I know this will work out." Libby watched his eyes for some sign.

"We'll give you a moment alone before we take him in," Agent Hudgins said, motioning to the other agent to step outside the door.

Libby nodded, putting her arm around her son. "Oh Robby, I'm so sorry. I'll call your father. We'll hire the best lawyers. You don't deserve to be treated like this."

"They want information," he told her offhandedly, as if he were talking about the sale of a car.

"I see," she said, admiring how reasonable he appeared. *It can't be that bad,* she told herself, even though she didn't understand corporate finance or what had transpired. Business matters were Ed's department. He would be able to make sense of Robby's dilemma, because he operated in a similar environment. Wiping the perspiration from her face, she reached for his hand. The cold metal of the handcuffs made her flinch momentarily. "No matter what happens, I love you. We'll get through this, son."

Agent Hudgins appeared in the doorway. "Okay, Mr. Marshall. It's time to go."

This was all a terrible mistake, Libby thought, nervously rubbing her sweaty palms together. *Had he been forced to commit these crimes?* she wondered.

109

She kissed Robby on the cheek and said, "I'll call your father immediately. We'll get our lawyers involved."

Robby nodded.

Despite his outer appearance of calm, Robby looked rumpled. With his two-day-old beard, stained shirt, creased pants, and scuffed shoes, he looked like a parody of the polished executive that he had always been. But her handsome son didn't look the part of the bad guy. He even smelled of body odor, she thought, wondering when he had last showered. Her motherly instincts kicked in. "Honey, are you hungry? When was the last time you had a proper meal? Can I bring you some food?"

"I'll be fine, Mom," he said as they took him away.

"Can I come with you, officer?" she pleaded.

"No, ma'am, I'm afraid that won't be possible right now. Your son is under arrest."

Libby froze at the harshness of his words. She wanted to say something snide, like he needed to mind his manners, but she was hardly in a position to be uncooperative. She followed them to the front entrance, but she couldn't summon any appropriate parting words.

She watched the agents put her son in the back-seat of their unmarked car as if he were a common criminal. As soon as they drove away, Libby snapped out of her daze and sprang into action. She scrambled to find the portable phone in the kitchen to call Ed. Her hands were shaking so hard, it took several attempts just to dial his number at work. The sound of her husband's voice triggered her pent-up hysteria. She relayed the events as best as she could.

"Slow down, Lib, and breathe," said Ed anxiously. "Everything's going to be okay. We'll do whatever it takes to help him."

"What if he goes to jail?" she cried. "I don't think I could bear it."

"We can't jump to conclusions, dear. We've got to remain logical and deal with this one step at a time. I'll call our lawyers, get home, and pack a bag. I'll be there as soon as I can. Maybe they'll let our lawyer see him tonight."

"Will he have to spend the night at some sort of detention center?" she asked.

"Probably," he said.

"Please hurry, Ed. This is a nightmare."

"I know. I'll meet you at Robby's in a few hours. Call me on my cell phone in about an hour and we can talk more. Why don't you make up some dinner?"

"Don't be practical at a time like this!" she wailed.

"We've got to take care of ourselves or else we're no good to him. Okay?"

"Sure," said Libby, allowing Ed's pragmatism to take hold. He always operated calmly in stressful situations. When they were alone, she often fondly referred to him as her rock.

In desperate need of something to keep her busy,

Libby began opening her son's kitchen cabinets. She removed several foam coffee cups from the counter, searching for the trash can. It took several minutes of pulling out drawers to remember which cabinet hid the garbage. Dirty ashtrays filled with cigarette butts littered the breakfast table. Lipstick was evident on several of them. She wondered what female had been here.

Several hours dragged on as she made her way into each room of the house, straightening up and dusting tables. Housecleaning was a balm for her troubled mind. A part of her wanted to descend into melancholy and dissect pieces of her son's childhood to figure out where the clues to this problem were buried. It would be so easy to just sit on the couch and cry, she thought, wiping dust from a tabletop.

Her cell phone rang. It was Ed, telling her that his lawyer had arranged to see Rob; he wanted to wait to find out if they would actually allow him to visit tonight. Ed promised to come to the house as soon as possible. Libby was relieved. Maybe he could make some sense of this mess. Libby went out to the car and retrieved her overnight bag, then went upstairs to settle into the guest room and wait. She tried to read a book, but the words kept blurring on the page as she pictured her son in handcuffs. Her intermittent breaks consisted of pacing the room, checking messages, and staring mindlessly at several television programs.

When Ed came in around two a.m., he looked worn out. Libby noticed a slight hunch in his shoulders. His eyes were bloodshot and his expression blank.

"How'd it go?" she asked, clicking off the television set.

"Not good," he replied as he sat at the edge of the bed.

"What does that mean?" Libby asked anxiously, her voice rising several notches. Ed looked at her, then glanced away. Libby watched him tense. He seemed lost in thought, probably trying to decide how much to tell her. "I want to know," she added quietly. "I need to know the truth."

Ed focused his eyes back on her. They were eyes she had trusted completely for forty-one years. She saw the disappointment. "He's definitely involved," he said in a monotone.

"What did he do wrong?" she exclaimed. "Is it fraud? Corporate theft? What?"

Ed took her hand. "He crossed the line, Lib. That's all I know right now. I don't whether it was for the money, the power, or the lifestyle. It was a huge error in judgment on his part."

"I just don't believe it," said Libby, her eyes welling up with tears. "Why would he do something like that? I taught him right from wrong. He knew better."

"He got caught up," said Ed evenly. "I don't think he acted alone. It was the corporate culture. All of the top company officials are going to be brought in for questioning."

"I don't think I can take any more. Does this mean he's going to jail?"

"I'm not going to lie to you, Lib. There's a strong possibility that he could get jail time if he's convicted. Things may get ugly."

Libby buried her face in her hands and began to sob.

The next morning, Libby prepared to face her worst nightmare, a trip to a federal detention center to see her only son. Her stomach was churning and her toast tasted like cardboard. After a few nibbles, she nearly gave up trying to eat. One look from Ed reminded her that she had to keep up her strength. They were in for a long fight.

She caught sight of a large sphere-shaped bowl with a rainbow of colors seemingly blown into its sides sitting on the sleek granite counter. She had seen work by this artist only in magazines, she realized, getting up to take a closer look. Running her fingers over the cold glass, she realized that this piece had cost a small fortune. Closing her eyes in disbelief, she wondered how her son could gamble his life away to acquire material things.

"It's by that artist with the 'Ch' name that sounds like a kids' game," said Ed, trying to break the tension.

"I thought so," said Libby. "And it's on the kitchen

counter no less," she exclaimed. "What was he thinking?"

"I don't know," said Ed. "I've been asking myself that question for the last twenty-four hours. I'm just as shocked and angry as you are."

"Seven years ago he became a millionaire; I know because he told me. He had a million before he was thirty years old. I was so proud of him and his accomplishments. Now, I wonder if he stole it." She caught herself. "Oh God, did I just say that?" She covered her face with her hands, ashamed of her outburst.

Ed came over to enfold her in his comforting embrace. "This is hard on all of us, Lib. I'm disappointed, too. I'm trying really hard to control my temper."

Libby leaned against Ed's comforting presence. "I know. I'm sorry I'm so emotional. I wish I were as calm as you in a crisis." She kissed him on the cheek.

He checked his watch. "We should probably head out now so you can see him."

"Let me use the bathroom first," she said, gathering up her pocketbook. The downstairs powder room was done all in marble with some sort of gold and red wallpaper. Libby peered at her own expression, clutching her stomach because it hurt so badly. She reached into her purse and pulled out the last of her antacid tablets, quickly chewing up two for good measure. Perhaps they could stop at the drugstore on the way home to pick up more. *Maybe even an entire case,* she thought wryly.

Lack of sleep had left dark circles under Robby's eyes. Libby was surprised when he lit up a cigarette. It was a disgusting habit, but she didn't feel now was the right moment to say anything about the smoke in her face, or mention how the acrid smell challenged her already upset stomach.

They were seated in a bare room with dirty white walls and hard metal chairs. A window faced the brick building next door. Everything seemed to have a filmy dark coating on it despite the fluorescent canned lights in the ceiling. The uniformed officer standing guard by the door had an expressionless gaze that reminded her of the guards at Buckingham Palace. Libby suppressed the urge to wave her hand in front of his face to see if the man would blink.

"Are they taking care of you?" she said worriedly.

"Taking care of me?" he said. "Oh, absolutely, Mom, I'm doing just fine. Really."

"When are they going to let you go?"

"They're trying to decide whether I'm what's known as a 'flight risk.' "

"What's that?" she asked. Libby looked down and saw Robby's hands, his fingertips covered in remnants of blue ink. It was hard to maintain her composure.

"In layman's terms, it means that if they let me out

of here, they want to be sure I'm not going to take off to someplace like Mexico."

"Have they given you any idea when a decision will be made?" asked Ed.

"The judge assigned to my case is supposed to return to town tomorrow. He'll have to read the reports, meet with authorities, and review the evidence before he can make a ruling. We're in negotiations so it's definitely going to take several more days."

"I hate this place," said Libby, nearly biting her tongue. "I mean," she corrected, "I can't stand the thought of you being held here."

He took her hand. "I know, Mom. I'm going to do whatever they want in order to get out as quickly as I can. I'm sorry that you're even sitting in a place like this."

"Don't worry about me," she said. "You know how much I love you, Robby."

Ed placed his hand on her shoulder. "I think our time's up," he said quietly.

Libby embraced Robby, unwilling to let him go. Despite his scratchy beard and thin frame, Libby wanted to scoop him up in her arms and carry him away; he would always be her baby. She wished she could soothe away his troubles, kiss him and make everything all right. Ed practically had to pull her away from him. Libby walked out of the police station feeling ill.

"I need to get some more antacid pills at the

drugstore," she said, climbing into their sedan.

"Fine," said Ed. "We're going to need to come up with a plan. I think you should come home with me and check in with the girls. I'm hoping we'll sleep better in our own beds. Besides, there's nothing more we can do right now."

Libby nodded.

CHAPTER 8

Ashley

On Monday morning, Ashley phoned Catherine to set up a meeting to purchase some new scrapbooks. The only time that worked for both of them was that afternoon. It seemed an enormous leap of faith, but she was compelled to try. On impulse, she also phoned Tara and asked her out to lunch. Much to her surprise, Tara seemed pleased to hear from her and readily agreed to meet that Friday.

As she contemplated the week's hectic schedule, Ashley suddenly felt exhilarated. With Steve's client dinner looming ahead, she asked around for the name of a good hairdresser. It had been a long time since she'd been to a salon. She also realized that she didn't have any nice high heels, so she would have to try to pick up a pair on sale. Ever since she had given birth to Tucker, it seemed as if everything about her was bigger, including her feet.

Ashley's excitement grew as she anticipated an evening out with her husband. It didn't matter that they would be dining with clients. The idea of going out, especially on a "school night," seemed like a novelty. Adult conversation was a novelty. Dressing up was a novelty. Preparations for their "date" became paramount. She did her nails, purchased stockings and a new lipstick, and borrowed an evening bag from a friend.

She managed to shower and do her hair before going over to Catherine's house to look at supplies for scrapbooking. She had made it clear that she was on a budget and she needed to be careful not to overdo it on the first day.

Catherine's guest room looked like a well-kept store, with an array of ribbons, beads, charms, colored paper, special scissors, stickers, colored pencils, archival paper, pens, different types of patterned paper, and, of course, multicolored scrapbooks.

"I know there's a lot to choose from," Catherine began. "So I've been thinking about how to make this easy for you. We've got this adorable white scrapbook with baby boots on it. Maybe this would be a good starting point for Sally, since it would give you less ground to cover."

Ashley agreed. "You're right. Let me see how I do on one book. I certainly wouldn't win any organization awards lately. Don't expect me to be your model client," she added with a laugh.

"Don't worry, have fun with this project. At least it'll help you get your baby pictures together. Let me show you something just to give you some ideas," she said. Catherine pulled out a stunning page with a picture of a baby in the center. "This was the winner of the 'Oh, Baby' page contest. I think it's always good to see what others have accomplished."

The page used a combination of patterned papers to create a flowered and polka-dot checkerboard background. Pink ribbon rosebuds were glued around the baby picture, and satin ribbon edged the corners of the page.

Catherine explained how the page had been put together with one-inch strips of patterned paper. She pointed out the various papers used, including green with white dots alongside the strips of pink paper. Beside the picture of the baby was a strip of vellum with a poem and the date of the photograph written on it.

"I may be able to do the ribbon and manage the dates. As for a poem, I'm not so sure."

Catherine laughed. "You'll eventually develop your own style. These are just ideas to get you started. Look at Tara's books. They're completely her own creation. Oh, before I forget, the meeting's at my house next Tuesday. I hope you'll come."

"I'm definitely going to try," said Ashley.

Ashley left Catherine's house with a bag of supplies, pleased that she had made the effort to start something new. She promised herself that she would continue searching the house for the rest of Sally's baby pictures. It occurred to her that a disposable camera had been left sitting in the kitchen drawer for the last two years; it probably contained pictures of Sally's christening and her first Christmas. Ah, well. She sighed, thinking that she would probably make everyone else in the group feel really good about themselves.

On Thursday, Steve called to confirm that he would pick her up at the house before dinner. That afternoon, Ashley wrote a to-do list so she could have enough time to get dressed for the evening and even manage some makeup. Her visit to the hair salon had apparently been a success, as all of the kids commented on her pretty new hairstyle. Ashley looked in the mirror, pleased with her new blond highlights. She had argued with the hairdresser, explaining that no matter what style he created, she had to be able to pull it back into a ponytail, which was truly a mother's hair salvation. They compromised and he had cropped it to the perfect length.

That afternoon, she ran carpools, helped with homework, and organized dinner for the kids. Ashley was nervous about being ready on time and scheduled the babysitter to come early so she'd have some time to dress. *This evening may turn out to be interesting,* she thought, assessing her new outfit with the low-cut top and pleated skirt. She slipped the dress over her head and twisted around to zip it up in back. It fit perfectly.

At the small, pricey clothing store last week, Megan had urged her to buy it, especially after the saleswoman pointed out that it showed off her full bust to perfection. There were some advantages to being plump, she had to admit. Megan had immediately cut off the inside tags, knowing that obsessing about the price and the size would have ruined her evening. "That's what friends are for," Megan had informed her. "You look great. You're not a number." Ashley was amazed that a simple piece of fabric could make her feel pretty again.

"Not bad," she said to her reflection as she put on a coat of mascara.

Sally barged into the room, crying. "Mommy," she wailed. "Cameron called me a stupid idiot."

Ashley was irritated that the babysitter had let Sally upstairs. All she wanted was fifteen minutes of peace to prepare. "That was not very nice. You know you're a smart girl, sweetie. Go tell your brother to apologize."

"He won't," she pleaded. "You talk to him."

"Sally," she said firmly, "give Mommy ten more minutes to finish getting ready and I'll come downstairs to help. Okay?"

"Okay," she said as she ran out the door.

Ashley finished her preparations. She was pleased with her efforts. She was anxious to see Steve and maybe have him notice her again. It had been such a long time since they had focused on each other.

When she came downstairs, the kids went on and on about how pretty she looked, her new hairdo, the black dress, the gold necklace, and her smile. Their reaction made Ashley feel she had indeed made a transformation, and it gave her some much-needed confidence.

Steve finally arrived, thirty minutes late. He walked in, put down his briefcase, and greeted the kids. When he looked up to see her, Ashley was shocked by his reaction.

"Wow," said Steve. "You look amazing." His smile was real, not forced. "Kids, doesn't your mom look awesome?"

Ashley felt her knees go weak. She hadn't seen that look of admiration in a long, long time. She felt the moisture in her eyes. Perhaps there was something left for them. For so long, it had been as if she were standing on a precipice, uncertain of whether they would make it. She remembered the little things: how Steve used to brush her hair back behind her ears, how he used to call her his sweet thing, the notes he left all over the house, the dinners they used to cook together, and how they used to say "I love you" regularly. Now, those words sounded as if she were speaking a foreign language. *Can we find each other again?* she wondered.

Suddenly, she imagined an announcer coming out of the pantry, saying "Now for another episode of *Can This Marriage Be Saved?* On the right, we have Ashley—a tired, overworked mother of four who is sick of doing all of the household chores. On our left, we have Steve—a stressed-out real estate broker who doesn't know how to be a good husband or parent anymore."

She returned his smile. "Thanks, honey. I appreciate the compliment," said Ashley. She didn't mention the fact that he was late.

"Give me just five minutes to put myself together and I'll be ready."

Ashley nodded her approval. She wasn't going to let anything spoil this evening. Sally approached her with sticky hands. "Careful of Mommy's new dress, sweetie," she warned.

"I want to touch it," she exclaimed, marching forward.

Ashley held up her hands for help. "Tucker, grab her!" Ashley watched as Tucker playfully picked up a kicking Sally.

"Thanks," she said with a wink. "I owe you one."

"I'd wait in the car," he suggested. "I don't know how much longer I can hold her." He had flipped Sally into a sideways position to keep her from kicking him in the face.

Ashley blew the kids a kiss, promised the sitter they wouldn't be too late, and made her way to the car. She could hear Sally's screams from outside the door. Ordinarily, she would have dropped everything to go soothe her, but she decided that Sally wasn't going to get her way tonight.

The air felt cool on her bare skin. Steve emerged a few minutes later to open the car door for her. "I'm surprised you made it out of there so quick," he said. "That's not like you."

Ashley thought for a moment. Rather than get defensive, she said, "I wanted us to have some time together, even if we have to include your client."

"I'm glad. Maybe we could go to that new French place for a drink afterward if you're not too tired."

"Sure," she said automatically, surprised by the invitation. They were starting to act a bit like the old Steve and Ashley, she thought, the couple that got married because they loved each other.

His car still smelled new. It was meticulously clean and neat. Ashley had forgotten how organized Steve had always been. She thought of her own brontosaurus-like SUV, filled with candy wrappers, juice boxes, and kids' paraphernalia. It was gross and she knew it. Perhaps she could ask the kids to help wash it and clean out their stuff tomorrow.

"So, who are we having dinner with?" she asked.

"Hank Anderson and his wife, Claudia. He's with Morris Industries, which is headquartered in New York. His firm is considering a possible reloca-tion to Belloix, because the cost of living here is so reasonable. It would be a huge bonus for our city if we could get a company like that here. There would be more job openings and development downtown."

"How many employees does Morris have?" asked Ashley, realizing that she hadn't talked to Steve about his work in ages.

"Six thousand. He's interested in potentially leasing the old Jenkins building and renovating it. It would be an enormous deal for me and my firm."

"That's exciting. I know how hard you work," she responded. "How can I help?"

Steve smiled. "He's going to have a lot of questions about the schools here, quality of life, kids' programs, that sort of thing. I'd hoped that you could share your experiences and feelings about the public school systems. You lived and worked in New York, so you'll be able to tell him and his wife about some of the transitions that you had to make."

"No problem," said Ashley. "I definitely wouldn't want to have to raise four children in New York. It would've been too expensive, and I would have worried about our kids all the time. Green grass is one of Belloix's top luxury items."

Steve laughed and reached for her hand. "I know he'll love you."

Ashley had received two compliments in the past forty-five minutes from her husband. *What a novelty,* she thought, looking down at her hand wrapped in his. "Thanks," she said shyly.

The restaurant was casually elegant. There were cozy booths with black leather cushions, a wood-beamed ceiling, and large vases filled with sunflowers. Ashley complimented Steve on his selection, comparing it to something they might find in New York. Anxious for the evening to begin, Ashley smiled up at Steve.

Moments later, they were seated in one of those cozy booths. Ashley ordered a very expensive glass of wine, feeling a bit decadent. She wished they weren't here on business and this warm, fuzzy feeling could continue all night.

Hank Anderson arrived with his wife, Claudia, who looked as if she belonged on the cover of a fashion magazine. Ashley took a huge gulp of wine, trying not to feel intimidated. She sucked in her stomach, praying that she wouldn't make a fool out of herself.

Claudia reached over to shake Ashley's hand, her fingers limp. In contrast, Hank was full of enthusiasm, giving her a kiss on both cheeks and thanking her for leaving the children on a school night. He even told her that she looked like a Southern belle. *This guy should be in sales,* Ashley thought, warming to his jovial manner. Despite Hank's being middle-aged, balding, and a bit paunchy, his personality made her feel like she was spending the evening with a rock star. No wonder he was one of his firm's top executives—everybody in the company must love him.

The waiter returned to take their drink orders. Ashley was relieved when Hank sat next to her. Out of the corner of her eye, she could see Claudia's diamond earrings and cocktail rings. Her dress was perfectly tailored to her small frame. Years ago, Ashley would have been able to name the designer instantly; it was clear that Claudia Anderson didn't shop off the rack. Desperately trying to curb her jealousy, Ashley glanced over to see if Steve was admiring her beautiful form.

"So," said Hank. "Steve tells me you're Superwoman, managing four kids on your own. That's pretty impressive. Claudia can barely handle our two. We have two live-in nannies."

"You're kidding," said Ashley. She caught herself. "I'm sorry, but I adore spending time with our children. It's not glamorous, but it's who I am," she added, looking him in the eye.

He smiled at her. "Tell me about the kids."

He made her feel comfortable. Ashley was delighted to share anecdotes about their kids' lives. She talked about how she was trying to play tennis with Tucker to help build his self-esteem, about Cameron's ability to play chess four levels above his age, about Janie's love of ballet and her shoe addiction, and of course, about Sally, the wannabe artist who thought their home was her own personal drawing board. Hank laughed at her jokes, often touching her hand in support.

"Did you hear that, Claudia?" Hank said. "Ashley carpools her kids and cooks dinner every night for them."

"Isn't that special," Claudia said coolly, turning her attention back to Steve.

Ashley bristled at her tone, thinking somehow she should try to smooth things over. "I know Belloix can never compete with New York in many ways, but it's so great for families. The school systems are wonderful, and so are the parks."

"I'm sure they are, dear, but it's so provincial. Not at all as sophisticated as city living. You wouldn't understand the differences."

"But I do. I used to live in New York. I worked for Anna St. Clair," said Ashley. "I understand both worlds."

"You worked for Anna St. Clair," said Claudia. "I don't believe it!" she eyed Ashley sharply.

Ashley took the blow, feeling as if someone had just leveled a clean slice to her midsection. After all, this was business. "I directed all of the firm's marketing activities for two years before we moved here to start a family," she explained calmly.

Fortunately, dinner arrived right after the exchange. Ashley had lost her appetite, knowing that Steve would be incredibly disappointed in her. She didn't have the polish to lure the Claudias of the world to do anything. After all, as far as women like her were concerned, suburban housewives didn't have anything interesting to say. Picking at her food, she spent the next hour answering Hank's questions as patiently and as honestly as she could. He wanted to know everything: names of private schools, local hospitals, her favorite stores, doctors' locations, and cost comparisons on groceries. He couldn't believe that a box of cereal cost less than three dollars in Belloix.

"That's amazing," he said. "You've been incredibly helpful," he said during dessert. "I can't thank you enough."

Ashley smiled weakly. She restrained herself from looking over at Steve, who was probably drooling all over Claudia. She was sure he was wishing his wife looked as good as her. She placed her fork in her dessert and moved it around a bit so it looked like she was eating.

As she stared at the melting ice cream on her plate, Ashley imagined various conversations that she could have started with Claudia to spark her interest in their small Southern city. They could have chatted for hours about designer clothing, but Claudia's insult had prevented Ashley from saying anything more about her experiences working for a major fashion house.

Ashley counted the minutes until the dinner was over. It seemed to take forever to pay the bill and say polite good-byes. As they headed out of the restaurant, Ashley sneaked a quick look at Steve, who seemed unfazed by the whole evening.

On the way out to the car, he took her hand. "You were awesome. Hank just loved you, which I knew he would."

"You're kidding, right?" said Ashley. "I thought Claudia . . ." Her voice trailed off.

"Claudia is a first-class witch. Hank even says it about her."

Ashley couldn't have been more shocked if he had told her that they were heading off to the moon. "I th-thought . . ." she stuttered.

"You thought wrong," he said. "She's awful, completely self-absorbed. Now, how about that drink you promised to have with me?"

Ashley's whole being lightened. She said, "I'd like that." Her cell phone rang. Trying to suppress her worry, Ashley calmed when she heard Tucker's voice.

"Mom," he said.

"Everything okay?" she inquired nervously.

"Sally won't go to bed. We've tried everything."

"Put her on," said Ashley. When she heard Sally's voice, Ashley said, "Sally, honey, you've got to get some sleep. Mommy will be home soon, I promise." Ashley then recited the Lord's Prayer and promised to check on her the moment she arrived home. Sally stopped whining.

Tucker got back on the phone. "I think that worked."

"Whew!" said Ashley, winking at Steve.

"You owe me, Mom, for helping the sitter deal

with her all night. You better be ready for tennis on Saturday."

"We'll do it," said Ashley. "Thanks, Tucker. You're a great kid."

Ashley whispered to Steve that she needed to go for a drink. It seemed that France was the theme of their evening out, or perhaps they were just drawn to French restaurants. They headed to Toulouse, a new spot that had a large orange awning in the front. Ashley checked her watch. It was nearly ten o'clock.

They were led to a corner table with a cushioned bench so they could sit beside each other. Ashley could feel the warmth of Steve's leg against her's.

"How about some champagne? I feel like celebrating," Steve said, ordering a bottle of something with a French-sounding name.

"Dare I ask the occasion?" quipped Ashley.

"It's the first time we've been alone in months. I don't have four pairs of hands in front of mine."

"Maybe we should do this more often," she said boldly. "I didn't think you enjoyed my company anymore."

"What gave you that idea?" he asked.

"I don't know, Steve. You work all week, then check out on the weekends to play golf. It's been tough."

He looked at her. "I'm sorry, Ash. Work is stressful. I need a break."

The waiter filled their glasses with champagne.

"Me, too," she said. "I don't want to dwell on the negative right now, if that's okay with you. We haven't had fun in a long time. I've missed you. I've missed us." Her eyes started tearing up.

"You're right. I think this is the first time we've had a real conversation in I don't know how long. You look beautiful tonight, by the way."

Ashley felt a tingle of excitement. She saw the look in his eyes. In that instant, she forgot where she was. He leaned over and kissed her. The kiss was passionate, a reminder of intimacy long buried. Their fingers curled around each other. He kissed her again, gentler this time.

They parted reluctantly. Ashley expected someone to tap them on the shoulder and say, *Get a room*. She giggled nervously, suddenly embarrassed by their embrace.

She cleared her throat. "Why can't we have a date like this once in a while? As much as I love the kids, I get tired of not having our private time." She saw the genuine surprise on his face. It was a step forward.

"Honey, I'm happy to do this every night if you want," he joked, reaching for her.

They laughed. They talked. They touched. Ashley thought she must be dreaming. She prayed that the kids would be asleep when they returned home. *Please,* she prayed, *just for tonight, don't let one of them be sick or crying or need something.*

"By the way, I saw what you did to the room off the kitchen. It looks great," he said.

"Oh, I'm glad you like it. I didn't realize you'd noticed. I'm going to turn it into an office. The kids have been helping me paint. As you can see, it's not done yet, but I've made a good start. And I've made some new friends, thanks to Megan. There's a woman named Tara whom I especially like a lot. We're going to have lunch tomorrow." She wanted to share her excitement over her new group, but decided it wasn't the right time.

"Whatever you've been doing, keep at it. You seem much happier."

"I am," she said. Ashley thought for a moment. Hadn't Tucker said the same thing to her last week? She didn't realize how lonely she had been for adult conversation, specifically with other women. It was a need she hadn't recognized until she found it again. She was really looking forward to next week's meeting.

"I have something I need to tell you," he said. "I keep waiting for the right time but there doesn't seem to be one."

Ashley gulped.

"I know you don't want to talk about anything too serious right now, but . . ." He paused. "It's important. I've wanted to say something for weeks."

Ashley nodded. She nervously took a sip of her drink.

"My dad's not been doing well. He recently had

surgery to remove a blood clot near his heart. He was pretty shaken up."

"When did you find out?"

"A few weeks ago. Mom called to tell me the news. She wants me to see him, patch things up. I've been struggling with what to do ever since."

"I'm so sorry," said Ashley, reaching for his hand.

"It's funny. I don't know what I feel, if anything at all. I've hated his guts for so long that it's weird. As far as I'm concerned, I never even had a father. You know I was only twelve when he ran out on us—younger than Tucker."

"Why didn't you tell me about his illness sooner? I'd have been there to listen."

"I know you would have. But I had to try and deal with this myself first. It's made me think a lot about things—about us, about our kids. Anyway, I just wanted you to know what was going on. I don't want to spoil the evening with any more talk about him."

"I'm glad you told me," she said. She had been curious about his change these past few days. This thoughtful person across from her was the man she had married, the man she fell in love with. So now she understood him a little more. Certainly they had a long way to go, but for the first time in ages, Ashley had reason to hope that things might get better between them. It was a start—a renewed connection.

Their rekindled intimacy was lost the moment

they opened the back door. Sensory overload descended so fast that Ashley felt as if she had just been hit in the head. Sally was screaming so loudly that it was impossible to hear.

"Be quiet, I want to go to sleep!" yelled Janie.

"Mom, she's okay," said Tucker.

Cameron was sitting on the counter, sobbing as if he were the one with the problem. The babysitter looked ready to pull her hair out. *Just another day in paradise,* thought Ashley.

"Okay," she said, reaching for Sally. "What happened?" When everyone tried to speak at once, Ashley waved her arms, signaling them all to be quiet. She was going to call on her babysitter, but the girl was clearly too frazzled to say much. "Tucker," she said calmly. "Go ahead, you tell the story of why everyone around here isn't in bed."

"Mom, everything was fine. We were all asleep until ten minutes ago. Sally must have fallen out of bed because she started screaming and woke us all up."

"Poor baby!" said Ashley, checking Sally for any signs of injury. Seeing nothing serious, she gave her another kiss. Sally snuggled against her, tucking her blond curls underneath her chin. "Mommy's home."

Ashley reached into her wallet and paid the babysitter, adding an extra few dollars in the hope that she might come back. Steve volunteered to walk her home.

After systematically tucking the children back into bed, giving them each a kiss on the cheek, she hurried to the master bedroom, hoping to salvage what was left of the evening before they both passed out asleep. Oddly enough, she wasn't exhausted. It occurred to her that she hadn't worn anything besides pajama bottoms to bed in ages. Maybe tonight would be different.

When Steve walked into the room, they stared at each other for a moment. It was a long moment, filled with speculation. The evening had definitely derailed, Ashley thought. Suddenly, they both started laughing.

"That was something," said Ashley, rolling her eyes. "Fortunately, no one was hurt."

"I can't believe how well you just did that. That was extraordinary, Ash. It was a complete circus when we walked in."

"Welcome to my world," she said.

He reached for her. She didn't hesitate. It felt so good to be appreciated, she thought, wondering what tomorrow would bring.

Ashley was in a bit of a daze the next morning as she made her way through the piles on her desk. She surveyed her kitchen and tried to neaten things up—picking up the kids' shoes, clearing the countertops of debris, and organizing her desk area. *A housecleaner* would *make her life much easier,* she thought. She made a mental note to discuss the possibility with Steve tonight.

The phone rang. She grabbed it, thinking it was Steve. "Hey there," said Ashley warmly. The voice on the other end of the line was not whom she expected.

"Ashley, it's your mother. I've only got a minute since I'm on location and it's about four o'clock in the morning here."

"Yes, Mother," she said politely. "What can I do for you? Don't tell me, you're calling because you've heard about some new diet that I might like to try." Her peaceful mood evaporated.

"No," her mother said. "I'm calling because I thought you might like to see your father's new television program. It's on CSBC tonight at eight."

"Daddy couldn't call me himself? Surprise, surprise."

"Sarcasm doesn't become you, dear," said her mother patiently. "Where's that sweet girl I know?"

"That sweet girl is sick of both of you," exclaimed Ashley. "I've got my own life now, filled with caring for my children. You wouldn't know much about that, would you, Mother? You and Dad were always too busy seeking the spotlight to think about anybody but yourselves." Her fury mounted. "By the way, Daddy doesn't even remember the last time he saw his own grandchildren. Doesn't that strike you as odd, Mother?"

"I'm not going to have a conversation with you when you're acting like this," she said. "At least

I'm trying to reach out to you. You're so busy try-ing to be the antithesis of me that you can't see things clearly anymore."

She bit her lip in frustration. She said good-bye and slammed the phone into the receiver. *She's the most shallow and superficial person,* Ashley thought. *How does that woman always manage to get to me?*

Ashley seethed with resentment. How dare her mother claim that her life choices were some sort of a rebellion? She was a good mother. Period. The problem was that she had let herself go. Her date night with Steve had proved that she needed to put more care into herself and her appearance.

Fortunately, today was her lunch with Tara, which gave her something positive to think about the rest of the morning. The promise of adult conversation would be a welcome relief from her angry inner tirade. Ashley was surprised to find Tara already seated at a corner table when she arrived with Sally that afternoon. A brand-new package of crayons and a coloring book were sitting on one of the placemats.

"That was so thoughtful of you to bring these," said Ashley, pointing to the art supplies. "Thank you so much." She watched as Sally scampered into her seat and reached for a bright blue crayon.

"Thank you," said Sally with a big grin. She im-mediately returned her attention to the coloring book.

"You told me she was a budding artist," replied Tara, smiling warmly. "I couldn't resist."

"I'm so glad this worked out," said Ashley as she sat down at the small wooden table.

"I love your new haircut," said Tara. "It really shows off your eyes."

"Thanks," said Ashley, picking up the menu. She planned to have a salad. Lately, some of her pants were fitting more loosely, which was encouraging. "You'd be proud of me. I got some more pages done on Sally's baby book. It's almost finished."

"That's terrific," said Tara. "What next?"

"I guess I'll start at the top and see if I can't organize a few of Tucker's baby pictures for our next meeting. But it's so overwhelming to think about how many projects I'd like to accomplish with my old pictures. So Cameron, my ten-year-old, has come up with a great idea for the future. He's going to show me how to load images from a digital camera onto the computer and make a scrapbook online. Digital scrapbooking isn't cheating, is it?"

"Absolutely not! You've got to do what works for your lifestyle. I think making books with the group and doing some books online is absolutely brilliant. I'm just glad you love to scrapbook! Are you going to Catherine's for the meeting next Tuesday?"

"Yes," said Ashley. "I went over to her house last Monday. It was pretty amazing. All of you have these gorgeous homes."

"First of all, I'm not married and I have no children," said Tara. "Keep in mind that Catherine's kids are older than yours and she only has two of them, so she has more time on her hands to decorate."

"Thanks for making me feel better. Well, in two years, Sally will be in kindergarten. That may change my entire life. I might be able to dress myself decently and have some personal time."

"Kindergarten," said Sally with a smile, holding up the picture that she had just colored in.

Tara reached for the crayon masterpiece and praised Sally. "You're really talented! I hear you want to be an artist."

Sally clapped her hands. "I love to draw," she said.

"You're so adorable!" said Tara. "I want one just like you!" She looked up at Ashley. "Whatever you're doing, keep it up! I can't believe how perfect this child is."

Ashley basked in the compliment. Sally did look particularly cute today with her blue-and-white checkered dress with dogs smocked on the front. A large blue bow was perched on top of her head, holding back the bangs from her side part. Her wide grin and bright eyes always won her immediate adoration from strangers, no matter where they went.

"You have no idea how much that means to me. I've had the week from hell. My mother claims I'm going overboard with my children just to spite her."

Ashley shook her head. "Imagine growing up in the shadow of the sixties sensation Marrie. My mother was considered the first real supermodel, known only by one name."

"You're kidding," said Tara. "How interesting! Was she that bad?"

"No," said Ashley. "It's not like she chased me around with coat hangers or anything. She was self-absorbed, that's all. Anyway, I vowed that unlike her I would stay home and raise my children, no matter what."

"I admire you for that. You have no idea how much empathy I have for you. My dad traveled a lot, so I rarely saw him growing up. We were pen pals. I'd receive letters from him from all over the world. I'm not sure things are much different now, but I'm older, so I'm able to accept him for who he is." She took a sip of her diet soda. "Actually, I'm flying to Washington next week to see him." She lowered her voice. "But the real reason I'm going is because I have a date," she said conspiratorially.

"Someone special?" inquired Ashley, not wanting to pry.

"Actually, yes. We've known each other for a long time. I'm really kind of excited about him. He also happens to be an expert on the artist Miró, on whom I'm writing my doctoral thesis, so we have no shortage of things to talk about."

"I hope you have a terrific time," said Ashley, looking back up at her friend. Most people thought that she was lucky to have celebrity parents, but Tara seemed to understand the loneliness that went along with it. Of course there were perks, but the instability was difficult to handle. There were so many times as a child that she had wanted to be part of a "normal" family, but it hadn't worked out that way. While she was distracted, Sally had reached into Tara's purse and started pulling out her keys and a book. "Sally, honey, no. That's private."

When she saw the book Sally had pulled out, she couldn't refrain from making a comment. "You're reading James's *The American*? That's one of my favorite books of all time."

"Me, too. I love his work so much that I wanted to read it again. I guess I can relate to feeling like an outsider."

"Funny you should say that. I had the same reaction. Who else do you read?"

"Tolstoy and Fitzgerald are my other favorites. But I also love biographies."

"Ooh, you're inspiring me," said Ashley. "I haven't picked up a good book in a long time. Perhaps I'll do so again in this century."

They both laughed. They chatted easily throughout lunch until Sally started to get restless. Ashley ordered her a cookie to keep her entertained for a few more minutes. After they had settled the check, Tara leaned over and gave Sally a big hug. "Sometime I'll babysit for you so your mama can have a few minutes to herself."

Sally gave her a big grin.

"I really enjoyed lunch," said Ashley.

"So did I. Let's do it again soon," said Tara. "I'll see you next Tuesday at Catherine's house."

"Have a wonderful trip this weekend," Ashley added. She couldn't help noticing the flush that came to Tara's cheeks.

"I will!" said Tara, waving good-bye.

Ashley knew she would be thinking about Tara all weekend. A romantic getaway sounded sublime. She couldn't wait to hear the outcome.

"Bye, Tara," said Sally. "Tara pretty, like Mommy."

"Aren't you a sweet girl," said Ashley, giving her daughter a kiss on the cheek. "I'm glad you like Mommy's new friend." Perhaps it was just serendipity that she had made a friend when she needed one most.

Sally nodded vigorously in approval.

"Mom, I'm home," Tucker called from the back door.

Ashley quickly composed herself, relieved to have something else to focus on. "Hey, honey, how was your day?" she said, coming over to greet him.

"Okay, I did a little bit better on my math quiz. At least I didn't flunk it."

"Not flunking is a good thing," she joked.

"I've got a ton of homework." He looked around.

"Where's all your stuff? Why is the house so quiet? This is unbelievable."

"I've gotten a lot done today," said Ashley. "Sally's over at a friend's house and so is Janie. Neither one of them will be home until dinner tonight."

"What about Cameron?"

"He's got violin practice. It's Mrs. Mather's turn to drive." Ashley looked at her watch, realizing that things were going to remain calm for another hour.

Tucker's face lit up. "Hey Mom, you owe me! Let's go play tennis."

Playing tennis was the last thing she wanted to do, but Tucker's enthusiasm changed her mind. "All right," she agreed. "But what about all your homework?"

"I'll get it done, I swear."

He looked so cute standing there with such an earnest expression, Ashley couldn't resist. "One hour, that's it," she said.

"Yes!" he said, running upstairs to change.

That evening, Ashley surveyed her almost neat-looking kitchen. Both girls had gone to bed early, so the house was quiet. Ashley was going through the piles on her desk when Cameron burst into the room.

"Hey, Mom, check this out! I've signed you up with this online company and we can make a digital album."

"You really are my techno-kid," she said excitedly. "Let me see."

At the computer, Cameron pointed to a photograph of Tucker, Janie, and Sally with the caption *Gates Family Pictures*. "I loaded all of the pictures we've taken this year in this file here. I think we've got about a hundred of them. You can pick which ones you like and make an album. It's really easy." He clicked on the icon. "The program almost does it for you."

"Very clever," she replied, watching him show her the right icons to select, including cover options, page format, and background. "How do we have a hundred pictures? I know I only took half that many."

"Well, I took some, too," he announced proudly.

"Great! Let's see what we've got," said Ashley, leaning into the computer screen. There was a photograph of Janie in her ballet costume executing a perfect leg kick. In another shot, Sally looked adorable posing with her favorite blanket and stuffed bunny. Then Tucker appeared with his mouth full of food. "That's gross," said Ashley. "You can just delete that one."

"Come on, Mom. It's funny," Cameron laughed.

"I'm not paying for an album with pictures of Tucker eating potato chips. No thanks," she said, pointing to the Delete button on the computer.

"What about this picture?" he said, breaking into a fit of laughter.

Ashley couldn't help herself. She laughed, too. "Poor Dreyfus," she said, adopting a firm motherly tone and looking at him in mock disapproval. In the picture, the kids posed with the neighbor's yellow Labrador, who was wearing a T-shirt and shorts. The dog even had a baseball cap flung to one side of his head. "Whose shirt and shorts are those?"

"They're Tucker's."

"Great," said Ashley dryly. "Okay, we can keep that one."

Cameron beamed in delight. He pointed to a heart icon. "You can create a separate file of your favorite photographs right here."

"I can't believe you figured this whole thing out," said Ashley. "I'm just so proud of you!"

He shrugged, clearly pleased with himself. "See, I told you this was a good idea!"

For the next hour, they selected photographs, wrote captions together, and debated background pages. It was such a breakthrough to give Cameron this kind of one-on-one attention, Ashley lost track of time.

"Oh no!" she said. "It's past ten and you've got to get to bed."

"Hey, we finished! Let me make sure it's saved. I'll bet your new friends are going to love it!"

"Yes, honey, I know they will," Ashley replied, giving him a hug. "Thanks again for your help. You're sooo awesome!"

"Ahh, Mom," he said bashfully. "I love you. G'night!"

"I'll be up in just a minute. Tell Tucker to wrap things up too, okay?"

She looked over at the clock and wondered why Steve hadn't called or come home yet. Rather than get upset, Ashley contemplated her lunch with Tara, tennis with Tucker, and what a good time she'd had with Cameron this evening. No matter what, she felt better about herself than she had in a long, long time.

CHAPTER 9

Tara

After an intense weekend of studying, Tara looked forward to Tuesday morning's meeting at Catherine's house. Armed with a diet soda and a suitcase full of supplies, Tara hoped to complete several more pages of an album about her favorite aunt, Tessa, who was her mother's older sister. She had turned seventy a few weeks earlier.

She pulled into Catherine's circular driveway just as Margy and Megan were emerging from their SUVs right in front of her.

"Hi, guys," said Tara. "I thought I was early."

Megan looked color-coordinated as usual in pink

cargo capris, a white shirt, and a funky patterned belt. Tara homed in on Megan's large pale pink tote bag with flower detailing and bamboo handles.

"Hey, where did you get that? That's great looking," she said.

Margy jumped in. "It's one of my new designs. Do you like it?" She carried a similar version in turquoise blue.

"I want one," said Tara. "I love how you've made this bag so stylish. You've really outdone yourself, Margy. I'll bet you could sell thousands of them as beach bags."

"I probably could, if I had a head for business. Right now, it's all I can do just to make twenty."

"Are there any left?"

Margy winked at her. "I may just be able to find one more for you."

Once inside Catherine's enormous dining room, Tara eyed the long serving table covered in the latest supplies, from stickers to custom-made paper. She placed her wheeled suitcase by her usual seat so she could look around and greet her friends.

Before long, Annie arrived with a red bag full of new photographs of her grandchildren that she couldn't wait to share.

"Where's Libby?" asked Tara.

Catherine put down her coffee. "She called and said she couldn't make it today. Something's come up with her son, Robby."

"Is he okay?" asked Tara.

"I think he's having a rough time now that Amvale is under investigation."

"I see." Tara knew how upset Libby must be over having her son involved in such a mess. Over the years, Libby had always shared what she referred to as her "Robby stories" about the celebrities he met or the women he dated. Though Tara had never met him, she had seen every single one of his baby pictures, which were beautifully cataloged in Libby's albums. "I hope everything's all right. I'd like to call her," said Tara.

"She sounded exhausted and upset. I'd go ahead and give her a call. I'm sure she could use all of our support right now. This has got to be tough."

The doorbell interrupted their conversation. Catherine ushered in a nervous-looking Ashley, whose eyes darted around the room, eventually coming to rest on the enormous crystal chandelier.

"Hi, everyone," said Ashley as she walked into the dining room. She tripped on the edge of the rug. Fortunately, she caught herself before she fell. "Whew! I made it," she said. Catherine headed to the kitchen to get her a cup of coffee.

Tara was pleased that Ashley had actually come today. There was something refreshingly honest about her. She spoke up. "I hope you'll sit next to me, Ashley. I'm dying to see pictures of your beautiful children."

"I'll sit there only if you promise not to laugh when I pull a mishmash of photographs out of the bottom of this bag." She placed them in several precarious-looking piles on the table. "Yes, the bag does belong to my daughter and that is a ballerina. But at least I made it here this morning!" she exclaimed.

Tara pulled out her own neatly organized supplies and put them beside Ashley. "Please feel free to use anything of mine," she said.

"You're assuming I'd know what to do with this stuff," said Ashley eyeing the nameplates, stickers, and pencils with a raised eyebrow.

"We'll all help you," said Catherine, taking a seat on Ashley's left.

Margy jumped up from her seat. "Oh, I almost forgot my fabric samples! They're still in the car." She headed outside and returned with an enormous clear bag. Turning to Catherine, she asked, "Where should I put them?"

"Maybe you should place some samples in that bowl on the center of the table? I'm sure everyone is going to want to use them."

"So how's little Sally doing?" asked Tara as she pulled several old photographs from a plastic bag.

"You should see what she did this week. She poured white rice all over the kitchen floor to make it look like snow!" Ashley removed a small leatherbound book and several pieces of paper from her bag.

"You're kidding." Tara laughed. "You've got to

write this stuff down. It's funny. You could even do a page with rice all over it."

"That's a great idea. There's probably still some left on my kitchen floor. I suppose I could call the page 'Sally's Spring Snowstorm.' "

"Very clever," said Tara with a wink. "Today is your first official day and you've already got a great idea. Next time Sally does something, why don't you grab a disposable camera and take a few pictures?"

Ashley nodded in agreement. She pointed to Tara's pictures. "Who's that?"

Tara smiled warmly. "That's my favorite aunt, Tessa. She's very eccentric but I just adore her. I wanted to put together a few pages on her today." Tara ran her hands over one picture and showed it to Ashley. "Look at this one. This is my aunt Tessa and me in Egypt riding a camel the year she turned fifty. I think I must have been fifteen or sixteen at the time." Tara pulled out another photograph. "Look at the funny picture of her in her scuba gear. She learned how to scuba dive at sixty."

"That's impressive," observed Ashley. "It was a big deal just for me to go on a school field trip in-state."

"I'm lucky to have someone like her in my life. My mother didn't like to go to foreign places, at least not outside Western Europe, where she's comfortable. Aunt Tessa is my mother's older sister and she's this huge feminist, scholar, and history buff.

She never married and she just loves to travel all over the world and embrace other cultures. When I was thirteen, she took me to Paris. We had such a good time that she took me somewhere almost every year after that. She's got two master's degrees and a Ph.D., and now she's in California teaching some history course on the Middle East. I miss her."

Tara got out a piece of paper and started jotting down her thoughts. It was hard to sum up in a few pages the impact this one person had on her life. Her approach needed to be different. She started writing phrases that came to mind about her aunt: *You taught me so much; I admire your independent spirit and your adventurous ways; I'll always remember my first camel ride when I thought I was going to pitch headfirst into the hot sand; you are such an inspiration to me.*

Tara started to envision her page with symbols that reminded her of their trip—a scarab, hieroglyphs, a pyramid, a mummy, and even a camel. She thought she might try a new technique of paper tearing to create a pyramid and maybe a sun. A camel might prove to be a real challenge to draw; maybe she'd use the outline of a horse stencil to get the basic shape.

Annie held up a page she was working on. It contained a backdrop of numbers and letters. "Will you just look at this picture?" she exclaimed. "Kelly just learned to say her ABCs and can count to one hundred. We're so proud of her!"

"How old is she?" inquired Ashley.

"She'll be two next month," said Annie. Seeing Ashley's astonished expression, she announced, "Only kidding. She's almost three and I think she's a real Einstein. I'm still trying to figure out how to lay out the picture," she said, eyeing her page. "Catherine, can I borrow you for a moment?"

Tara looked up from her camel sketch to watch as Catherine and Margy helped Annie angle the photograph in the center of the page. Margy pulled a green plaid piece of fabric from the center of the table, suggesting Annie use it as a border. "Hey Annie," she said. "Any news?"

"The mayor just fired his twentysomething secretary for this thing called blogging. Apparently, the young woman kept an online journal of all the activities in his office, calling herself 'Mayor Girl,' referring to her boss as 'overbearing and rude' and the office as 'a closet full of stupid people.' I wonder how she thought she wasn't going to get caught. Anyway, she was fired yesterday."

"I can't imagine 'Mayor Girl' is going to have an easy time finding another job."

"But, on a more interesting note, Tom and his colleagues have enjoyed lengthy debates on how to reduce this country's dependency on foreign oil. They've initiated a long-term program to upgrade the city's buses. I think it would be marvelous if we could bring back that old trolley that used to run along Main Street downtown. That would definitely cut down on traffic."

"I'm all for the trolley and new buses, but I think we need to explore other energy sources like solar power or smaller cars, for that matter. Although I'm just as guilty as everyone else of oil consumption since I drive an SUV. Perhaps I need to think about changing that," said Margy.

Ashley leaned over to Tara. "I can't live without my SUV, so I'm not going to say a word."

Tara returned her attention to the page in front of her. She spent the next few minutes sketching, then looked over to see Ashley struggling with her pictures. "How's it going?" she asked.

"I can't figure out whether to show this ugly picture of me pregnant or not. I look like a house," said Ashley, surveying the picture. "Or the side of a barn, however polite you want to be. I had a figure like yours once, but it was a long time ago."

Tara wasn't sure what to say. "You were about to give birth. Don't you think you should give yourself a break? I'd love to have a child."

"That's the boilerplate answer," said Ashley. "Look at my fat ankles," she continued with a laugh. "They look like tree trunks."

Tara took the picture and surveyed it. "I still don't get it. See how pretty your face looks?"

Ashley cocked her head to one side, ignoring her compliment. "May I borrow those scissors?"

"Sure," said Tara. She watched as Ashley started to crop her legs off. "I see you're determined," she said. "But may I make a suggestion?"

Ashley stopped in midcut. "Yes?"

"Before you amputate, you should think about how much Sally might enjoy seeing you pregnant with her," said Tara. She reached for two other photographs of Ashley holding Sally as a newborn and another baby picture. "Let's position these three pictures on the page like this. You could cut out a piece of vellum and stick it around you to deemphasize your shape if it bothers you." Tara reached for a border. "If you place this pink background around the other two pictures, it may offset the problem."

Ashley smiled. "You're good at this."

Tara watched as Ashley pondered her suggestion and started adding her own ideas with stickers. Tara noticed how Ashley carefully sketched a huge pink daisy and started cutting. She leaned over and said, "See, you do have a feel for scrapping."

"What's scrapping?" asked Ashley.

"It means the same thing as scrapbooking, only it sounds more official. Seriously, that looks terrific." She watched Ashley's face light up as her page started coming together.

"You were right. I don't look half bad."

Tara looked at her watch and realized that several hours had gone by and she hadn't once thought of Peter or the coming weekend. That was nothing short of a miracle. When the group decided to start packing up, Tara gathered her things.

Later that evening, when Tara turned on her bedroom television, a breaking news report confirmed that several of Amvale's top executives were being questioned for securities fraud. Though the report didn't mention Libby's son specifically, Tara was almost certain that she recalled Libby saying that he was in charge of the firm's financial operations, and therefore must somehow be involved. If ever Libby needed a friend, it was now. Checking the time, she picked up the phone only to get Libby's machine. She left a message.

Moments later, the phone rang. Thinking it was Libby, Tara was surprised by the sound of her father's voice.

"Tara, darling," he said. "I'm glad I caught you. Roberta told me that you were coming to town."

Pleased that he had phoned her directly, she said, "Yes, sir. I was hoping that you could meet me for lunch on Friday."

"I've checked my schedule and I can make it then. There's a wonderful restaurant around the corner from the station. Is everything all right?" he questioned. "Roberta told me that this lunch was more than a social call."

Tara gulped. How was she possibly going to tell him about the letter? "Oh, yes, I'm well," she replied. "I've got the first part of my dissertation completed. I hope to finish in a year. The news I have to tell you is, well . . . personal."

"Oh, I see," he said, sounding relieved. "Very good then. Why don't you come by the station around two o'clock? Look forward to it," he said.

"So do I," said Tara. "See you then," she added.

When she hung up the phone, Tara bit her bottom lip. Would she have the courage to ask him for the truth? Even worse, what if the truth was a secret that she was better off not knowing? Her head began to ache as she took the letter out and read it again.

CHAPTER 10

Libby

Her home seemed foreign. Robby's arrest had forever altered her world. Part of her wanted to scream and rage; the other part felt like running upstairs to hide. She spent hours on the phone, talking to Caroline and Pamela and helping them calm down as well as allaying the fears of close friends, who called to offer support. The gossip mill, she surmised, could have started and the fate of her son would be the topic of many conversations in this small community. She refused to dwell on it. After all, Robby was a good boy. Her heart refused to accept anything but his innocence.

She spent the next couple of days after Robby's arrest in a daze. Things were so chaotic that she lost all track of time. She and Ed drove back and forth to Atlanta trying to see Robby and talk with lawyers. In the midst of the crisis, her most pleasant surprise was a message from Tara, asking if she could help. She finally managed to call her back, expecting to get her machine. But Tara answered the phone, and after they spoke for a while, Tara insisted on bringing them some supper. Libby was too tired to refuse.

As soon as she hung up the phone, she wandered into the sun room to lie down on the sofa, promising herself that she would rest for just a moment. A knock on the back door woke her. Scrambling to get to the kitchen, Libby greeted Tara, who was holding a large basket and a shopping bag. Libby was touched by her thoughtfulness.

"I'm so sorry," said Tara. "Did I interrupt you?"

Libby smoothed back her hair, hoping she didn't look like a complete wreck. "You couldn't have come at a better time," she said politely. "Will you stay for a quick glass of iced tea?"

"Are you sure?" she asked. "I don't want to intrude."

"I'd love the company," Libby said. "Really."

Tara walked into the kitchen and placed the basket on the counter. "I brought you something along with dinner," she said shyly.

"How kind of you," said Libby. "Please forgive my appearance. I'm afraid it's been a long twenty-four hours."

"I'm not going to stay long," insisted Tara. "But I thought you might like to see—"

They were interrupted by the doorbell. Libby excused herself and walked to the front hall to open it. Her friend Mae was holding a terra-cotta pot filled with a lovely gardenia.

Before Libby could invite her in, she said, "I've got the car running and I need to go. We'll talk tomorrow."

"Thanks for thinking of us," Libby called after her. This show of support was just what she needed. Her close friends knew how much she loved flowers. The sweet-smelling plant made Libby feel better. She brought it back in the kitchen to show Tara.

"Now, where were we?" asked Libby, stirring some sugar into their tea. She watched as Tara reached into her shopping bag and pulled out a present wrapped in blue-and-gold-striped paper. "Tara, dear. Dinner was more than enough."

Tara smiled. "Open it and you'll understand."

Libby gingerly untied the ribbon and peeled away the paper to reveal a glossy cover. "Oh," she exclaimed, examining the book. "This is incredible. Wherever did you find it? You're such a clever girl. I can't tell you how much I appreciate this."

"A friend told me about it. It's supposed to be the

most comprehensive book on photography out there."

Libby got up from her chair to embrace her. "I can't thank you enough. What a welcome distraction. I'm trying to stay positive, you know?"

"Believe me, I understand," said Tara thoughtfully.

"You're a gem," said Libby. "I'll read every word. Now tell me what I missed on Tuesday. Everyone met at Catherine's, right?"

Libby listened while Tara shared some of the latest tidbits of information: Annie's story about Mayor Girl; Margy's new fabric samples; Catherine's update on her family's recycling efforts; Megan's trip to the pediatrician because of Hannah's stomach flu; Catherine's saga over trying to find a discontinued fabric to upholster her family room chairs.

"And how about you?" she inquired.

Tara hesitated. "Well, I'm okay," she said.

Libby raised one eyebrow.

"The truth is," said Tara, "I'm confused about a relationship right now."

"Someone new?"

"Don't I wish," said Tara with a heavy sigh. "There's a man in my life that I've known for some time now. We've been very good friends. We have so much in common, a passion for art history, music, European history. The list goes on and on. I guess I'm trying to decide whether to stay away."

Libby thought for a moment. "What's holding you back?"

"He's involved with someone else," said Tara.

"Has he given you any indication that he's unhappy with this other person?" Libby knew better than to ask if the gentleman in question was married. Her instincts told her that it was probably the case.

Tara nodded. "Absolutely. In fact, I'm sure of it."

"Don't worry, these things have a way of working themselves out," she offered. She wished that Robby had found someone like Tara. Perhaps it would have changed things. Wishful thinking, she told herself.

Tara smiled. "I hope so," she replied. "Enough about me. I forgot to mention that Ashley Gates also joined us for our meeting. I think she enjoyed it."

"I'm going to make a point to call her soon and volunteer to babysit those children," said Libby, taking a sip of her tea. "You know what fun I'd have."

"I'm the one that should be offering assistance. You've got enough going on. We're meeting again in a week at Margy's place. I hope you'll be able to come for a little bit."

"I'll try," said Libby. "Things are uncertain right now."

"I know what you mean," said Tara.

That night, Libby crawled into bed and dozed, but woke up a short time later, frightened and worried about Robby. She turned over to see Ed sleeping.

The room was completely dark except for the small light emanating from the nightlight she kept next to their bathroom. As her eyes adjusted to the moonless night, she smoothed back the tangerine-colored down comforter. Rolling onto her back, she faced the ceiling, contemplating the future. Just last week, she had envisioned their retirement years filled with family vacations, hobbies, and new projects. The thought of Robby behind bars made her feel sick to her stomach again.

She reached for her antacid pills by her bed. Popping several into her mouth, she quickly chewed them. Her glass of water was in its usual place on her nightstand. She gulped down several sips and stretched her shoulders. Slipping out of bed, she trudged downstairs, not sure of how to occupy the early hours of the morning. Making her way into their family room, she flipped on the light and sat down in one of her comfortable armchairs.

Pondering what to do next, she couldn't help but envision the cold, dark room where her son was spending the night. Tension made her shiver, so she tightened her white terry-cloth robe around her. She hated feeling so helpless. As she looked around the familiar room for comfort, family photographs caught her eye. Each picture was a colorful reminder of a special time in their lives. Seeing the faces of her children and grandchildren helped Libby relax for a moment.

She smiled at the sight of Robby's prom picture,

the one that she refused to take down despite his embarrassment. *His white tuxedo wasn't that horrible,* she thought wryly. Not like his date, the homecoming queen, whose dress was cut down to her navel. Without realizing it, she dozed off, comforted by images of her happy son around her.

The phone rang. Libby was startled and nearly tripped on her robe when she jumped up to answer it. Picking up the receiver, she heard Ed's voice already engaged in conversation with the lawyer. Libby announced that she was on the line, feeling a bit like an intruder. Realizing that it was difficult to conduct a three-way conversation, she stayed on only a bit longer before hanging up. Ed would fill her in on how things were going.

She raced upstairs. Ed was still on the phone, so she sat down in her flowered armchair to wait to hear the news. He looked alert, tense, and ready for business despite wearing only his pinstriped pajama bottoms. When he hung up, Ed met her gaze squarely.

"What?" she cried. "What now?"

"It's worse than I thought," said Ed, scratching his head. His hair stuck up on one side.

Libby hugged herself. "What did he do?"

"I don't know the whole story," said Ed. "But in short, he made some deals with his clients in order to get them to do business with Amvale. He wanted to ensure the company projected specific earnings."

"Why?" she croaked, her voice sounding hollow.

"Money! He wanted to make sure he got his three-million-dollar bonus! I'm so furious I could clock that kid on the head."

"Ed, stop."

"He was price fixing, Lib. Robert made illegal deals so that he could make more money. His motive was greed, pure and simple. How could he have done such a thing?"

Libby instantly thought of her son in his Batman costume. She had always believed that they had instilled the right values in him. How did he get so caught up in his company's corporate culture? This all seemed so oddly nightmarish, almost like something that happened to other people. "Maybe there's more to the story. I know Robby."

"Stop calling him that," Ed snapped. "His name is Robert. More important, he's a grown man soon to have a criminal record." He stormed off into the bathroom and slammed the door. She heard the sound of the shower running.

Libby was terrified. Ed's high blood pressure couldn't take this kind of stress. Somehow she was going to have to stay calm enough to mediate between father and son. Her Robby—Robert, she corrected herself—had made a terrible mistake. She still loved him unconditionally, but Ed would not be so forgiving. A sharp pain jabbed at her stomach. Calculating the time, she went to get her antacid tablets, chewing a couple of the berry flavor.

Twenty minutes later, Ed emerged from the bathroom, looking contrite. Libby said nothing.

"I've got a meeting this morning," he announced.

"I thought we had planned to go see him together. You were going to drive us back to Atlanta."

"Caroline can take you," said Ed, putting on his navy blazer.

"What's that supposed to mean?" Libby cried. "He's our son. You can't just abandon him now. He needs us."

"I'm not going today," said Ed in a clipped voice. His cheeks were flushed. "I'll get there another time."

"When?" she demanded.

"I don't know."

"This isn't like you," she said. "You've got to support him. He knows you. If he thinks for a minute that you're not behind him, it may change things."

"Change what?" he snapped angrily. "He knew I didn't like Amvale. I always suspected something was wrong. I told him so on several occasions, but he always laughed and told me that he could handle things. Look at what a fine job he's done," said Ed, unable to keep the sarcasm out of his voice. "You were always too easy on him, never allowing me to spank the kids if they did something wrong. Now look."

"Don't you dare blame me for this!" said Libby. "This is not about whether he got a spanking for bad behavior at five years old! You're being

166

absolutely ridiculous. I need you, Ed. We all need you. You're the one that can get our family through this, deal with the lawyers. He's our son and always will be, no matter what."

Ed sat down on the edge of the bed. "I never thought we'd be in this position."

Libby walked over to sit next to him. "Neither did I, but we're going to have to cope."

Ed hugged her tightly. "I'm sorry, Lib. It's not your fault. You were a great mother, and still are."

"I couldn't sleep last night, so I stared at old photographs of Robby," said Libby.

"God, I didn't even hear you get up."

Libby wasn't surprised. Ed's hearing wasn't what it used to be. "I needed something to occupy my mind. I'm so worried about him. He's a young man with his whole life ahead of him." She couldn't bear to discuss the possibility that Robby could get jail time.

"Not if he's convicted for securities fraud," exclaimed Ed, standing up.

Libby nearly covered her ears. She said, "We can't think like that. There must be something we can do."

"Okay, I'll go down with you today and have a talk with him. He'll need to cooperate fully with the police, which means giving away corporate secrets. It's his only chance. I know Robert well enough to know he won't like it. He was never one to tattle about anything, so it'll be tough on him. But he's the one who knows all of the company's financial dealings. He can help them nail the other executives."

Libby saw the look of determination on Ed's face. She didn't know how she would ever get by without him. She stood up and took his hand. "I think that makes good sense. Maybe the government will reward him for his help," she added hopefully.

"I don't think *reward* is the right word, honey. Robert's only hope is to reach some sort of plea bargain with the authorities. Perhaps they'll give him a reduced sentence."

"Reduced sentence," repeated Libby, her hand instantly going to her stomach.

"Lib, you've got to face reality. Our son is in serious trouble." He hugged her. "I'm sorry but I've got to head into the office for a few hours. I'll pick you up at ten sharp."

Libby nodded, unable to speak.

CHAPTER 11

Tara

Thoughts of Peter swirled in Tara's brain as she made her way to Washington. It still registered that this meeting was bad form on her part. He was her married thesis advisor, after all. But despite her misgivings, her attraction carried her forward as she pictured them strolling through Georgetown, enjoying a late-night dinner, or visiting the Corcoran to talk about Impressionist art. These romantic fantasies were mitigated by visions of a tense meeting with her father. Her anxiety levels grew as she glanced into her purse to make sure the letter was safely tucked into the side pocket.

As she rolled her black bag to the taxi stand, Tara felt guilty about not having told her mother she was coming into town for the weekend. At the very least, she should give her a call to say hello. Her mother's office wasn't too far from the hotel, so she could still stop in for a quick visit on the way. Pleased with this new plan, Tara managed to get hold of Martha, her mother's longtime personal assistant.

"Tara, how are you? How's your doctorate going?" said Martha.

"Hi, Martha. Things are going really well. Thanks for asking. You're not going to believe this, but I'm in a cab right now heading your way. I decided last minute to come to D.C. to hear a lecture. What does my mother's schedule look like?"

"Actually, you're in luck. She's just wrapping up a meeting with Senator Wilkins and I know she'd love to see you. I'll bet by the time you arrive, she'll be free."

About ten years ago, her mother had decided to

devote her time and energy to creating a foundation to help underprivileged kids. She came up with the idea for "Mentors on the Hill" because she wanted to give bright kids from the inner city of D.C. a chance for more opportunities. The foundation had a team that selected roughly one hundred fifty kids each year from inner-city schools to help them socially, emotionally, and professionally. Her mother had enlisted dozens of volunteers to teach these kids how to build self-esteem and achieve their life goals. Once they had completed an informal training program, they were paired with a leader on the Hill and given valuable job experience.

"Thanks so much, Martha. Tell her I'll be there in fifteen minutes."

"I'll let her know you're coming. She'll be thrilled to see you. Bye."

From the backseat of the cab, Tara observed the familiar monuments, the last few errant cherry blossoms on the trees, and the inevitable parade of businesspeople making their way across Connecticut Avenue. It really did feel good to be back in a more vibrant place.

Tara would have adored spending more time with her mother, but everything about this visit was already awkward. No, this idea of just a brief meeting was right. She promised to come back and stay with her mom on her next trip. Besides, the letter felt as if it were burning a hole in her purse pocket. Her mother was an incredibly intelligent and competent woman; it was hard to believe that her father might have betrayed her. *There is just no way.*

What a difference her mother had helped make for hundreds of teenagers, Tara mused, comparing her mother's self-effacing manner to her father's ego. Opposites must attract, she thought wryly. She spotted her mother's office building on the corner of K Street. Her mother was very clever, managing to secure office space in this newly renovated building thanks to a generous donation from a wealthy friend. In her usual way, her mother refused to disclose the name of the person; Tara concluded that it was yet another admirer of Candice's brilliant mind.

When Tara walked into the foundation's reception area, Martha greeted her with enthusiasm. "Your mother can't wait to see you. Go ahead in. Can I get you some coffee or anything?"

"No, I'm great," replied Tara, waving at Charlotte, another long-term associate of her mother's and an incredibly energetic former social worker who was the backbone of the organization. Tara smiled at several new faces as she walked by, not sure whether to introduce herself.

"Mom," said Tara as she pushed open the door. She was filled with an unexpected rush of emotion and suddenly was very glad she'd come.

"Tara, darling," said her mother, standing up to give her a hug. Her black pantsuit, pearl choker, and white blouse were simple and elegant. "I can't believe you're here. How long are you staying?"

"Just the weekend. I've got to work, which is why I didn't call you before," she said, hating herself for the white lie. "But I just couldn't stand the thought of being in the city and not seeing you. My thesis advisor is giving a lecture this evening so I need to be there. There are a few important people in the art world he wants me to meet this afternoon. He can open a lot of doors for me," she added, hoping her mother wouldn't question her any further.

"Of course," said Candice with a smile. She looked into her eyes. "You look as beautiful as ever, but a bit tired. Are things going well?"

"Absolutely," Tara replied too quickly.

"Come on in and sit for a minute," said Candice, putting her arm around her and leading her to a chair.

For an instant, Tara desperately wanted to confide in her mother about everything. Part of her wanted to leap into her mother's arms and ask for comfort, but her self-discipline prevailed. She wanted to tell her mother about the letter, about Peter, and seek her mother's wise counsel. After all, Candice was a born problem solver; she'd always had a knack for taking complex situations and simplifying them into a workable program. *I wish she could apply this skill to my life,* Tara thought. For the first time ever, Tara wanted her mother to tell her what to do. Instead, she said, "Martha said you were meeting with Senator Wilkins. How'd it go?"

Candice's brown eyes lit up. "Well, he wants to help me raise funds to expand the program. He really thinks that we can find jobs and mentors for fifty more kids so that Mentors on the Hill can be a prototype for other cities across the country." Candice thought for a minute. "I'm definitely interested in expansion, but my resources are stretched to the limit as it is. There just aren't enough hours in the day. To make matters worse, he wants me to go with him to talk with the secretary of education and the first lady about what we're doing."

"Mom, that's great!" said Tara. "I'm so proud of you."

Candice sighed, looking down at her hands. "I'm just not sure if I'm the right person to run this national initiative. The whole idea is a bit overwhelming right now."

"You can't be serious! Everyone on the Hill knows you're a leader. You're the absolute best person for the job. That's why people want to work with you. You get things done."

"Thanks for the vote of approval, honey, but that's enough talk about me. I'm so glad you're here. I want to know what's been happening in your life."

Suddenly, there was a persistent knock at the door. "Yes?" said Candice, looking at Tara.

"I'm so sorry to interrupt," said Martha. "Senator Wilkins is on line one and insists on speaking with you. He says it's really important."

"Tell him that my daughter just arrived and I'll call him back shortly."

Tara jumped in. "No, Mom, it's okay. I've got a meeting this afternoon and I'm already running late."

"Are you sure?" said Candice.

Tara nodded, relieved to have an excuse to leave. So the visit was brief and impersonal. Her mother was always busy. If she stayed to chat, she was afraid her mother might sense that something was wrong.

"It's so wonderful seeing you," said Candice, giving Tara a hug. "I'm so sorry I have to take this call. Let me know how things go, okay?" Candice reached for the phone.

"Absolutely," replied Tara, waving as she walked out the door. Tara was relieved that she'd gotten what she wanted, but this feeling of loneliness was all too familiar.

A short time later, Tara was headed down M Street to her hotel in the heart of Georgetown. Her father had arranged for her to stay here; that was one of the many perks of being Kent West's daughter. The front lobby was decorated with gilt-framed paintings, oriental rugs, leather chairs, and mahogany furniture. Checking her watch, Tara calculated that she had enough time to browse through the charming shops and galleries outside on M Street before Peter's lecture. At the reception desk, she was informed that her hotel stay had been paid for by a

Mr. West. *That's a pleasant surprise,* thought Tara. Hopefully, he wouldn't regret the warm welcome after their talk.

"Hi there," said a male voice as she felt a tap on her shoulder.

Tara turned around to find Peter standing there. Her breath caught in her throat as she looked at him. He seemed completely at ease in his jeans, blazer, and loafers with no socks.

"Hi," she said nervously. "I really didn't know you were staying here."

"What a perfect coincidence," he said.

"Yes," she said, sensing that her voice was sounding a bit too breathy. *He's just a man,* she reminded herself. There was absolutely no reason to feel awkward in his presence. After all, they had known each other for more than a year.

"Have you had lunch?" he inquired. "I was just heading out to get something. Will you join me?"

"Sure," she said, thinking she could win an award for one-word answers. "I mean, that sounds great. Let me put my things in my room and I can meet you back here in, say, ten minutes?"

"Certainly," he said. "I'll be waiting over there. Wake me up, if you must." He pointed to a large tufted leather chair in a quiet corner.

Tara headed upstairs to her room. It turned out that her father had booked her into a suite with a full living room area, dining table, mini-kitchen, and bar. The marble bathroom with double sinks made it even more luxurious. *Perhaps I should come visit him more often.* She chuckled to herself, trying not to think about the cost per night or the fact that she had ended up at the same hotel as Peter. It really must be fate, she decided.

She didn't want to keep Peter waiting, so she just washed her hands, brushed her teeth, and made a quick change into jeans and flats. Checking her appearance in the wall-size lighted mirror, she removed the tangles from her shoulder-length hair and added some lipstick.

He was still waiting for her in the lobby. Tara wanted to pinch herself. Once outside, he put his arm around her as they strolled down the street. She could smell his aftershave, which had a slight citrus scent.

"There's a wonderful little Italian place just down the way. They make their pasta and breads fresh every day, so the food is sublime."

Once they were seated, Tara looked around at miniature ceramic pitchers filled with wildflowers, yellow tablecloths, and displays of brightly colored plates decorating the white stucco walls. The place was utterly charming.

"What time are you speaking tonight?" she asked.

"Around seven. They told me the evening is sold out. That comes as a great relief. You never know if people are going to show up at these things or not." He glanced at the menus in front of him. "Would you like a glass of wine?" he asked.

"Yes," she said. "You choose."

"Very well then," he said, turning his attention to the waiter. He ordered them a bottle of pinot noir.

"Fortunately, I got my ticket for tonight and for the exhibit tomorrow morning online, so I have nothing to worry about."

"You're very meticulous. That's one of the things I enjoy so much about you. Your writing is the same way, very precise and very clear. If all goes well, I would hope your dissertation would be the basis for a wonderful book."

"I think this is the first time you've ever told me you liked my writing," she said. "So you get some perverse pleasure out of red-penning my manu-script even when you like what I have to say?" she said, with a hint of challenge in her voice.

"Absolutely," he said. "I've got to keep my wits about me to stay one step ahead of you."

"Your humility intrigues me." Tara basked in Peter's compliment.

The waiter brought their wine, pouring them each a glass. They ordered their lunch. Tara asked for mixed greens with balsamic vinaigrette along with goat cheese ravioli. Peter had the Caesar salad and spaghetti. A large basket of freshly baked bread was placed in front of them, along with a large bottle of olive oil.

"This stuff melts in your mouth," he said, tear-ing off a piece of the bread. When he held it for her to try, she had a vision of Tess of the D'Urbervilles eating that strawberry. She thought of Ashley, who she knew would be amused by the comparison. Tara took the slice from his hand.

They lingered over the wine, talking about Miró and Calder. Peter expressed his excitement at seeing Calder's circus animals at the exhibit. When he was a boy, he explained, he tried to bend coat hangers into animals. He was completely disappointed that despite many earnest attempts, he couldn't create anything like the ones Calder made. At twelve years old, he was smart enough to realize that he didn't have a chance of becoming an artist like Calder. Tara realized that this was the first time Peter had ever shared anything so personal about himself. The conversation was more intimate, Tara thought, as the tension between them steadily escalated. When his leg brushed against her knee, she nearly flinched but caught herself.

"I can't wait to show you one of my favorite pieces in the exhibit. It's one of Calder's wire portraits of a Medusa head hanging from the ceiling. You should see what happens when the piece swings in the air. There's this whirling shadow on the wall beside it. It's an absolutely brilliant technique. David Murray, the museum's curator, and I walked underneath the figure several times so that it would move a bit for us. Too bad we couldn't have a fan in the exhibit so the figure stayed in motion. I'll make a note to talk with him about that."

Tara laughed. "I'll look forward to seeing it. Will

they let us into the gallery after your talk?"

"I think I can arrange that," he said silkily.

"So we'd be alone with millions of dollars of art. How romantic," she shot back. "We could get arrested."

They both laughed. He reached for her hand and began to caress her fingertips. It sent sparks of pleasure through her nervous system. She liked the feel of his hands on her skin. His movements were fluid and easy.

"I'm so glad you came," he said softly.

"I am, too," she said.

If ever she wanted to be kissed, it was at that moment. But they were interrupted by the waiter, who had come to refill their wineglasses. Tara looked around, noticing that the lunch crowd had all but disappeared.

"Why don't we go walk around?" suggested Peter, who paid the check despite Tara's protestations.

By the time they stepped back outside, the skies were overcast. They peered into the window of an antique shop, debating the merits of an English chest of drawers. A gallery with a colorful painting of a seascape enticed them both inside. Tara looked around the shop, feeling completely at home among the abstract paintings.

One picture caught her eye. She was instantly reminded of Miró's work, as the forms had a way of drawing the viewer into their world. The painting was royal blue with several large abstract shapes painted across it in green and brown.

"I love it," she said aloud.

A woman dressed in a tailored brown jacket came over to her side. "Isn't it magnificent?" she said. "This artist recently had his first museum show here in town. His reviews were excellent. I think he's going to be a national name before we know it."

"How much does his work sell for?" asked Tara, praying that the price wasn't too horrible.

"This particular painting is about thirty thousand. I have smaller works for less."

Peter came up to stand beside her. "I think that painting is great; the abstract shapes remind me of Miró."

"That's just what I was thinking," said Tara. "Though there are a few more zeros on the price tag than I had hoped."

He checked his watch. "It's almost five thirty. I think I need to head back to shower and change for tonight. I don't think David would appreciate me showing up in jeans."

"I agree."

They headed back to their hotel rooms, holding hands. Tara didn't want to let him go. He walked her to her room. Finally, Peter bent down to kiss her. *Reality is so much better than my imagination,* Tara thought, when their lips touched for the first time.

"I'm looking forward to tonight," he said.

Tara nodded. She watched him walk back down the hallway, noticing how well his tailored jacket fit his broad shoulders. After this afternoon, she was sure that she'd made the right decision in coming here.

It occurred to her that she needed to get word to her father that she had arrived safely and to confirm their lunch tomorrow. She wondered if she actually might receive his undivided attention for a whole hour. Rather than dwell on his inadequacies as a parent, she decided to stay positive and thank him for the gift of her stay in such a lovely place. At that moment, she wasn't sure she wanted to confront him about the letter. It was sobering to realize that her actions were certainly no better than his. She played with the ring on her index finger.

As usual, Peter had been acutely modest about the potential crowd that would gather to hear him speak. The auditorium was overflowing with people holding his book, hoping to get an autograph. She overheard people talking about him, using words like "brilliant," "insightful," and "charismatic speaker." It was thrilling to know that she had had a private audience with him this afternoon and would receive his undivided attention tonight over a late dinner.

Around seven o'clock, an older man with a British accent came to the podium and introduced himself as Dr. David Murray, the curator for modern and contemporary art at the museum. He spent several minutes giving Peter a lavish introduction, praising him for his insightful biography on Miró as well as his contributions to the art community.

"I'd also like to recognize Peter's lovely wife, Rosalyn Bergen, who is a distinguished teacher of Latin at Lakefield Academy. Now, you're in for a real treat. . . ."

Tara felt ill. How could she have been so stupid? Wanting to crawl under her seat, she looked around for a way out, wondering if she could leave without anyone noticing her. She heard Peter's voice thanking Dr. Murray. Feeling like a trapped animal, she glanced at each of the exit signs. Her hands felt clammy. It seemed as if her only option would be to wait until the question-and-answer period, when she could quietly slip away.

She reminded herself that she had always known he was married. She shouldn't be so shocked. After all, this was part of the deal. If she had a relationship with Peter, she would have no claim on him at all. Suddenly, Tara wasn't sure if she was cut out to handle such a thing.

What were her feelings for Peter? It all seemed so convoluted. She had kissed him passionately this afternoon, waiting for the promise of fulfillment tonight. His wife's arrival felt as if someone had poured a bucket of ice water all over her. Peter, it seemed, was clearly unfazed. She listened to him highlight several pieces of art in the exhibit that were particularly special. She was counting the minutes until he finished, trying not to listen to his insights into several of the works in the collection.

At the sound of massive applause, Tara finally managed to make her way out. This was certainly not how she had wanted the evening to end. She walked several blocks in the drizzle, looking for a cab to take her back to the hotel. It was a somewhat pathetic moment, she thought, like living a scene from a bad made-for-TV movie.

Once inside the safety of her hotel room, she bolted the door. Wishing she were more tired, she wrapped herself up in the hotel's white terry-cloth robe and settled down to watch a movie.

The knock on the door woke her. It had just the right level of force, enough to make a point that someone was out there who wanted to talk with her. A confrontation was inevitable, she decided, hoisting herself up out of bed. She pulled the robe tightly around her small form.

"Who is it?" she said.

"Me," said Peter. "I want to talk to you."

"No," she said. "There's nothing to say."

"Yes, there is," he commanded. "Meet me down in the bar in fifteen minutes. I'll be waiting."

Tara debated what to do. She didn't have to go. Pacing the room, she flipped on the light and began to dress.

When she came downstairs, he was waiting for her, seated at a table with a glass of wine at her place. She glanced around to see several small groups of people gathered around tables. The bar was dark with mahogany paneling and leather furnishings. Several portraits of presidents hung on the walls. Her father would be right at home here, she thought.

"Look," she said, taking a seat across from Peter. "I'm incredibly embarrassed by my actions today. I can only assume your wife is around here somewhere, but I promise to stay away. Don't worry, I've had all evening to think about things and I can find a new advisor."

"Stop it, Tara. I'm the one who should be apologizing. I didn't know she was coming. She's gone now. I'm sorry you had to go through that." He paused. "If you think this is comfortable for me, then you're wrong. I didn't anticipate this happening either, but I can't help how I feel."

Tara took a sip of her wine. "Neither can I," she said quietly. "But I realized tonight that I can't play second to anyone else. I want more from a relationship."

"I understand," he said. "But I've got commitments, obligations. You know that."

"I do know that. I did know that. The rational part of my mind went on vacation. It's back now."

"I'm crazy about you," he said. "I can't think straight when you're around."

"Me, neither," she said. "Which is why I should say good night."

He reached over to take her hand. "I want you," he said quietly.

"Don't," said Tara, snatching her hand back. "Don't make this any harder on me."

"Why do you think you're the only one in this relationship? This is hard on me, too. We're both involved, whether we like it or not. I can't control how I feel any more than you can."

"I need to go now," said Tara, standing up. "I need time to think. All I know is that this doesn't feel right."

"Fair enough," said Peter. "Time won't change how I feel." He stood up. "May I walk you to your room?"

Tara shook her head. She didn't trust herself. "Good night," she said weakly.

"Where does this leave us?" he asked, running a hand through his dark hair.

"I don't know," she replied. It would be so easy to just let things happen. She turned to look at him. *He was hard to resist,* she thought.

It was a long night. Tara tossed and turned, wishing she could shut off her feelings for Peter. Even worse, this decision affected her life's work. After all, he was an expert on Miró. How was she going to continue working with him while pretending this weekend hadn't occurred?

Around seven a.m., the phone rang. It was her father, wanting to reschedule lunch. A high-ranking foreign diplomat had come to town unexpectedly, he explained. It was his only chance to get an interview.

"You know I'd love to see you, darling," he said, "but I'm absolutely swamped again. Can you make breakfast tomorrow morning?"

Tara knew she should be accommodating, but she was stressed out and sick of his work commitments. "I'm sorry, Daddy," she said sweetly. "Something's come up in my schedule as well, so that won't be possible. Another time, perhaps?" she added for good measure.

"Oh," he responded quietly. "I was really looking forward to seeing you. Can't we figure something out?"

"Sure. I'll give you a call next time I'm in town," said Tara easily. "Sorry we missed each other. Bye."

"Good-bye. Sorry, again."

As soon as she hung up the phone, Tara actually felt liberated for once. She had never, ever refused an invitation from her famous father. As a child, she was always willing to accept whatever crumbs of affection he gave her. It finally dawned on her that she was an independent woman with choices.

The letter was still hidden in her purse. She was trying to decide whether to drop it off at his office with a note that said something like, *This note came to me. Would you care to explain it?* She laughed aloud, knowing her father would find some clever way of evading the issue. He was a master story-teller.

Tara imagined herself appearing on a daytime talk show. As Kent West's daughter, she could do a segment on famous fathers and the children they'd abandoned. Even better, she thought, she could title her dissertation "Why I Can't Have a Normal Relationship."

For a fleeting moment, Tara thought about calling her mother for support, then discarded the idea. Her mother always defended him no matter how hard she tried to get her to admit the truth. To her, Kent West could do no wrong. It annoyed her how much Candice put him up on such a pedestal. That's what made this whole situation with the letter so difficult. Candice was an idealist, and she always saw the best in the people she loved. Groaning aloud in frustration, Tara paced the floor.

With a sudden burst of energy, she decided that she would do things for herself today. She absolutely wasn't going to run home and feel sorry for herself. She ordered from room service and began to plan her day. When the knock came at the door, she opened it for a waiter who carried a tray.

"These were the largest cups we had, Miss West," he said with a laugh. "So I brought you three of them."

"How lovely," she responded easily, signing the check.

He placed the tray on the table, thankfully not commenting on her meal of diet soda and dry toast.

Her morning was surprisingly enjoyable. She spent the better part of the day touring the Calder and Miró exhibit at the National Gallery, where Peter had spoken the night before. Her only moment of weakness came when she spied the Medusa head he had talked about over lunch. When the security guard wasn't looking, she walked below it several times to generate some air. Peter was right. They needed to hook up a fan.

After immersing herself in art all day, Tara was pleased to have accomplished so much. Around dinnertime, she returned to the hotel, ready to take a hot bath and order from room service. When she opened the door to her room, she was alarmed to find that all of the lights were on. Then she saw him.

"Daddy, what are you doing here?" she asked.

Kent West turned around to face her. Tara had to admit, he was a striking figure in his navy blazer with a pocket handkerchief. His hair was gray only at the temples, probably thanks to a bit of hair dye. He looked, as always, camera ready.

"I came to take you to dinner," he said nonchalantly. "This is my usual suite. I've known the hotel manager for years, so he was kind enough to let me in so that I could surprise you."

Suddenly, Peter walked into the room. "I thought *I* was taking you to dinner," he said forcefully.

Just think, I have my distant, globe-trotting father

and my married boyfriend together in the same room. Isn't this just great? Tara dropped her bags on the table. "Peter, this is my father, Kent West. Daddy, this is Peter Bergen, my thesis advisor."

"Kent West is your father?" said Peter incredulously, walking over to shake his hand. "Kent, I'm Peter Bergen. You did a story on me several years ago."

Kent shook his hand. "I remember," he said. "Your biography was exceptional. You were one of the youngest men ever to win the National Book Award."

"That's right," said Peter. "And you won the National Press Award for coverage of the crisis in Kuwait. You gave this country one of the most outstanding examples of reporting I've ever seen."

"Why don't you two have dinner together?" asked Tara, torn between anger and amusement.

Both men laughed.

"Really," Tara sighed. "I'm not sure I can take much more of this." She meant it. She ought to kick them both out of her room.

"Come on, darling," said her father. "I've got reservations at this marvelous restaurant downtown. We'll catch up there. I can't wait to tell you about my interview today. It was superb." He turned to Peter. "Will you join us?"

"Peter was just leaving," offered Tara, trying to assert herself. As much as she loved her father, he always seemed to have a way of using his celebrity to get exactly what he wanted. It was irritating, yet, like everyone else, she had always been a bit in awe of him. As for Peter, Tara thought angrily, he was just as unavailable as her father. A tiny voice reminded her again that she had known he was married when she came here. "We'll talk later," she said to Peter, staring at his handsome face, feeling a tingle of excitement. She secretly wanted him to come, but she told herself she was right to keep her distance; it would be downright stupid to get involved with him, no matter how much she wanted to.

Peter turned to her father. "I'd love to come."

Tara paused for a moment, wavering over whether to succumb to the wishes of both men. It was hard, she thought, disgusted at her own weakness. Did she really want to spend the evening by herself in the hotel room? It wasn't a very appealing option. Sighing heavily, she glared at Peter to let him know she wasn't pleased. When their eyes met, he looked at her with such intensity that it made Tara catch her breath. Tension crackled between them. His gaze lingered on her face, and Tara felt herself softening.

Her father held up his hands. "I never involve myself in Tara's personal life. I'm sure you two can forget about your differences long enough to enjoy a meal together?" He winked at her. His laissez-faire attitude was part of his charm.

"You're too busy to involve yourself in my life,"

Tara muttered under her breath. "I need a few minutes to freshen up," she announced more loudly, wishing she could haul herself over the balcony and escape.

When she emerged from her bedroom, she found both men involved in a spirited conversation about the current administration's handling of the war.

"It's a bloody mess over there," said her father.

"I can't imagine having to film out in the desert," said Peter, catching sight of her.

Her father immediately tempered his remarks. "You learn to sleep sitting up. Very relaxing," he added. "I think we should head out. My driver's waiting downstairs."

For the next two hours, Tara felt as if she were participating in a match of verbal volleyball. It was an intellectual challenge to keep up with such fine-tuned thinkers, both experts in their respective fields. She refused to feel inferior.

"What do you think of the new Supreme Court nominee?" asked Peter.

"Brilliant," raved her father. "One of the finest legal minds this country has ever seen. I'm hoping to interview him next month."

"I agree," said Peter. "He understands both party lines but follows the law."

"I think the president should have nominated a woman," declared Tara. She launched into a diatribe about women in leadership positions, especially the country's need for a female president.

"What do you make of the sale of that van Gogh for a hundred million last week at Sotheby's?" asked her father, moving the conversation to safer ground.

"It certainly means art is a serious investment that won't lose its value," responded Peter.

"I think it's absolutely outrageous that someone would pay that kind of money for one painting. It doesn't bode well for the marketplace," countered Tara, glaring at both men.

When the waiter came to take their order, both men requested steaks. Tara had the fish. Silence descended over the table.

Not one to be deterred, her father seemed determined to make dinner interesting. "Anyone heard the reports on Amvale? Those guys are a bunch of crooks. I fear for what it's going to do to our economy."

"I think greed is an integral part of our corporate culture," added Peter.

"How do you know they're all guilty?" asked Tara.

"Don't be naïve," said her father. "They overstated their profits by millions of dollars to raise stock prices. I hope they crucify those guys to set an example for the rest of the corporate thieves out there."

Tara winced, thinking of Libby and her son. She would never admit to her father that she knew anyone involved. He'd be after an exclusive interview in a matter of minutes. "It may not be as bad as they're reporting," she said.

"My sources tell me that the SEC is hot on the case. They're going for blood. I've been talking with several of the lawyers. We want to break the story before an indictment is made."

"How wonderful for you," said Tara dryly. Her fish felt heavy in her stomach. What ridiculous notion had possessed her to come out to dinner tonight? She must not have been thinking clearly. How could she have let herself get swept away by the two charismatic men with her? It was utterly nauseating how they were fawning all over each other. "I've had enough." She sighed, getting up from the table. "I'm sure the two of you won't have any trouble continuing the conversation without me." When Peter stood up, she warned, "I'm going back to the hotel alone."

As she was leaving Tara could hear her father telling Peter that she'd always been a bit of a spitfire. Tara had a good mind to march back to the table and start screaming. Her good sense prevailed and she managed to get to the front door on her own. Just as she finished speaking to the hostess about a cab, Peter walked up. He put his hands up in mock surrender as he approached.

"Don't worry, honey, you can head on. I'll finish up with your father."

"I think you should divorce your wife and marry my father," snapped Tara. "It would be an ideal match. You could debate the world's problems forever."

"I think I should divorce my wife and marry you," he offered.

"Very funny," said Tara.

"I wasn't kidding. I'm crazy about you and you know it."

Tara faced him. "That's not fair."

"It's the truth," he said.

Her resolve was weakening; she could feel it. She stared at his face, wanting to believe him. Suddenly, a woman dressed in black came up behind them to tap Peter on the shoulder.

"Peter, is that you?" She kissed him on the cheek. "What are you doing in D.C.? Is Rosalyn here?"

"Marissa," he said. "How are you? No, sorry, she was but she didn't stay. I'm here working with David over at the National Gallery." He eyed Tara nervously.

"Hello, I'm Tara West," she said, extending her hand. "I'm one of Peter's students, here to do research for my doctorate." The words flowed easily from her lips. "We've just finished a, shall we say, challenging dinner with my father, Kent West, who covered more issues at the dinner table than he does on television each night." She motioned toward the table where her father was talking with yet another admirer.

Marissa's eyes widened. "How marvelous, I adore his show. Don't tell me that you're in the middle of writing another prize-winning biography?" she asked Peter.

"You caught me," he said with the appropriate laugh. "I'm at work on another project, but I'm not ready to talk about it just yet."

"Fine. No more questions." She gave him another hug. "So nice to meet you, Tara. Good night." She headed out the door.

"You handled that well," he told her. "Marissa Bevins is one of Rosalyn's old college room-mates."

"How special," she said, backing away from him.

"How about one last drink back at the hotel?" he asked, inching closer to her.

"Don't count on it," she said firmly, knowing her words rang hollow.

Tara was wracked by indecision on the way back to the hotel. Peter was hard to resist. Was one drink so awful? Maybe she wouldn't feel a thing when she sat across from him tonight, and then all of this nonsense would simply fade away. Perhaps if she faced her feelings, she would see that Peter was most definitely wrong for her. Okay, so he was extraordinarily attractive and brilliant. The memory of their kiss lingered on her lips. Suddenly filled with self-disgust, Tara eyed her purse with the letter tucked inside.

With new resolve, she decided the best course of action would be to simply take a detour for a few hours. Where could she go to kill time and avoid the inevitable confrontation with Peter? Checking her watch, she saw that it was nearly eleven o'clock. Going alone to a movie at this hour was out of the question. When she was growing up, one of her favorite places to visit was Union Station—the train station was always a hub of activity and a relatively safe place for a single woman. Certainly Peter's ego would get the better of him and he'd refuse to wait up for her.

Tara walked into the domed building, trying to decide where to go. Several shop windows had already turned off their lights so she turned left, spying a brightly lit bookstore. Luckily the local Barnes & Noble didn't close until midnight. Visions of Peter clouded her brain, weakening her resolve. A little voice inside her mind told her that it would be so easy to meet him back at the hotel. That love only came once in a lifetime. Peter was so incredibly perfect, she thought, trying to search her brain for some flaws. Maybe he had bad breath in the morning; or, even worse, maybe he had been a terrible son to his mother, abandoning her to some nursing home. Perhaps he was a total slob who refused to help out around the house. Yet even as she compiled a list of Peter's supposed foibles in her mind, her legs moved her toward the nonfiction section of the bookstore so that she could check out Peter's picture on the back jacket.

"Tara, is that you?" said a fashionable woman with blond, shoulder-length hair.

"Nancy?" Tara replied, delighted to recognize the familiar face of a childhood friend. "What are you doing here?" Nancy's interior decorating business kept her busy, and it had been months since they'd last seen each other.

"I was just in Baltimore for the day and had the longest client dinner ever. This couple argued over everything from what shade of blue to paint their bedroom to bathroom accessories. I'm so frazzled I can't see straight. Needless to say, I was going to console myself with a couple of trashy magazines before bed. I wish I'd known you were coming to town. I'd rather have had dinner with you than the bickering dynamic duo."

"I'm so sorry I didn't call, but I planned this trip at the last minute. I barely even saw my mother yesterday. I came to hear this expert speak on Miró last night."

"Fantastic. So where are you off to now?" asked Nancy, glancing at Tara's evening clothes.

"Actually, nowhere," said Tara. "I just had dinner with my father, and I didn't want to go back to my hotel because, well, I'm having trouble with a . . . boyfriend who's not my boyfriend. Does that make sense?"

"Sort of. I have a live-in boyfriend who's waiting for me at our apartment and I'd rather be here at the bookstore."

"I wish I could say the same. I'd much rather be with my totally sexy nonboyfriend, but . . ."

"But?"

"He's married and I just don't want to go there," said Tara, needing to confide in someone, and knowing Nancy would support her. After all, she and Nancy had shared all of those teenage firsts together, and that counted for something.

"Good for you. You're way too brilliant and beautiful to settle. Come on, let's go have a drink and I promise we won't talk about *him*."

"Thanks," said Tara. "I can't wait to hear about your life and all of those famous clients."

"You're not going to believe how cheap many of them are," said Nancy with a giggle. "Now, we'd better be able to find an open bar somewhere so Nathan will be fast asleep when I get home."

Tara welcomed the distraction. For the next two hours, they talked fashion, decorating secrets, hair, celebrity gossip, and, of course, the inevitable rehashing of high school boyfriends. Tara learned that Jack Fleming, her total crush in ninth grade, was now a nationally ranked professional tennis player. She made a mental note to look for him when she watched Wimbledon. After two hours of reliving their childhood, they decided to call it a night and share a cab back downtown.

Her spirits renewed, Tara nearly forgot all about Peter when she walked back into the hotel lobby. It came as quite a shock to see him waiting for her in a leather chair.

"Hi," she said sheepishly, noticing his rumpled

hair and unshaven face. His sleepy expression made him even more irresistible.

"Hello there," he said calmly. "So, there must have been a lot of red lights on the way home. Right? Didn't you think that I might be worried about you? I left you a couple of messages on your cell."

"Sorry, I was out and turned my phone off. I'm fully capable of taking care of myself," Tara said defensively. She really wanted him to blow up or demand to know where she had been. Then she'd have the evidence she wanted to prove that he wasn't right for her.

"Fine," he said casually. "If you want to pretend there's nothing between us, then you're kidding yourself. I never thought you'd be such a coward."

Tara felt as if he had struck her. "Coward?" she lashed back. "You know I'm not the type to have some sleazy affair. Your wife was just here last night and I lied to that Marissa woman. I just completely lied," said Tara, looking around to see if anyone was listening.

"Can we continue this conversation elsewhere?" he said, holding out his hand.

Tara wanted to slap away his hand, but controlled herself and felt his firm grip on hers. "Fine," she said.

"You know, it would be easier to talk in private upstairs," he suggested smoothly.

"All right. We'll go to my room for fifteen minutes," she agreed. She felt the warmth of his hand in hers, but refused to succumb to the tingling sensation that his touch aroused.

"I can do better than that," he quipped, raising an eyebrow at her.

"Not funny," she shot back, amazed that his sexual innuendo could make her stumble in the middle of a fight.

Her hands trembled slightly when she opened the door. She could smell the tangy scent of his after-shave and she knew she was in dangerous territory. Flicking on all of the lights, Tara marched over to the sofa. "Okay, let's get something straight. You win. I'm attracted to you and I won't try to deny it. It's so hard because I've never met anyone like you before in my life. It would be so easy to let things happen, but I would never forgive myself. I'm just not going to wreck your marriage."

"My marriage is over, Tara. I wouldn't be standing here with you if I were in love with my wife. I'm crazy about you. Why not take a chance?" Peter moved over to stand next to her and brushed his hands through her hair. "You know it would be worth it," he said quietly.

Tara's heart hammered in her chest. When he leaned down to kiss her softly, Tara nearly melted into his arms. They certainly had chemistry. Of that, she was sure. "I want more than tonight," she said.

Peter let her move a few inches away from his embrace. "So do I," he said, idly rubbing her back.

"I don't believe you," she said, with a narrowed

glance at his muscular body. "Prove it," she challenged, certain she would regret her own words.

"Fair enough," he replied, stepping away from her. "I'll wait until you're ready. No matter how painful that may be," he added, with a mocking grin as he sat down in a beige velvet side chair.

"Very funny," said Tara primly, going over to stand beside him. How many times could she respond to him with "very funny" and "not funny"? She was sure she sounded like she was in eighth grade. When she looked at him, her rational thought seemed to go on vacation.

"I can assure you I'm not laughing right now." Peter gently pulled her onto his lap and held her close. "You have no idea how crazy I am about you."

"Crazy enough to play by the rules?" she asked, sitting up to look him in the eye.

"I'll do whatever you want me to do," he replied smoothly. "Within reason, of course. But for right now, I think I'll go to my room and take a nice cold shower." He gently motioned for her to stand up.

Tara was secretly thrilled that he was willing to wait; it made her all the more smitten. " 'Night," said Tara sweetly, following him to the door.

"Don't I get a kiss good night?" he asked.

Just as Tara reached up to give him a chaste peck on the check, Peter captured her lips with his and kissed her soundly. Tara felt as if someone had knocked the wind right out of her. She was breathing rapidly when he pulled away.

"Good night," he said when he left.

When the door closed behind him, Tara scanned the elegant room which suddenly seemed empty and lonely. Biting the nail of her index finger, Tara longed to call Peter back. Desire was dissipating all of her rational thought. Just as she was about to reach for the phone, Tara spied her purse with the letter in it, a cold reminder of why she was really here.

CHAPTER 12

Libby

One Month Later

I don't like anyone staring at me, Libby thought, trying to avoid the gaze of a woman whom she had met socially a few months ago. Because she and Ed were well known in the community, word had spread that her son worked for Amvale. She was certain that local speculation about Robby's fate was rampant. It didn't help matters that the national news had labeled the once-lofty executive branch of Amvale as "a clever bunch of cheaters and liars."

Libby avoided eye contact as much as possible when she went to the grocery store, the dry cleaner, or the gas station. It was easier that way. There were days when she didn't go outside the house. She wanted to post a sign in the front yard that said, *My son is a good boy. Leave us alone.* How sad, she thought miserably, that this scandal had invaded their daily lives. In the wake of the investigation, ordinary tasks were difficult to accomplish.

"It'll pass," Ed told her every time she complained.

"When?" she asked. "I don't know how much more of this I can take."

At least her students knew nothing about Amvale or securities fraud or accounting malpractice. The second- and third-graders at the local elementary school were the reason she was able to get out of bed on the days she was a substitute teacher. Within the confines of her classroom, she felt safe and able to react normally for a few hours. Otherwise, she and Ed existed in a state of anxious limbo as they worked closely with their lawyer to clear Robby's name. Each day was a fight with no indication of how things might work themselves out.

Ed urged her to keep things as normal as possible. Libby knew she had lost too much weight, but it was hard to eat and sleep normally when she feared that her son faced jail time. Knowing that Ed watched her closely, Libby scattered her scrambled eggs around the plate so that it looked like she had taken a few bites.

"I have some good news," he said, taking a sip of coffee.

"I haven't heard you say anything like that for weeks. What's happened?"

"Robert wore a wire yesterday and was able to record some valuable information against Amvale's CEO."

"How come I knew nothing about this?" she asked.

"I didn't want to alarm you," said Ed.

"Ed, I'm not a child. You promised to keep me informed."

"Since we didn't know whether the operation was going to be successful, I didn't want you to be disappointed. That's all," he said. "We're hoping that the tapes will prove that his boss was guilty of fraudulent practices. We need to show that he was a major force in creating a corporate culture based on deceit. It's the first positive thing that's happened in this investigation. If Robert continues to cooperate, the authorities will present his case more favorably."

"So you still think he'll do jail time?" asked Libby cautiously.

"It's a possibility," said Ed. "He may end up with a reduced sentence of, say, six months in a minimum-security facility. Adam and I have discussed his options if he is sentenced. There's a place a couple of hours from here where it would be easy for us to visit him."

"Now you're talking to Adam about prison options! What else haven't you told me? How could you do this to me, Ed? I *trusted* you."

"Calm down, honey."

"No, I won't calm down. You're to include me in every single discussion with Adam, is that clear?"

Libby stood up to carry her plate to the kitchen sink. She scoured the plate with a scrub brush.

"Yes," agreed Ed quietly. "I'll keep you informed. But only if you agree to see Dr. Robbins for a checkup."

"I'm fine," said Libby. Her movements were swift, causing hot water to spray her face. She quickly wiped the offending drops away with the sleeve of her robe.

"Let the doctor decide." Ed cleared the table carefully, depositing the salt and pepper shakers on the side counter where they didn't belong.

"I'll see if I can get an appointment this week. I could use something to help me sleep. Now, that's enough about me. Where do things stand with Robby?"

"All I meant to say was that we need to be prepared for all outcomes. Certainly, the best-case scenario is a suspended sentence and community service. Robert would certainly never be allowed to hold any kind of position in the corporate world again. That's a given."

"No matter what, he'll be devastated. He loved his career."

"That's for sure. He's going to have to rethink his life's priorities when this is all over. Clearly, he's made some bad choices."

Suddenly, Libby had an idea. It was too early for her to discuss the possibilities, but she filed it away in the back of her mind.

"What are your plans today?" asked Ed.

"I don't know," she said.

"That's not like you. It's Tuesday. How about spending the morning with that scrapbooking group that you love?"

"I haven't been feeling up to it. There's some laundry around the house that needs to be done. I was thinking of polishing the silver in the dining room."

"Look, Libby, you've always loved working on those books. When was the last meeting you attended?"

"I haven't been back in over a month. I keep thinking I'll go, but it hasn't worked out that way."

"You need something to take your mind off Robert. We're doing everything we can to help him. Our lawyers are working closely with the government. I think yesterday was a real breakthrough. You've got to take better care of yourself. Look at you, you've lost so much weight. Come on, Lib, go out and see people. You're not helping our son by wasting away with worry. Will you please go?"

"I'll think about it," she replied weakly. Ed was right. Worry was eating her up inside and they were still a long way from a resolution. She was frazzled, tired, and constantly numb with fear. Perhaps an afternoon with her friends would help. But then she instantly dismissed the idea as frivolous. After all, she shouldn't be thinking about herself.

After Ed went to work, Libby straightened up the

kitchen, folded laundry, and checked her e-mail. When the doorbell rang, she was annoyed.

"Who is it?" she called. There was no answer.

She opened the door to find seven women standing on her doorstep, holding a poster that read *We Love You, Libby!* decorated with pictures of her friends. It was suddenly hard to see through the buckets of water gathering in her eyes.

"We're not going to take no for an answer this week!" announced Annie, walking boldly into the house. "We're your friends, Libby."

"What's all this?" Libby asked, seeing Catherine and Megan carrying boxes.

"We're having our meeting," said Catherine nonchalantly, as if this event had been planned for weeks.

Libby felt the beginnings of a smile forming on her lips. "I never thought . . ."

"That's right, my friend. You didn't think about how much we missed you or the fact that we're here for you."

"Things have spun out of control. I didn't feel like I wanted to burden you all with my problems."

"Why not?" said Margy. "All of us have relied on you dozens of times. Erin still claims you got her through fifth-grade math."

"I'd never tell my mother what I tell you!" quipped Tara.

Annie stared hard at Tara. "You know, Tara, you have been awfully secretive lately. I think you may be the one with the story this week." Tara flushed bright red.

"I'm counting on you to babysit!" exclaimed Ashley.

Everyone laughed.

"I think she means it," said Catherine.

Tara placed a cup of coffee in Libby's hand, ushering the women into the sun-filled family room. Catherine walked in with a tray filled with muffins and fruit, passing it around to everyone. Libby reached over and helped herself to a large blueberry muffin.

Catherine took the lead. "We had an interesting meeting last week."

Everyone laughed.

"You see, Libby, things became confused because each one of us had a different idea of how we could show our support. And I must say, every single suggestion was fantastic. Little did I realize that no one here can follow directions, so we've ended up with an abundance of gifts. Okay, who's going first?" Catherine asked, looking around the room.

Annie jumped up. "Libby, darling, what you don't realize is that politics is full of scandal. Why, it's our middle name. You're just not accustomed to it. So I talked to Tom about how to best help you ride out the storm, so to speak." Annie reached into a small bag and pulled out two pins. One read *Vote for Tom Griffin.* "You see, Tom's always thinking about himself. Now, seriously, the first thing you need when you go through a crisis is a happy face." She walked over and stuck the other pin on Libby's lapel. "Now, there, doesn't that look better?"

Libby admired the bright yellow pin. "I love it!" she exclaimed.

"Well," said Margy. "I have the perfect complement to that pin. I made this tote bag." Margy pulled out a black tote bag with ten images of Kermit the Frog stamped across each side. She whispered to the group, "Okay, so I stole the idea, but the rest of the Muppets will never know! Anyway, Miss Piggy was very upset that she wasn't selected."

Libby took the tote bag. "You remembered!" she said.

"How could I forget that scrapbook you made for your grandchildren? As you may recall, we discussed the merits of every single Muppet during that project."

Catherine came forward. "Who's next?"

Libby realized that she had already consumed nearly half of her muffin. She looked down to see Kermit smiling at her.

"I can't compete with Kermit," said Megan. "But I had Hannah draw you a couple of pictures." She gave her several brightly colored pictures of a garden with rainbows and birds in the background.

"These are so lovely," said Libby. She was at a loss to say more. It was one thing to enjoy the company of your friends, but it was another to have them help you when things were really difficult.

Libby was so touched by this show of support that she felt that words were insufficient; somehow, she would have to find a way to show everyone how much this moment meant to her.

"I had a similar idea," said Ashley. She held up a beaded bracelet. "Janie and Sally made this, with a little help from Mom!"

"And I've been meaning to give this to you for ages, but of course I never got around to it. This is something special from us to you," said Tara.

Libby opened the box. It was a framed picture of the group from the previous Christmas. In the photo, they were all wearing red sweaters. "This is terrific," she said. "You have no idea what this means to me."

"We're going to take our gifts back if you don't make it to our next meeting!" said Catherine.

"I'll be there," she said. "I promise."

A week later, Robby met his parents at his house. He greeted them nervously, his handsome features showing the strain of the past few weeks.

"Thanks for coming, Mom and Dad. I know this hasn't been easy on anyone."

"We're doing just fine," said Ed, winking at Libby.

"Sure," said Robby with a nervous laugh. "We can just think of this as a kind of large yard sale. I've got the list from the judge of what I'm allowed to sell. Everything has already been appraised, so I guess it's a matter of selecting the right pieces."

"It would make sense to try to sell the artwork

first," said Ed. "Let's take a look at your art collection. We were lucky to get Stephanie, an art dealer, to handle the sale discreetly. We'll want to take the things with the highest value first. Okay?"

"Yeah, let's do this. Lawyers need their money," said Rob sarcastically. "Perhaps I should have gotten my law degree instead of an MBA."

"Perhaps," said Ed. "Then maybe you would have learned right from wrong."

"Ed, that's enough," warned Libby.

"No, it's not enough," he retorted. "Robert, I still can't believe you would be involved in something like this! Did you learn nothing from us?"

Libby grabbed her stomach.

"You know, Dad, don't give me any of your self-righteous garbage!" shouted Robert. "You weren't there. You don't know the pressure I was under. They threatened me to keep me quiet. It got really tough."

Ed's face went white. "What are you talking about, son?"

"Nothing," said Rob, storming away.

Libby stepped forward to place a hand on Ed's shoulder. "Why don't you let me handle him?" She waited for his response. "Please," she added quietly.

Ed nodded, and then turned away.

Robby's words hovered around her, validating all of her worst fears. She knew the pressure on him had been intense. Somehow, he must have fallen under the spell of Amvale's corporate ideology. Now that the firm's financial dealings had been exposed to public scrutiny, Robby had been humiliated by all of the accusations of wrongdoing. Amvale executives were the punch line for the late-night comics, the subject of ridicule from the press and scathing editorials in the papers. Everyone seemed to have an opinion.

Surely, she reasoned, the investigators would realize that his role in the scandal was not entirely for self-reward. He had somehow gotten caught up in the corporate game, and things had escalated to a level where he had no control. The stakes were high. Hundreds of millions of dollars of assets were on the line, assets that belonged to shareholders, employees, clients. It was a big mess.

As Libby went in search of Robby, she noticed the tags on furniture items. His place had the look of a department store. They would have to sell almost everything in order to pay the legal fees and his bail money.

She found him on the rear terrace, sitting under a magnolia tree. It looked as if he were hiding out behind the thick green leaves, shielding himself from reality for a few moments. She could see patches of his clothing: red shirt, blue jeans, and worn loafers. He looked more like a boy than a man. The strain was evident as he leaned his head back against the trunk of the tree. His pain seemed to emanate across the lawn. Her heart ached for him.

"May I join you?" she asked, bending down to make eye contact. He nodded. She sat down beside him, hoping her presence would offer him the moral support he so desperately needed right now. It was hard to know how to comfort him. Breaking the silence, she cleared her throat to get his attention. "Robby, do you remember when you were ten years old and we were about to move to Europe for Dad's business?"

He shrugged. "Mom, I know you're trying to help, but it's hard to take these kid stories seriously when my whole life is falling apart."

"Aha!" exclaimed Libby. "You said the same thing back then. You thought the absolute worst of the situation. You complained relentlessly about someone else living in your room and taking your friends. You figured that the school was going to be horrible because they made you wear a uniform. You were absolutely miserable for several weeks."

"Okay, I sort of remember. So what did I do?" he said.

"You came home from school one day and said, 'I've realized that I'm going to learn a lot, so I'm okay with going.' That was it. You never looked back and we had an incredible two years abroad as a family."

"Mom, I've screwed up. I can't turn this one around. I can't ever work in the securities industry again. I'll be poor. What woman is going to want to attach herself to the infamous Rob Marshall of

Amvale? People know who I am and think the worst. You don't know what it's been like."

"I've had an idea. You're going to think I'm crazy, but I want you to think about it just the same." Libby prayed that she could get through to him.

"Don't tell me," he said. "I can change my name and move abroad, is that it? I've already thought about it. Believe me, the concept has its advantages. I'm not sure I'm going to stay in the country after this is all over." He folded his arms.

"Robert Marshall, you can't just run away from who you are. You've made some mistakes, but you've also done the right thing in cooperating. That should count for something in your mind, and hopefully, the authorities will take your efforts into serious consideration. More important, I want you to consider keeping a journal of your thoughts and feelings each day."

"Mother, I'm not one of your third-grade students!" he said, a hint of a smile forming on his face. "There will be no report at the end of this project."

"Robby, you were always a gifted writer until you went into the corporate world. You were an English major, remember? You can tell this story. You've certainly got a lot of material. It'll help you rebuild, maybe prevent somebody else from going down the wrong path." Her idea sounded perfectly reasonable. She thought it completely sound, if not brilliant. It would give him back his ego and an ability to make a good living if he was successful. After all, Robby did like the fine things in life.

He took her hand. "Mom, I appreciate what you're trying to do. Really. But I'm not there yet."

Libby was undaunted by his lack of enthusiasm. "It doesn't have to be an autobiography. You can make it a work of fiction. Call Amvale something else, like Worldwide Telecommunications. That's up to you. I'd like you to think about it."

"So, where's my cookie?" he asked with a wink.

Libby smiled. "Cookies and milk are in the kitchen." She looked him in the eye. "But only if you promise to consider what I've said," she offered gamely.

"Okay, I'll give the project some consideration." He paused. "By the way, Mom, thank you for everything. I don't know what I'd do without you."

She leaned over and gave him a hug. "I love you, Robby."

"I love you, too, Mom."

A few days later, her daughter Caroline picked up Libby to go shopping at a downtown children's clothing store. Sarah's tenth birthday was coming up, and they were in search of the perfect party dress.

"Grandma," said Sarah from the backseat of the car, "you should see this place. They have really cool stuff."

"By that, she means there are no embroidered

dresses or traditional party attire," explained Caroline.

"What kind of dress are you looking for, dear?" asked Libby.

"I want lots and lots of sequins," said Sarah. "And some shoes with high heels like the other girls wear. Maybe even a halter top."

"Oh, my," said Libby, recalling the plain, square-necked dresses she used to buy for Caroline.

"Grandma?" said Sarah.

"Yes, Sarah," said Libby, putting on her sunglasses.

"Why is Uncle Robby in trouble? Mom won't tell me."

Libby swallowed hard. "Uncle Robby made some mistakes at work, but he's doing what he can to fix things. Everything is going to be just fine." Libby rummaged through her purse for her antacid tablets.

"Aren't you angry with him?"

Caroline frowned, then looked out the window.

Libby didn't know how to answer the question. It was all very awkward. She thought for a moment. "Both Grandpa and I were disappointed, but we've forgiven him. I think there are lots of ways that he can make something positive out of this situation."

"Like going to church and stuff?"

"Church would be a great place to start. He could also do things for the community."

"How can he go to church if he's in jail? Do they

216

have churches in prison?" Sarah sat up in her seat, looking over at Libby for answers.

"That's enough, Sarah," said Caroline. "We can talk about this another time. Now, what color dress would you like?"

"But you won't," whined Sarah. She seemed to catch her mother's warning stare, then settled back down. "Something with an animal print. Like a cheetah pattern."

"I'm not sure you're going to be able to find a sequined, animal print, halter-top dress that looks good," suggested Caroline, rolling her eyes at Libby.

Libby gave Caroline the expected weary smile, even though she felt ill. Somehow she would have to find a way to get through the next hour of shopping without revealing her upset at a ten-year-old's curiosity. Rubbing her forehead, she suppressed the urge to tell Caroline that she needed to go home. Instead, she told Sarah how much she loved the store, marveling at the low-hanging colored light fixtures and racks of colorful clothes. She spotted a blue suede seat near the dressing room and headed for it.

A young salesgirl was nodding eagerly at Sarah, seeming to grasp exactly what she wanted.

Caroline came over to sit beside Libby.

"I'm going to let the salesgirl over there take over. Sarah doesn't really want my opinion just yet. It might cramp her style. Are you okay, Mom?"

"I'm fine," said Libby. "I just can't believe that Sarah knows so much."

"She's almost ten, Mom, and very curious. I'm sure she's heard us talking about it. I just wish this whole mess would go away," said Caroline. "Fortunately, most people at Sarah's school don't connect us with the name and the scandal."

Suddenly, Libby imagined herself drowning. She fought for self-control. "I hope this will all be over soon and things will get back to normal." The words rung hollow. Things would never be normal again.

"It's Tuesday morning," said Annie cheerfully over the phone. "We expect you at Margy's house by nine."

"I'm really not sure," protested Libby. She wanted to go back to bed.

"I'll pick you up, so you have no excuse," insisted Annie. "See you in an hour."

Reluctantly, Libby got out of bed to take a shower. She got herself a cup of coffee, and went in search of her black bag full of supplies. Perhaps today she could get something done on one of her books.

Her friends welcomed her into their circle; Catherine rushed to get her coffee, and Margy put some fruit and a muffin on a plate for her. Libby sat down at the enormous wooden table in Margy's workroom. Each had a coffee mug at her place, except Tara, who held a large bottle of diet soda. Handbags lined the shelves, and clear plastic bins were filled with fabric. Margy had decorated the room with framed posters of glamorous women carrying her handbags, which added a touch of whimsy to the environment.

Libby pondered what she wanted to work on. For the first time in weeks, she felt safe among her friends. She carefully laid out her supplies.

"Tara, you're positively glowing these days," said Annie. "Who is he?"

"Well," she said. "His name's Peter and he's terrific. We've been spending a lot of time together lately. I think he's the most amazing man I've ever known."

"It's about time for you to get married. I'm thrilled for you," said Annie.

Tara blushed. She began nervously cutting a photograph. Libby noticed that her hands were trembling.

"You're lucky," said Tina. "You get to choose whom you want to marry. I didn't."

"What are you talking about?" asked Megan.

"My parents arranged my marriage from birth. I didn't have any say in the matter."

"But this is the twenty-first century. You're American now. How can that be?" asked Margy.

"I was not going to go against the wishes of my parents. And, in my own way, I've learned to love Nigel. We share the same values and the same Indian heritage. That is the way things are."

"That's unbelievable," said Margy.

"To you, maybe," said Tina calmly. "But I have a different way of looking at things. I'm happy with my life."

Libby thought about the past forty-one years with Ed. She had been lucky in many ways. Theirs was a true love match. As she reached for her scissors, she realized that even the younger women had to face tough issues. It wasn't as if she was the only person whose life was complicated.

"I used to think marriage was easy. Now, I'm not so sure," said Ashley, taking a sip of her coffee. "It's a hell of a lot of work. Nobody tells you that when you're picking out that white dress. Back then, the whole concept of marriage seemed like one big party. I'm not sure I really understood the 'for better and *for worse*' part."

"I thought things had improved with Steve," said Megan.

"They have," said Ashley. "I've even got a house-keeper back at the house right now. Yes, someone else is actually helping clean once a week. That's been the biggest breakthrough."

There was an awkward silence. Libby sensed that all the other women were thinking about her immediate crisis. "I wish I could get a housekeeper to clean up the mess in my life!" she quipped.

Everyone laughed, breaking the tension.

"Ashley, I'll gladly come over and scrub dirt. At least you don't feel like you're wearing it."

"Has it been so awful?" Annie asked delicately.

"I'm not going to lie," said Libby. "It's been pretty bad. I feel like I can't go out of the house without people watching me. My granddaughter wants to know why Uncle Robby is in trouble with the law."

"I'm sure she didn't mean it," said Annie.

"It hurt just the same," said Libby. "This is not exactly what I was planning on for this time in my life. I was supposed to take a photography class, work on my scrapbooks, and enjoy spending time with my children and grandchildren. You know, normal things. I never expected my retirement to be so complicated."

"Well, my life is just as messy," said Tara. "Believe me, we all face tough times." Tara looked flushed and uncomfortable.

Libby leaned over and gave her a hug. "Thanks for making me feel better."

"Anyone want to see the new designer paper that just came in?" asked Catherine.

"Great idea," said Tara.

"You guys are such wonderful friends," said Libby, dabbing at her eyes. She looked down at her paper, figuring out where to start. She wanted to put her focus back on her grandchildren for a few hours. Pulling out an envelope full of photographs, Libby laid them all out in front of her, trying to decide which ones she wanted to highlight.

A photograph of her four grandchildren on Easter Sunday caught her eye. That had been a joyous day, with all the girls running around the backyard searching for hidden eggs. She would spend the next few hours capturing some of their positive moments from this past spring.

Libby returned home feeling significantly better. She had just put her things down when a sedan pulled into the driveway. Rushing to the back door, she saw Ed and Adam, Robert's attorney, getting out of the car.

"Ed," she called. "I wasn't expecting you."

"Didn't you get my message?" he asked, coming forward to greet her.

"No, I'm afraid I just walked in the door." Remembering her manners, she greeted Adam, then looked anxiously at Ed. "Is everything all right?"

"Fine," said Ed. "Let's go inside."

Libby went back into the kitchen along with Ed and Adam. Looking somber, Adam put his briefcase down.

Ed directed him to the breakfast room table. "I don't want to talk about Robby at work. We thought you should sit in on this meeting."

Ordinarily, Libby would have offered Adam some iced tea. At the moment, she was too nervous to do anything but take a seat at the table. "What's going on?"

"The assistant U.S. Attorney has made a decision on Robert," said Adam.

"Oh my God," said Libby, her hand reaching for her throat.

Ed reached for her hand.

"Please tell me. I don't think I can take much more of this!" Libby listened carefully as Adam explained the terms.

The news was better than what she had expected. Rob wasn't going to jail, but he still had a number of problems to resolve with the authorities: a year of probation, a thousand hours of community service, and the repayment of his legal debts. Holding corporate office was no longer an option.

"What a relief!" she exclaimed as she squeezed Ed's hand.

CHAPTER 13

Ashley

Ashley watched Cameron scan the crowd before he took his seat to play the semifinal round of a junior state chess championship. Her heart sank when she saw the look of disappointment cross his face. His father wasn't there, after he had sworn he would make it. Anger consumed her. She dug her fingernails into the palm of her hand to try to get hold of herself. At this moment, she despised Steve more than she could bear. *He's a terrible father and nothing is going to change that fact.*

Ashley told Tucker to watch Janie and Sally so

that she could go out into the hallway and call Steve's office, again. *Stay calm,* she told herself. It wouldn't do any good to yell or scream at him. The rational approach always worked best.

"Melinda, it's me again," said Ashley firmly. "Any word yet from Steve? The competition is just starting."

"No, Ashley," Melinda said quickly, her irritation palpable. "I told you before, he's in a client meeting and can't be disturbed."

"I'm sorry to call again. Can you please have him call my cell as soon as he's free?"

"Sure thing," she replied before clicking off the line.

Melinda's tone of voice irked her. *She could have been more helpful,* Ashley thought, as she paced the floor feeling completely helpless. How could Steve just not care about his kids? It was amazing to her that this man had fathered four children, yet took no responsibility for their lives. Sure, he paid the bills and gave them a few crumbs of affection. But he wasn't *involved* in their lives at all.

Ashley quietly shuffled through the crowd to return to her seat to watch Cameron play. It was such an honor that he had gotten there in the first place. Whenever the door opened, Ashley's eyes darted to see if Steve had shown. Although the event was out of town, it was no excuse for his indifference; he could have at least called to wish his son luck. As the hours ticked by, Ashley watched the concentration on Cameron's face as he contemplated each move. She fed Janie and Sally way too much candy to bribe them both to sit still and watch their brother. Finally, it was over. Cameron had done it and made it to the finals. The crowd cheered and Ashley was bursting with pride.

When Steve came home that night, Ashley didn't say anything to him. She pretended to be asleep as he got into bed beside her. Part of her had wanted to get up and leave the room, but it would mean having to talk with him. Instead, the next morning, she had told Steve about the match, listened to his excuses, and watched as he went into Cameron's room to congratulate him on his victory. Disgust seeped through her veins.

Seated at the kitchen counter at lunch, Ashley picked at her unappetizing salad. A nagging fear kept running through her mind, like the circling of a nasty mosquito on a summer day. She wondered if Steve was cheating on her. His transformation from do-nothing husband to Mr. Romance that night two months ago had lasted for a few short weeks. Certainly, things had been better for a while, but lately he had begun his disappearing act again. She thought of Steve's many business trips and how often she didn't know where he was. It had never occurred to her before that he would be unfaithful, but lately she wasn't so sure.

Ashley was the only full-time parent. The kids depended on her completely for their emotional well-being. Like a retro 1950s couple, she was the housewife and Steve wrote the checks. Anger swept over her as she thought of how many nights she had taken total responsibility for the children. She had planned to have a family life that incorporated some sort of division of labor; instead, she felt more like a single parent.

Ashley bit hard on her nails, nervous over what to do about her racing thoughts. After all, she could be imagining something that had never occurred. Or had she finally come to her senses about her marriage? It was hard to know the right thing to do. Were they all better off with him or without him?

How do I go about confronting him? she thought. It wasn't as if she could say, "Pass the salt, and by the way, did you sleep with another woman?" Ashley began to pace the kitchen floor. After all, she had no real proof. It was just a nagging suspicion that had lodged itself in her gut. But her instincts had generally served her well.

Ashley got up from the kitchen counter and walked into the downstairs powder room. She tried not to notice the crayon on the wallpaper. Staring at her own reflection, she puzzled over whether she had become so consumed by her kids at the expense of herself. Her mother's words rang in her ears. Was she really that furious with her attention-seeking model mother that she had become the antithesis of her by letting herself go?

She thought about the women in her scrapbooking

group, who pursued other interests outside their families: Margy made handbags; Tina worked at the museum; Catherine ran an actual scrapbooking business; Annie was always involved with politics; Libby was a substitute teacher. They proved that the possibility existed for her to carve out more dimensions to her life. Who said that she had to be a full-time stay-at-home mother? Her turbulent thoughts were making her feel a bit queasy. It crossed her mind that a chocolate bar might make her feel better, but she decided that food wasn't the answer.

On an impulse, she phoned Margy, surprised to get her on the line in the early afternoon.

"Ashley," said Margy. "This is a pleasant surprise. How are you?"

"I'm good," she said. "I loved being in your studio the other day. It was such a treat. I'm calling because I've wanted to talk with you about an idea of mine. I don't know if you'd be interested."

"Sure thing."

"Would it be possible . . ." She paused. "I mean, could I come over and see how you make your bags? Maybe even help with something?"

"I'd be happy to show you what I do, anytime. It's not the most professional operation, with three kids running around, but I love it."

"That'd be great. I realize how much I miss being creative. I'm looking for a direction or maybe even some inspiration. Do you think I'm nuts?"

"No way, I completely understand where you are right now. Five years ago, I felt the same way. That's when I began taking some design classes. We can talk more when I see you. I'm just thrilled you like my work enough to call me. How about tomorrow afternoon around one o'clock?"

"Sure, if I can bring Sally. Is that okay? I promise to get her to behave."

"Honey, Sally can cut and paste to her heart's content in my workroom."

"Great. See you tomorrow after lunch."

"I'll look forward to it."

"Me, too."

Ashley suddenly felt energized. She wasn't sure what she hoped to accomplish, but Margy seemed so together. Somehow, she would find a way to care for the kids, organize the house, do the chores, and get more help. After all, she was entitled to some time for herself.

Her thoughts went back to what to do about Steve. She wasn't sure whether to confront him about her suspicions or just wait and watch.

After a hectic afternoon of driving the kids to after-school activities, helping with homework, and making dinner, Ashley finished cleaning the kitchen. Exhaustion was beginning to take over as she wiped the countertops. What was she thinking, planning to go to Margy's studio tomorrow? She didn't have time to do anything. Suddenly, she remembered her mother urging her to get an au pair to help with the children. Ashley had been offended at the time, but now she was beginning to think that it wasn't such a bad idea. Her mother had even offered to pay all of the expenses.

For the first time in a long time, she missed her mother. It was an odd thought, but she realized that she had shut her completely out of her life. Her father was never there; that was a given. But, honestly, her mother wasn't *that* horrible. She was trying to make amends, wasn't she?

"Mom," said Janie. "Will you read with me?"

"I'd love to, in about ten minutes. Cameron has a math problem he needs me to work on with him. Can you ask your dad?"

She shook her head.

"Please," said Ashley. "I've got to get Sally to bed and I need to finish what I'm doing."

She watched as Janie sat on her father's lap while he read her a story. It seemed normal, she thought. For a moment, she wondered if Steve wasn't as bad as she believed. A short time later, Janie returned to find her, indicating that Daddy had stopped reading to take a call on his cell phone. Ashley told Cameron to wait just a second.

When she spied Steve out on the back terrace, Ashley crept outside. He was speaking in hushed tones. When he saw her, he immediately hung up.

"Who was that?" she asked.

"Just Melinda. We were talking about a new client," explained Steve.

"I thought you were going to read with Janie for a few minutes," said Ashley.

"I did," he said innocently. "I finished the story."

"Oh, I see," said Ashley sweetly. "Sorry to bother you."

"No problem," he said with a smile.

Ashley remained calm. So he had taken an evening call from Melinda. She knew Melinda was a tall, leggy brunette who was endlessly fascinating. Fear nagged at her, but this time Ashley resisted the urge to comfort herself with food. Somehow, she would figure things out.

The following day, as she prepared for her meeting with Margy, Ashley noticed that many of her pants were too big. She went to the middle section of her closet to find a black pair with a single-digit size. It had been years since she had worn anything this small. Despite her now constant worries about Steve, at least she was no longer embarrassed by the way she looked. Anxiety had its benefits. Preparing to go to Margy's, she brushed her hair and applied mascara and lipstick as if she were going to a real job interview.

As she stood in front of the full-length mirror, Ashley was pleased with her appearance. Suddenly, she bit her lip in sadness. Did her husband's love depend on her weight? *Stop it,* she told herself.

"I am more than my dress size!" she said aloud to her reflection, wishing Steve were in the room to hear.

"I stopped loving you for a while, but now I'm back," came his imaginary response.

"Why did you change?" she wanted to know. "Is it because I look better now? Where were you when I needed you so much? It's so hard to be a parent. Why didn't you help me more?"

These questions ate at her soul. Beauty was such an amorphous concept; her mother had spent the bulk of her life in a quest for physical perfection. Ashley wanted more for herself and her children, especially her daughters. Wasn't it important to be a kind and generous person, live up to one's potential, and make a difference in the lives of young people?

"I'm so glad you're here!" exclaimed Margy, giving both her and Sally a hug.

"Thank you so much for making time for me," said Ashley, suddenly relaxing. Glancing around the house as they walked through it on their way to the studio, Ashley noticed that things were neat, but not pristine like Catherine's or Tara's homes. The place was painted in earth tones and had an inviting lived-in look. "I wish you could come over and do this to my house. Everything looks so cozy here. Did you ever work in the design business?"

"Actually I did, in another lifetime. I'm always willing to help my friends with their houses."

"Do you think I could bribe you to come take a look at mine?" asked Ashley hopefully. She pointed to a hand-painted armoire. "Oh my, where did you get that?"

"I bought it at a yard sale for fifty dollars and refinished it myself."

"Really! And that chair with the lime-green velvet cover is so unusual."

"Another yard sale find. I go about once a month. I'll call you next time if you'd like to come along."

"I'd really like that. I need to put more effort into my house. It looks like a yard sale inside. However, I did start cleaning out one space, and the kids helped me paint it." Ashley paused in front of Margy's shelves lined with rows of wicker baskets. They made the studio look so orderly. Ashley thought something like that would look great in her new workspace.

"Even better, I have a college student who does odd jobs for me. He's always looking for work. He's very detail oriented and inexpensive."

Ashley followed behind Margy, listening to her talk about the different classes that she took and what stores in town were now buying her bags. She showed Ashley some sketches of designs she was working on for the fall line.

"I'm so impressed with what you're doing," said Ashley, running her hand over an orange patterned bag lying on her worktable. "It really makes me want to fix up my house and pull my act together." Ashley put Sally down and watched as she ran immediately to see the coloring book and crayons

Margy had cleverly placed on a small table in the corner. "Thanks," she said, watching Sally immediately flip open the book and start coloring.

"She's so cute!" said Margy, turning her attention back to Ashley. "Don't be so hard on yourself." She pulled out a bar stool for her, then sat on the one beside her. "You're doing great. Four kids is a lot of work. Think of what you've done since we met. You started to find your creative side again with our scrapbooking group. My hunch is that it was just a beginning for you."

"At first, I thought it was absolutely ludicrous, given my time constraints. But I've really connected with the group and you're right, I love it. It's given me something to look forward to each week. I don't know what's next," said Ashley, looking at Margy's buttons, which were organized in clear plastic boxes on the table. "Oh no!" She immediately ran over to stop Sally, who was trying to pull all the fabric from one of the drawers.

"It's fine," said Margy, remaining in her seat. She seemed unfazed by the mess Sally was making. "Don't worry about it, Ashley, let her have a good time. My kids used to tear this place apart on a regular basis. Anyway, I think you're smart to gather ideas for the future. You'll eventually have more time and figure things out. In the meantime, I'd love to see your house and maybe make some suggestions."

"You'd do that?" said Ashley.

"Sure. It's fun for me," said Margy, swinging off of the bar stool to open the door of a closet. She appeared to be looking for something.

"I hope the piles of junk don't offend you," explained Ashley, knowing on some level that Margy wouldn't care.

"I love a challenge," said Margy, returning to the worktable with an armload of materials. She spread everything out on the table for Ashley to see. "Just pick a time and we'll make it work. Speaking of challenges, let me show you one of my latest ideas. It's a sort of mother's tote. I want to design a hip-looking diaper bag. I'd also like to make something fun for mothers with toddlers. There could even be pockets for juice cups and crackers. Then I have these patterned tote bags with the bamboo handles that can be washed."

"What a great idea!" exclaimed Ashley, picking up a piece of fabric with a cheetah print. "You could make the diaper bag in that hobo style that's so popular now. It would look more like a purse."

"That's a terrific suggestion," said Margy, jotting it down on a yellow Post-it pad. "You used to work in the fashion industry in New York, right?"

"Yes," said Ashley. "But my specialty was actually gathering publicity and figuring out how to launch collections. You'd need a write-up in a national magazine like *Vogue* or *Harper's Bazaar*. Of course, a celebrity endorsement would be the ultimate coup." She had been pretty good at that, Ashley thought, thinking of her mother's friends in the modeling industry.

"That's great experience," said Margy. "Perhaps we can talk more about that at some point?"

"I'd like that," said Ashley.

A few days later, she got a letter from her mother begging for another chance to get together. Ashley decided that she'd held on to her anger long enough. She asked her mother to come for a visit on Friday, assuming she could book a flight.

The Tuesday morning meeting of the scrapbooking group was at Tara's house again. Ashley came with a shopping bag full of photographs to sort through for her next album. She wanted to work on something for her mother. Perhaps it was only a small peace offering, but she thought she might like to arrange some family photos to give to her.

"Good morning," said Tara, sitting beside her. "You look like you've come up with a plan." She eyed Ashley's large bag.

"Plan? I'm not so sure. You should see this mess. There are about a hundred pictures of my parents in this bag that have been sitting in a closet for years. I thought I might try to sort through them and tackle a few pages." Ashley reached for a cup of coffee.

"You look great, by the way," said Tara with a smile. "Any pictures of your mom in there?" she asked. "I'd love to see them."

Ashley took out a photo of her mother in a printed minidress with white boots.

"Oh, your mom's so pretty!" exclaimed Margy, peering at the photograph. "She looks like that model from the sixties, Marrie. I used to love her."

"My mother *is* Marrie, actually," said Ashley.

"You're kidding! How incredibly cool. That's so exciting!" said Megan. "Marrie was up there with Twiggy."

Ashley dug into the bag to pull out another old black-and-white photograph of her mother. She passed it around for the group to see. Libby was noticeably absent. "How's Libby today?"

Annie shook her head. "She left me a message saying that she had some important business. That she'd be in touch by the end of the week. I hope everything's all right."

"Me, too," said Tara. Ashley hoped for Libby's sake that her son wouldn't have to stand trial.

Annie picked up the photograph of Marrie. "Will you look at that dress! I haven't seen those wild geometric prints with wedge shoes in years!" she exclaimed. "It's priceless. I once wore a skirt almost that short."

"And that hair," said Tina. "I can't believe that people could walk around like that."

Ashley reached into her bag to lay out more photographs on the table. She put out five or six pictures of her mother and then a picture of both parents.

Tara looked over to see her photographs. Her eyes widened. "Who's that with your mother?" she asked, her voice taking on a higher pitch. She grabbed the photograph and stared at the couple.

Ashley was confused by her reaction. "It's my father."

"That's impossible," said Tara, looking more closely at the photograph. Her face paled.

"What do you mean, impossible?" Ashley laughed. "Tara, why are you looking so strangely at my parents?"

Tara abruptly left the room. Ashley was completely baffled, curious as to why a picture of her parents could have made Tara look so ill. After all, everyone knew her famous parents: her mother the supermodel and her father, who was a regular figure on television.

The usually poised Tara returned to the room holding a large leather-bound album. Beads of perspiration were forming on her forehead. Her hands trembled as she placed it in front of Ashley.

"What's going on?" said Ashley.

"That's what I'd like to know," said Annie. "Tara, honey, you look like you've just seen a ghost."

"Open the book, Ashley," said Tara. "Look familiar?"

Seeing the look on Tara's face, Ashley flipped to the first page. Tara pointed to a photograph. It was a wedding photograph of a dark-haired woman . . . and her father. She shuddered in disbelief. "Oh my

God, I don't understand. What's my father doing? I mean, why are they posing together? Was my father married to that woman?"

"He *is* married to that woman," said Tara. "She's my mother. Her name's Candice."

"How long have they been together?" asked Ashley in confusion.

"More than forty years," replied Tara. "How long have *your* parents been married?"

"Forty years. This doesn't make any sense," said Ashley. "I don't understand," she cried. The room started to spin and she felt physically ill. She could hear people around her, but it was hard to focus on anything concrete. She needed to get hold of herself, but she couldn't. She saw things turn black before she lost consciousness. She awoke with a cold compress on her head. Six pairs of eyes stared at her. "I'm sorry," she said weakly.

"Please don't apologize, dear," said Annie. "I think we need to stay calm and piece together what we know. So Ashley, you're saying that your father is Kent West?"

"Yes." Ashley sat up, rubbing her aching head.

"How can this be?" Tara cried. "I mean, I knew he was hardly home, but I always thought he was researching some story or something. Do you realize that this makes him a bigamist? He's obviously been leading a double life for decades. What was he thinking?" She still held Ashley's family photograph in her hands.

"Before we jump to any conclusions, I think you both need to make sure you have your facts straight."

"How are we supposed to do that?" asked Ashley. "I don't know what to do." She shook her head in disbelief. "He was never there for my mother and me. He spent most of his time on the road. I stopped speaking to both of my parents a while ago. In fact, I'm seeing my mother for the first time in months this Friday. What am I supposed to say? By the way, Mom, your husband is really a fake?" Ashley thought she might be ill again. She looked over to observe Tara's pale features.

"But something doesn't make sense. If your parents are both public figures, how did he avoid being photographed with your mom?"

Ashley thought for a moment. "I do know that they attended very few charity or media events together. They've always kept a close circle of friends who they socialized with for dinner parties or small get-togethers. Dad used to claim that he desperately needed his privacy and longed for time away from the spotlight. My mother always supported his wishes. So they kept mostly to themselves when he came to visit."

"This is surreal, but it would explain a lot of things," said Tara.

"On a bright note," said Megan. "It would mean that you both are sisters, which is kind of great."

"Wouldn't it be half sisters?" asked Margy.

"Who knows?" said Ashley. "I'm really confused

right now. I already felt unsure of things. This is too much to handle."

"I'll pick up Janie and Sally this afternoon," offered Megan. "I'll call on Tucker and Cameron and make sure they can go home with Linda."

"Thanks," said Ashley. "I think I just need some time to recover." She tried to bring some moisture to her dry mouth.

"Me, too," said Tara, sitting down on the chair across from her. "I'm still in total shock.

"Perhaps the rest of us should go and leave you two alone," suggested Catherine.

"Don't worry about word of this getting around," said Annie. "If I told anyone, they probably wouldn't believe me!"

The women laughed nervously.

"Are you all right?" asked Tara, leaning over to look at Ashley after the women had departed.

"I guess. What do we do now?" asked Ashley.

"I have no idea," answered Tara. "This is really bizarre."

An hour later, Ashley headed home, still feeling completely shaken. *To think, the famous Kent West may have been leading a double life for almost forty years. Even worse, he knew that both of us were now living in the same small city. Okay, so Belloix has a million people, but . . .* Ashley didn't know what to do next, so she decided to be practical. A long, hot shower was definitely in order.

Water pounded the back of her head, and she

couldn't control the rush of tears that came to her eyes. Her father had never been there for her. He might be famous, but he was also a liar. Was this all some sort of game to him? Having two wives, two families, must have kept him on the edge at all times. Perhaps it was time to get even; this story would make national headlines.

As she scrubbed her hair and skin clean, Ashley realized that the reason she craved stability and some sort of domestic tranquility was to compensate for her parents' lack of support growing up. Yet by picking Steve, she was subconsciously re-creating it; Steve was never there for his family, just like her father. Why had she settled?

Tara had looked just as shaken. Still, Ashley wondered if *she* was the daughter who'd been neglected. Perhaps her father had adored Tara and showered her with attention. Maybe he even re-membered her on birthdays and holidays. Maybe she was the favorite. Ashley tried to control the inevitable swirl of negative thoughts as she envisioned Tara as the center of attention.

None of this was Tara's fault, Ashley reminded herself. *She's as much a victim of this situation as I am.* Ashley recalled how her hands had shaken when she leafed through the photographs. Sud-denly, she had an idea. Certainly her father was going to find some way to deny the whole thing. Perhaps she and Tara should put their pictures together.

"Mama," yelled Janie. "Where are you?" She burst into the bathroom just as Ashley put on her towel. "Your friend Megan said you were sick. Are you okay?"

Seeing Janie's sweet innocent face turned up to her in concern, Ashley felt so much love pour back into her heart. "Honey, I'm okay. Don't worry about me. It must have been something I had for lunch."

"Mommy!" cried Sally. "I missed you." She tore off Ashley's towel in her effort to scramble into her arms.

"Hold on, sweetie. Let Mommy get dressed. Where are the boys?"

"Tucker said he would cook up some pasta for dinner. Cameron is setting the table," she added.

Ashley got dressed, feeling so incredibly proud of her boys. She was certain that Megan must have coached them, but maybe not. To think they were downstairs trying to cook dinner to help her out. She expected to find chaos when she arrived in the kitchen; instead, Tucker was pouring some pasta into a strainer as if it were something he did every night.

"I think you've got yourself a new job two nights a week," said Ashley with a wink.

"Really?" he said. "This is pretty fun. I don't mind doing it."

"How about if I give you five bucks extra a week to help with dinner and clean up?"

"Awesome!"

"What about me?" asked Cameron. "I'm doing a good job, too."

"Yes, you are. You can set the table for breakfast and dinner each morning and night, too, for a three-dollar increase. You're also going to both add seventy-five cents extra to the money you give to charity. Agreed?"

"Sure, Mom!"

"Cameron, go ahead and pour the milk. I'm going back upstairs to talk to your daddy for a minute. Does anybody need me for anything else?"

"No," said Tucker. "We're doing just fine."

Ashley went back into her room and closed the door. Thinking she didn't want to be interrupted, she turned the lock. Taking a deep breath, she called Steve at work, which was something she rarely did. After a short delay, he got on the phone.

"Hi," she said. "What time do you think you'll be home tonight? Something's happened and I need to talk with you."

"I'm sorry, Ashley. I've got a meeting on the schedule until ten. We can talk about it tomorrow."

"No, we can't," she said firmly. "I have a problem that I'd like to discuss with you. It's important."

"I'll see what I can do," he snapped. She could hear the impatience in his voice.

"You know what?" she shot back. "Don't bother, Steve. I've had enough of you! As a matter of fact, don't bother coming home tonight. I don't need you anymore." Ashley slammed down the phone. It felt good.

I'm so sick of him, she thought. *Let him spend the evening with Melissa or whatever her name is.* Ashley picked up the phone to call Tara.

"Hey, Tara, it's me."

"How are you doing?"

"Well, I took a shower, which was a good thing. I just told my husband not come home tonight, which was a bad thing. And I want to shoot my father. How's that?"

"At least you're clean."

"Seriously, what I called to say was that even though this is a nightmare for both of us, I'm glad that we may be related."

"You're so sweet. I feel the same way. But I think we need to come up with some sort of plan to deal with this. It's overwhelming."

"How about murder in the first degree? Or we could embarrass him and have one of his competitors break the story."

"I've thought of that, but the price is too high. You've got your children to think about. And I value my privacy too much. This would be a media circus. I don't want to be in the tabloids. We also have to think what it would do to our mothers. I can't speak for your mother, but my mom is so traditional; this is going to be really hard on her."

"My mom, too. She loves him."

"So does my mother. What a complete mess!"

Tara sighed heavily. "Can we meet for breakfast tomorrow morning? We can both think on it tonight and share ideas. Sound good?"

"Sure," said Ashley. "I'm not expecting to sleep."

"Me either. I feel so stupid. There were so many clues that something wasn't right and yet the reality is kind of hard to take."

"But neither one of us could have ever come up with such a crazy scenario."

"No kidding. I'm starting to think it would have been easier not knowing."

"Maybe, but I'd rather know. A lot of things make sense now."

"We'll see. I'll call you in the morning."

Ashley didn't want the children to see her upset. She did her best to carry on the evening as usual. They depended on her to keep things normal, so she answered homework questions, filled out school forms, cleaned up the kitchen, and put everyone to bed.

Divorce, she thought, was such an ugly word; both for her and for her mother. Things weren't supposed to be this way. But she wasn't going to stuff her face to cope tonight. She remembered the time Steve had seen her in the kitchen surrounded by wrappers; his look of sheer disgust had angered and embarrassed her. He didn't have enough compassion to see how much she was hurting. Even now, those ice cream bars were tempting. Glancing at the refrigerator, she steeled herself. Hard physical labor, she thought, would help relieve some of her anxiety.

She went down to the basement and brought up the paint. She figured she would work all night to finish the room off the kitchen. The room was only half done, but it had so much potential. If she put in the effort, she knew she could make it beautiful. The task seemed daunting as she surveyed the unfinished walls, but Ashley was determined. The hours passed by as she rolled a fresh coat of aqua on the walls. By the time she was finished it was past midnight, her arms ached, sweat poured from her skin, and her hands were bright aqua.

The welfare of her children was paramount. If she separated from Steve, how hard was it going to be on the kids? Despite his overtures of romance these past few weeks, she realized that their physical intimacy didn't make up for his having been an absentee father. Watching him ignore his kids on a regular basis had slowly eaten away at the love she had once had for him. Somehow, she would cope without him.

That was when Steve walked into the room. "Ashley," he said angrily. "What are you doing painting in the middle of the night?"

"What are you doing here?" She whirled around to face him. "I told you not to come back. What I do now is none of your business!" she said, putting down the brush.

"I came home like I always do," he replied.

"Let me guess, you had a momentary pang of guilt

so that you thought you'd drop by. Do I look like a complete idiot to you? I'm sorry it's been such a chore for you to leave what's-her-name to see your wife and children."

"What's gotten into you? I've never seen this side of you. You used to be so sweet."

"I used to be in love with someone who cared about me and made me laugh. Someone who I thought would make a great husband and father. Not the self-absorbed fool that you are now!"

His face blanched, but he recovered quickly. "Well, I never expected the woman I loved to become a fat pig after we got married."

Ashley felt as if someone had stuck a knife through her heart. "Do you have any idea how hard it is to have a baby? Let alone four? You were just a sperm donor. I've done everything for these kids. They're my life. You think your father abandoned you? You're no better a parent than he was. Now, I want the truth!" Tears blurred her vision. "There's another woman, isn't there? Someone who works with you. And don't lie to me anymore."

"Give me a break, Ashley. Is there something in those paint fumes that's making you crazy?" he said, stuffing his hands in his pockets.

"Nice try. Don't try to deceive me anymore. Please give me a little bit of credit. You checked out of this marriage years ago. I just know that you haven't been faithful. I can feel it."

He looked away and paused, "I . . ."

Ashley saw the guilt in his refusal to look her in the eye. "Go on," she prodded, stealing herself for the truth.

"It wasn't planned or anything. It just happened one night."

"That's enough," she said. Even though she had been certain, it hurt. "I knew it but I don't want to hear any more. Get out!"

"Ashley, wait. This is getting out of control. We need to think of the kids."

"Since when have you ever considered the welfare of your children? You heard me—I said get out! I hate you," she said. "I really do."

Steve turned away.

"Mom," said Tucker, standing in the doorway. "Are you okay?" His eyes were filled with tears.

"Honey, I'm so sorry," said Ashley, covering her mouth. "You shouldn't have heard any of this." She reached for him.

"Tucker," said Steve. "I . . ."

Tucker faced him, his face a mask of rage. "You heard Mom. Get out. We'll be just fine without you."

Ashley saw the look of shock on Steve's face at Tucker's words. Perhaps it should have given her some sense of perverse satisfaction, but it didn't. In an odd way, she felt sorry for him. After Steve slammed the kitchen door, Ashley and Tucker held each other for a long time.

"I'm so sorry," she said. "You should not be a part

twenty-four hours. She checked the time; she had less than an hour before Ashley arrived.

Rushing to the drive-thru, Tara veered into the lane between two other vehicles. She was annoyed that she had to wait. She stopped at the microphone and ordered two supersized diet sodas for good measure. Scrambling to get her money, she saw the boy with the braces, her usual drive-thru server.

"Miss Tara," he said. "You're breaking tradition! Two diet sodas?"

"I need the extra kick," she explained.

"Do you know you have the most amazing blue eyes?" he said.

"How sweet," she said as he handed her the first drink. "Thanks," she said as she grabbed the second one. "How old are you again?"

"Old enough to know you're the most beautiful woman in the world," he shot back.

She looked over at the rearview mirror to observe her puffy face, wrinkled shirt, and sweatpants. Were all men liars? she wondered as she accelerated out of the drive-thru. Taking a long sip of her soda, she allowed the cold liquid to wake her up.

Ashley arrived, looking completely depressed. Her face was just as puffy as Tara's, and her hands were blue.

"Good morning," Tara said politely, sipping from her second huge soda. She'd probably have to go to the bathroom all day long at the rate she was drinking.

"What's good about it?" groused Ashley, stepping inside.

"Well," said Tara. "It's not raining, for starters." Seeing Ashley's sullen expression, she tried another tack. "What's with the blue hands, Picasso?"

"You're not going to make me laugh now that my whole life has fallen apart. Anyway, I spent the night painting my office. Steve and I had a huge fight and I kicked him out. I think he cheated on me with his secretary, who's gorgeous, like you!"

"Hey, don't bring me into this! I've got enough problems of my own! And for your information, I'm not nearly as pretty as you. My mother wasn't Marrie, the most sought-after model in the world."

"Oh, give me a break, Tara. You're perfect."

"That's why I'm one hundred percent single and longing for children," said Tara dryly.

"Well, you're technically an aunt to four children, so you've got two nieces and two nephews now."

Tara's eyes welled up with tears. "Really?" she said. "I honestly hadn't thought of that. That would be the best thing in the world to me."

Ashley smiled a bit. "I'm going to need a lot of help. It's not so easy being a single mother with four children."

"I'd be a great babysitter."

They stopped talking and hugged. They broke apart to look at each other.

"Do you really think I'm pretty?" said Ashley. "Last night, Steve called me a fat pig."

"You've got to be kidding. I'm outraged that the father of your children called you such a horrible name. You're gorgeous! You look a lot like your mother. I mean, you have her bone structure and everything. Steve is a complete jerk!"

"*Self-absorbed fool* is the precise term I used last night."

"He's obviously insecure and controlling. After all, if he can make you think you're not good enough, you'll never leave him."

"Thanks for the vote of confidence," said Ashley. "You have no idea how much that means to me. At least some good may come out of this mess. I'm starting to feel glad that we're related. But do you have any caffeine around here? I feel like I'm going to drop dead." She walked into the kitchen.

"Sure," said Tara. "Give me a minute." They spent the next few minutes in companionable silence as Tara fiddled with the coffee maker. "Okay, so I don't know how to work this thing. I always drink diet soda in the morning."

"How about tea? Do you have any of that, or a muffin?"

Tara opened the refrigerator to reveal bare shelves except for a carton of milk, mayonnaise, bread, and some ketchup.

"You really are single!" exclaimed Ashley. "I'll take that soda over there." After taking a sip, she scrunched her nose in distaste but said nothing.

"So what do we do now?" said Tara, sitting down at the table.

"You're the big sister, you figure it out. I'll follow you."

"So, a few months qualifies me for the big sister role, huh? I like that. But, it certainly doesn't say much for dear ol' dad," she added. Tara thought about her father's personality for a moment. "I think we need to confront our father, tell him that we know, and ask for some kind of explanation. I also think he ought to be the one to tell both our mothers. Though I'm not sure we're going to get a full confession. After that, I can't be sure."

"It sounds reasonable, but first we have to find him. He could be in the Middle East for the next month, for all we know. Second, are you sure he won't have a heart attack if we walk into the room together?"

"One of us can call Roberta now and talk with her about his schedule. I was just up in Washington a few weeks ago. He met Peter, so perhaps he'll be more responsive if he thinks this visit is about my boyfriend troubles. As for the heart failure, if he can weather desert storms and gunfire, he ought to be able to handle a visit from both of his daughters. But, more important, who's going to take care of your kids if we go to D.C.?" She hesitated. "I'm just thinking out loud, but we could ask Libby. I'd trust her in a minute. She's been through such a tough time, she may even welcome a diversion."

"Terrific," said Ashley. "My mother was supposed to visit on Friday, but I think I'll put her off for another week. I'll just have to tell her the truth . . . or part of it, anyway. That Steve and I have got some serious problems and we're probably going to get a legal separation." Ashley choked up for a minute. When she saw Tara's look of concern, she said, "I'm okay, really. I mean, I'm incredibly sad, which I think is normal, but I want more from my relationship. Steve isn't a good father and I hate him for that." Ashley accidentally knocked over her soda. "Ohh, I'm such a klutz!" she muttered, looking for something to wipe it up and offering repeated apologies.

"Stop being so hard on yourself!" said Tara, placing several dishtowels over the spill. "It's no problem," she assured her, wiping up the mess. "I wish I had something brilliant to say to make you feel better."

"I'll get through this. I may have to wire my jaw shut to keep from overeating," said Ashley, pointing to her tummy. Sensing Tara's disapproval, she said, "It was a joke. Really. I do think I'm strong enough to cope without food."

"I know you'll be fine. You deserved better and I'm sure you'll find it."

"Come on, Tara. I'm not an idiot. There isn't a man alive who'd take on a woman with four kids. I'm starting to think that, subconsciously, that's why I stayed with Steve for as long as I did. I thought something was better than nothing. But after a while, I realized that I'd prefer to be alone. At least I have the children, who give me a reason to get up in the morning." Ashley avoided meeting Tara's gaze.

"Don't sell yourself short. You're a wonderful person with four great kids." Tara wanted to shake her so that she'd see things differently; she couldn't stand Steve, who sounded like an egomaniac.

"I do have terrific kids, so I should count my blessings. I loved Steve once, but now I think that love isn't enough. You also need to be friends and be able to help each other out."

Tara thought about Ashley's remark about love not being enough. In her case, it really wasn't. The reality was that she shouldn't be seeing Peter at all. It was all wrong and too complicated. She looked at Ashley. Her sister. "We've got to take care of a few details, but I think we should head to D.C. as soon as possible. Maybe it'll bring some clarity to this situation."

"How can you say that?" asked Ashley. "I'm inclined to think that things are going to get worse before they get better."

"I thought you were an optimist," said Tara, studying the planes of Ashley's face.

"Not at the moment."

"Where's Libby when we need her?" asked Tara, realizing that her hands were trembling. The caffeine was getting to her. "She was the one in the group who always had a cheerful outlook on things."

"Well, if her son goes to prison, I'm not so sure she's the one we should lean on to brighten our day," said Ashley dryly. "Anyway, I can't wait to see dear old dad again."

"Not funny," said Tara.

"It wasn't meant to be."

Several days later, Tara ushered Ashley into the same fancy hotel where she had stayed on her last visit. Memories of Peter made her cheeks grow warm. She decided not to tell Ashley that their father had picked up the tab for this trip. When they walked into the luxurious suite, Ashley grew really excited.

"Wow!" she said, flopping down onto the bed. "Luxury for a day! Absolutely no one needs me right now. I hereby nominate Libby for sainthood."

"She was delighted to help. I knew she'd need the diversion." Both Libby and Ed were staying at Ashley's house.

"Look at this!" said Ashley, wandering around the suite. "A real marble bathroom with double sinks. Steve and I have been bumping into each other for years. Boy, I forgot about all this stuff. It's been so long since I've been away."

"Clearly, you should get away more often."

"There was no one to take care of the kids," said Ashley.

"Well, now you have Libby and me. We'll help you."

"You know, some of this martyrdom is my fault. I finally realized that I was so angry at my mother for being so consumed by her looks that I wanted to be the perfect mother—you know, never take time for myself, do everything for the kids. In many ways, I now realize that it was kind of stupid. We all need a little help. To my mother's credit, she's offered to pay for help in the past, but I always turned her down." Ashley walked over to stand at the window and look at the view of the city. "You know what, you don't need to hear any of this. I must be boring you."

"It's okay, I'm not bored. You have a lot to be proud of. You're a great mother."

"How come you're so logical and calm all the time? You always know the right thing to say and—"

"Please," begged Tara. "Don't even suggest for a minute that I'm perfect. I'll tell you one of my secrets to alleviate any fears that you may have in this area."

"What?" laughed Ashley.

"I have the worst-smelling feet. I have to wash them all the time. It's awful by the end of the day. Do you think I'll find someone who finds that cute?"

"I get your point and I'll shut up," said Ashley with a grin.

"Good. Now I have plans to meet Dad at his office in a few hours. Let's go walk around the shops and get something to eat."

"I'm too nervous to eat," said Ashley. "I've always been a bit afraid of him. Seeing him on television all the time made him seem not real, kind of like he didn't belong to me anyway. What's he going to do when we walk in? Scream? Yell? Is this going to be a melodrama like a bad movie? Or even worse, maybe he won't care." Ashley bit her lower lip and suddenly looked incredibly young. Tara could see what she must have looked like in elementary school.

"He'll care. He owes it to both our mothers to tell them the truth. He's got to do something to make amends."

"Yeah sure, knowing Kent West, he'll hop off to Utah or Africa to explore the concept of multiple wives in a searing documentary. He'll probably go on air and talk about his experiences both in his personal and professional life. Then he'll win an Emmy for outstanding broadcasting."

Tara rubbed her aching head. "I hate to say it, but he's very clever. He'll figure out a way to capitalize on the whole thing. He could even write a biography called *My Double Life*. He'd have no problem generating press, or book sales for that matter."

Ashley cringed. "If he does that, then I'll write my own story and call it *The Father Who Went South*. Catchy, isn't it?"

"No," said Tara wryly. "Let's go."

Tara reached over and put her arm around her sister. She'd never realized before how much she had hated being an only child. It was amazing to think about what it meant to have a real blood sister in her life. Unfortunately, she was sure her mother wouldn't see it that way.

They headed outside to the streets of Georgetown, stopping for a bite to eat at a bistro. Everything Tara saw reminded her of Peter, but this time she was overwhelmed with guilt. Thinking about her mother and looking over at her sister and what she had suffered because of Steve's infidelity made Tara feel even worse. She had almost ruined a marriage and she was deeply ashamed. Suddenly, she decided to end things with Peter. Seeing Ashley's pain made her decision very clear.

They took a cab to the CSBC building. Tara trembled as she paid the driver, not really knowing what she was going to say or do next. Greeting the security guard, she introduced herself as Kent West's daughter. The guard called and spoke to Roberta, explaining that Mr. West's daughter was in the lobby. He handed Tara the phone. Tara calmly explained to Roberta that she wanted to surprise her father with some personal news; fortunately, Roberta didn't question her further. After that, the guard issued temporary identification, then sent them upstairs for their meeting.

The elevator smelled of stale smoke and coffee. Just as Tara was mentally congratulating herself on their smooth arrival, Ashley cried, "I can't do this. I'm too nervous."

"Oh, yes, you can," ordered Tara. "It's the only way. We have to talk to him about it. I'm not going to yell or scream or make a scene. I just want him to know that we know. After that, I'm not sure what else to do." Tara noticed the beads of sweat on Ashley's forehead.

"I feel sick," Ashley said.

"Don't you dare fall apart on me!" said Tara. "We've got to face him together!"

Ashley took several deep breaths. "You're awfully bossy for someone who's new at being the big sister!" Tara grabbed her hand and squeezed it tight. "Ouch!" she exclaimed.

Tara laughed. "See, I am new at this. I'm not trying to hurt you." Relieved that the color was returning to Ashley's face, Tara stepped outside the elevator to talk with the receptionist, securing directions to her father's new corner office.

Their first stop was in the restroom, though, which luckily was empty. Something about stepping inside the bathroom's lounge area calmed Ashley's nerves. Perhaps it was the carpeted lounge area, or the vase of fresh-cut flowers, or the black-and-silver tiled floor, or the mirrors that allowed her to fuss over her appearance as a distraction.

"I'll head into his office first. Give us a few minutes alone before you join me."

"I feel like a criminal," said Ashley. "It sounds as if we're plotting some big heist."

Tara worried that Ashley wasn't going to follow

her plan. She could easily start getting sick in the bathroom or just leave. Tara considered her options, realizing that she didn't have much choice. "Do you promise me you'll come? I can't do this alone."

"You know I hate this, but I'll see it through. I think it's time."

Tara made her way down the hall and into her father's office. He was seated at his computer, probably tapping out some breaking-news event. She watched his profile as he frowned at something he read on the screen. The lines on his face gave him a weathered look, which made him all the more endearing to his viewers. As always, she felt like a guest in his life.

"Daddy," she said nervously, feeling suddenly queasy herself.

"Ah, Tara, darling," he said, getting up to give her a hug. His charming demeanor always caught her off guard. "You're right on time. Punctual as always. You look lovely today, my dear."

"Thank you," she said, feeling her legs tremble beneath her. "I won't beat around the bush. I want to talk with you about something," she said.

"Indeed, you mentioned that Peter fellow that I met. If you ask me, he's quite fascinating."

"He's married. It's kind of a problem."

"Is it?"

"Yes, it is," said Tara, seeing the side of Ashley's leg. "But he's not really why I'm here. There's someone I want you to meet," she said. She watched his expression carefully as her sister walked in. She saw a fleeting look of surprise before his face returned to normal.

"Hello, Dad," said Ashley.

"So," he paused. "It's Lee. What a pleasant surprise." His eyes narrowed as he walked toward them. "What happens now? You planned this little ambush. I knew the possibility existed that you two might meet, but I'd assumed you ran in different circles," said Kent, walking over to shut the door. He casually returned to his chair and glared at them.

"What do you mean?" exclaimed Tara. "We found each other by accident. How could you have done what you did?" *So Ashley was the Lee in the letter,* Tara realized.

"I have no regrets," he stated simply, daring them both to contradict him.

"But what about our mothers?" cried Ashley. "They're bound to be destroyed."

"They're both mature adults. They could handle it if the need arose. However, I don't think it's necessary to inform them of your little discovery."

"Am I missing something here?" said Tara. "This is a crime, Dad. You can't be married to more than one woman in this country."

"I realize that," he responded smoothly.

"My mother's going to be devastated," said Tara, sitting down. "Does she have any idea?"

"She may suspect that there's someone else, but

we've never talked about it. I love her too, but I wanted more from my relationship. If you study other cultures, some people believe that it's not natural for a man and a woman to have just one partner."

"This is not a documentary!" Ashley exclaimed. "These are our lives! You've led this double life for over forty years."

"Don't be so melodramatic! That's *my* job," he said arrogantly.

"I have a sister, and we would have never known about each other!"

"This is a delicate situation," explained Kent. "There were pros and cons to telling the truth. Sometimes, a confession such as what you're suggesting can be worse than a deception." He turned to Tara. "Besides, now that you're in a similar situation, you know what it's like to have your personal life get complicated."

"Wrong, Dad," said Tara passionately. "I'm not like you."

"Yes, but you'd be lying if you told me you didn't have feelings for him despite the fact that he's married. I watched you with him. We can't always control our feelings, can we? I love both women, each for a different reason."

"Oh, please," said Ashley. "You make this all sound so civilized, and it isn't! I hated my childhood. You were never there for me, just like my soon-to-be ex-husband."

"Lee, listen to me," said Kent. "I do love you both. I never meant for anyone to get hurt."

"But I did get hurt," said Ashley. "You may be able to pretend that nothing is wrong, but I can't. I wanted more. I needed more."

"Your mother and I adore you, Ashley," he said. "Most kids don't have that to count on. Why do you make me out to be some criminal?"

"Because you are," said Ashley. "It's illegal to be married to two people at the same time!"

"Lee, keep your voice down! This is my workplace," he reprimanded her. "I'll send you both packing if you don't stop this nonsense."

"We're right, Dad. I think you ought to talk with Mom and Marrie." Tara folded her arms across her chest.

He looked away for a moment, then returned Tara's challenge. "You know, girls, I'm delighted that you came today, but we need to wrap it up. I go on the air in two hours." Swiveling his leather seat back to the computer, he began typing.

Unwilling to be dismissed, Tara said, "You can't just pretend this problem doesn't exist." She went to stand in front of his desk.

"Why not?" he countered, turning his seat back around to face her. "Why don't we follow your own logic through to the end. Your mother will be heartbroken, and so will yours, Ashley. Do you want to take responsibility for that?"

"But it's the right thing to do," said Ashley, coming forward to stand beside her sister.

"What makes it so right? I'm happy, they're happy, and now, you've both found each other. I'd say it's not so bad."

Tara knew that his response shouldn't surprise her, but his pompous attitude was just too much to bear. "I can't listen to this," said Tara. She looked over at Ashley. "Are you ready?"

"Sure," she said.

"What are you going to do when we tell our mothers the truth?" Tara challenged.

"You wouldn't dare," he said acidly. His face became a cold mask of disapproval.

Tara backed off. "I can't believe millions of people admire you. You have no conscience."

He gave her a penetrating smile, revealing a charisma that attracted people to him like flies. "Why do you think I'm so successful, darling? You can't afford one in my line of work."

Tara ushered Ashley out in front of her and then shut the door on Kent West. She motioned Ashley to hold her feelings in check until they left the building.

"Can you believe that?" said Ashley, once they were a safe distance away. "He's got absolutely no remorse!"

"I didn't expect much from him," said Tara. "But he's right on one count. The truth doesn't always work."

"Are you saying that you're going to keep his secret?"

"What choice do I have? Maybe his logic isn't all that incorrect. I know my mother would be devastated."

"Tara!" exclaimed Ashley. "He's wrong and he's trying to justify his bad behavior by appealing to your logical side."

"But didn't you hear him? I'm no better. I've had feelings for a married man that I couldn't help."

"But you didn't act on them!" said Ashley. "Did you?"

"Sort of. I mean, I wanted to. But, this incident with Daddy and well, you, has made it clear that it's not the right path for me."

"What are you going to do?"

"Take the coward's way out and write him a good-bye letter," said Tara anxiously as she thought about what she was going to say. *I've made a terrible mistake. My admiration for your work became confused with more personal feelings, which I now realize was wrong.*

"Good for you! I have to be honest and tell you that you're doing the right thing by breaking it off with Peter. You should know that I sensed Steve was cheating on me, and it hurt. The pain was often too intense to bear. I tried to hide it, cover it up, and swallow anything with sugar in it to make myself feel better. But it didn't work. There was always this little voice in the back of my mind telling me that I was worthless for allowing someone to lie to me all the time. Okay, so I'm still not deliriously happy, but there's something good about facing the truth, no matter how ugly it is."

"I know," said Tara quietly.

"But let's get back to dear old Dad. If you're refusing to live a lie, why allow your mother to do the same?"

"I don't know," said Tara. "I need to think about this one over a supersized Diet Coke. So you're going to tell your mother, aren't you?"

"Yes," said Ashley. "I am."

CHAPTER 15

Libby

Libby had thought Robby would be pleased with the verdict, but his mood seemed darker than ever. After the judge handed down the terms of the sentence, she and Ed had invited Rob to stay with them for a few weeks while he figured out a new direction for his life. Since his arrival, Rob seemed to have become someone she barely knew, shunning all responsibility and household rules. Conversation was tough, even when it pertained to mundane events. Libby wasn't sure if they had made the right decision in allowing him to visit. Perhaps being in his childhood home and temporarily relinquishing his independence had taken an even worse toll on his self-esteem.

After two weeks of Robby's bad behavior, Libby had had enough of living with an overage teenager who was rude and disrespectful. That night, she finally approached Ed about her feelings.

"I don't know how to help him," she said in frustration. "He's not himself. He sleeps until noon, goes out drinking with his friends until all hours, and has taken no steps forward in obtaining some sort of gainful employment."

"You're absolutely right," said Ed, scratching his head. "I mean, he can't just do nothing each day. I was hoping that he'd have come up with an idea by now."

"So was I, but it hasn't happened yet. What do you think we should we do? I've made several suggestions, but he didn't seem interested. It's as if he's turned into a completely different person, unmotivated and lazy. I don't do any activities during the week that would be appropriate for an ambitious thirty-five-year-old man." Libby placed her potted orchid in the sink to give the plant some water.

Ed took a seat at the counter. "In his defense, he's just been through a major crisis. Maybe he needs time to reassess his priorities."

"Since when have you been so patient? I don't think he'll find answers at the bottom of his beer mug," said Libby sharply, rinsing the sink. "He needs to be productive again." Libby didn't want to mention her other fear—that Rob could end up with a drinking problem if he didn't find some sort of purpose. She had allowed him to get away with doing nothing to help around the house, but she would make sure that changed the next day. "I'll help him figure it out," she promised.

Tough love, she told herself. She didn't like it, but she was going to have to force him to abide by their rules. Their tacit acceptance of his behavior wasn't helping any of them. Libby was still exhausted from worry, but since the court's decision, she had gotten her appetite back. She had also sworn off antacid tablets indefinitely.

Libby got up the next morning and made some phone calls to gather information on graduate-level English courses. She phoned Tara to get her thoughts.

"Tara, dear, I need your help. This is a bit awkward because I know how busy you are. I'm wondering if you could talk to my son Rob about graduate-level courses at the university. I mean, he was always a talented writer but chose to get his MBA instead of pursuing a career in journalism. Would you mind?"

"Of course," replied Tara politely. "I'd be happy to share with him what I know. There's a professor named Dr. Sarah Michaels who heads up the English department. She's terrific and I could also put him in touch with her."

"Would you?" said Libby. "I can't tell you how much I'd appreciate it. If it's all right with you, I'll give him your number."

"Sure thing," said Tara. "He can also leave a message on my cell; let me give you the number."

"Thank you," said Libby, hunting for a pen. "You're such a gem."

Rob came downstairs around noon. Libby's fury erupted when she saw that he hadn't shaved and he smelled like the inside of a barroom. Enough was enough.

"Robert Marshall, if you think you're going to act like an overgrown teenager and live in my house, then you've got another thing coming." Libby placed her hands on her hips.

"Not now, Mother!" he said. "I'm not in the mood."

"Don't you dare talk back to me, son! You haven't been in the mood for anything in weeks. Get upstairs and clean yourself up. I'll be waiting!" she demanded. She watched as he followed her instructions. *Not bad,* she thought to herself.

Thirty minutes later, Rob returned to the kitchen clean shaven and dressed in khaki pants. He looked at her sheepishly. "Sorry, Mom. It was a late night again last night."

"Drinking yourself into oblivion isn't going to change anything."

"Is there any coffee around here?" he asked.

"I've made you a proper lunch," she said, pointing to the table. "You've got to do something productive with your time. Here," she said, handing him Tara's number.

"Who's Tara West?" he said, taking a bite of macaroni and cheese.

"She's a lovely young woman in my scrapbooking group. She's in the process of getting her doctorate and would know what's happening at the university. I just spoke to her and told her to expect your call today. She'd know about getting an MFA in English or taking some courses in journalism. You used to love to write when you were a child."

"I'd have to go through an admissions process," he argued. "And it's already too late for next fall."

"You can start by auditing some classes and using that brain of yours again. I'm surprised it hasn't pickled at this point," she added dryly.

"Hey," he said with a wink. "You're funny."

"I didn't mean to be. Dry out and pull your act together, son. Your father and I are very worried about you. Will you please think about it?"

He nodded, but said nothing. His silence was painful. But Libby decided it was better not to push him any further. She had made her point; the next step was up to him. She prayed he would start taking some steps forward.

Libby didn't see Rob for the rest of the day, but he left her a message not to worry about him for dinner, that he'd be home at a reasonable hour. It was a step in the right direction.

"Lib," said Ed that night, "how'd it go?"

"I'm not sure," she said, thinking back over her confrontation. "He did indicate that he would be home this evening. That's good, isn't it?"

"You're doing everything right," said Ed, taking her hand.

Libby felt so uncertain. "Do you think so? I told him that he had to find something productive to do with his time. I also think it's odd that he hasn't had much contact with any of the women in his life." She laughed. "You know, Robby always had swarms of girls around him."

"I disagree. I think it's good that he reevaluate the kind of women he used to date. Clearly, those model types only cared about him when he was wealthy. Where are all those so-called friends now?" Ed took a bite of his meat loaf. "This is the best stuff in the world!" he exclaimed, loading up his fork again.

Libby frowned. "Tomorrow night, it's going to be organic vegetables."

"Yes, Major," said Ed with a wink. "I hope our son will find a woman as wonderful as his mother."

"You're a good man, Ed Marshall," said Libby. "But your kindness is not going to get you a third helping of mashed potatoes."

"Wanna bet?" he said.

For the next few days, Libby watched and waited for Rob to say something about their earlier conversation. He didn't bring up any of her suggestions. *At least his behavior is better,* she thought. He had come in before midnight the past few nights. She

273

made a deal with herself not to say another word about his professional life for another week. After all, she didn't expect him to change overnight.

The following Friday morning, Rob was up early. Libby noticed that he was showered and shaven, wearing pressed pants and a collared shirt. He smelled of aftershave, not beer. She wondered if she was dreaming.

"Good morning," she said cheerfully, trying to hide her surprise. "There are muffins on the counter, and juice. Can I get you anything else?"

"No, thanks, Mom. I've got a meeting. I'll just grab a cup of coffee." He kissed her on the cheek as he headed out the door.

Libby was dying to ask him where he was going in such a rush, but she simply smiled and said, "Will you be in for dinner?"

"I'm not sure yet. I'll call you this afternoon."

"I'd appreciate that. Have a good day," she said automatically, feeling like a sales clerk.

That morning, Libby decided that this was a good time to try a new recipe. They were having Pat and Larry, their oldest friends, over for dinner the following evening. It would be the first time that they had entertained since Rob's indictment. Ed had convinced her that they needed to resume their social life. Sharing a meal with their closest friends seemed like a good place to start.

Oddly enough, Libby was excited about preparing an elaborate dinner. She found cooking a wonderful form of relaxation—and, of course, it distracted her from thinking about Rob. She'd allow Ed to sample some of her sautéed chicken to lessen the pain from the plate of vegetables she had planned for his dinner tonight.

Sometime after lunch, Rob burst through the door carrying a large bouquet of sunflowers.

"Hi, Mom," he said cheerfully, handing her the flowers.

"These are lovely," she exclaimed, taking them from his hands. "You didn't need to do that."

"Well," he said shyly. "These are just my small way of saying thanks for everything. I met with your friend Tara West the other day. You neglected to tell me that she's beautiful and brainy. After our talk, I realized that your suggestion of writing a book was my best option. Anyway, I gave Dr. Michaels a few pages of my writing to review. We met this morning to go over them and start the process of outlining for a book."

"And?" Libby said, grasping the counter for support. She was not going to cry in front of her son.

"The good news is that she thinks I write well. She wants me to talk about how my experiences at Amvale changed my perspective on having money. She's also agreed to do some editing for me."

Libby ran over and hugged him. "I knew you could do it, Robby. I just knew it!"

"Mom," he said. "You're choking me!"

"Oh, sorry," she said, releasing her grip. "That's

such wonderful news!" She clapped her hands in delight, suddenly feeling like a cheerleader at a football game.

"I've got several hundred pages to write, so I'm not ready to celebrate, but it's the first positive thing to happen in my professional life for a long time. But I really appreciate your faith in me. I know I haven't exactly been a model son."

"Robby, in my eyes, you'll always be absolutely perfect just the way you are."

CHAPTER 16

Tara

"Hey, Tara," said the male voice on her cell phone. "It's Rob Marshall, again. Are you free for lunch? I've got something I want to talk to you about."

"Sure," she said. "I can think about something else besides Miró for an hour. Where shall I meet you?" Tara was caught off guard. She hadn't expected to actually *like* Rob when he came over to ask her a few questions last week. Sure, he was Libby's son, so she had planned to be polite, but he was so charming that she had found herself won over by him.

"I thought I could meet you at the library around one o'clock. Isn't that your home away from home?"

"That works perfectly," she said. "I'll see you in a few hours."

"Great," he replied. "See you then."

What a pleasant surprise, she thought as she gathered her things together. She wondered what Rob wanted to talk to her about. He seemed rather serious. No, that wasn't the right word. *Earnest* was the way she would have described him. For someone who had just come through a life crisis, Rob appeared desperate to make a fresh start. It was the least she could do to help him out, she reasoned. He was certainly easy on the eyes, Tara had to admit. She'd seen hundreds of Libby's pictures, but they'd failed to capture the sparkle in his eyes or the dimple that formed on his right cheek when he smiled.

On their first meeting, Rob must have caught the look of surprise on her face when she had opened the door to greet him. When he had held up the bright yellow "Get Out of Jail Free" card from Monopoly, Tara had burst out laughing. The rest of the conversation had been easy and relaxed. She was actually looking forward to seeing him this afternoon.

Tara paused from her studying around noon to head outside and take a break. Rob wasn't due for an hour, but she was irritated by her search to document a particular reference. Peter had criticized everything about her previous submission, making their last meeting extremely tense. Tara had filled out the paperwork to find another advisor, but she knew it was going to be impossible at this stage.

Just as she stepped outside, Peter was coming her way with a serious look on his face. Tara braced herself for the inevitable confrontation.

"I was just coming to find you," he said curtly.

"Don't tell me," she shot back. "You've got another problem with my latest chapter."

"As a matter of fact, I do. Let's head back to my office and discuss it."

"I can't wait," she said under her breath. He must have heard her. When she saw the look of anger cross his face, she got really nervous. She wanted to apologize, but realized it probably wouldn't go over very well.

His office felt like a tomb. Why had she once been completely spellbound in that cramped dark space? So far, they had managed to keep things somewhat polite, but Peter looked too out of sorts for this meeting to go smoothly. When he closed the door behind him, Tara wanted to flee. She watched as he took a seat across from her.

He pursed his lips and said, "There's a major problem with your analysis of Miró's work. I'm not sure it can be fixed."

"What?" Tara said incredulously. "You can't be serious."

His eyes narrowed. "Oh, but I am," he replied with a smug expression.

"What's that supposed to mean?" she asked.

"It means that your paper is going to be hard to defend."

Tara felt as if he had slapped her. "You're not going to trash all of my hard work just because I didn't . . ." She was so shocked she couldn't even finish the sentence.

"Sorry, Ms. West. You're giving yourself way too much credit. The paper is flawed and I've written you several pages of comments on how you might fix it."

"I see," she said quietly, unable to look at him. So Peter was going to punish her by destroying her chances to get her doctorate. He was also a powerful man in the art world, so she was sure that many doors would also now be closed for her as well. Tara took the pages from him. "So this is how it's going to be," she said sadly.

He nodded.

"Thank you for all of your help," she said sarcastically as she made her way for the door.

"Anytime," he replied.

Tara practically ran down the hall, trying to keep the tears from streaming down her face. She was so filled with hurt and rage that she had a hard time thinking straight. Running across the lawn, she wanted to scream aloud at what a snake Peter Bergen had turned out to be. Her only consolation was the fact that she hadn't let things go too far. She should have known that any man who would so casually cheat on his wife was capable of far worse. A vision of her father came to mind, but she quickly shoved it aside.

She parked herself underneath a tree near the library. It all seemed so unfair. All of those years of hard work were going to amount to nothing if Peter had his way. Certainly she could fight him, but it was going to be tough. He clearly had the upper hand, and his reputation was impeccable; Peter Bergen was highly respected and admired at the university.

Wiping her nose on her sleeve, Tara cried harder, feeling completely alone. Who was going to believe her? She wanted to just curl up in the fetal position and disappear.

"Tara," said a male voice. "Are you all right?"

"Oh Rob, I'm so sorry I forgot all about our lunch." She covered her face with her hands. "How did you find me?" When she thought about how loud she must have been, she added, "Wait, don't answer that."

He sat down beside her under the tree. "Here, you can use this if you'd like." He handed her a blue bandanna to help her wipe her face.

"This is so embarrassing. You have no idea," she said, peering over at him.

"As a matter of fact, I think I might be an expert on the embarrassment and personal crisis front."

Tara couldn't help herself; she laughed. "Well, I'd say my life's a mess at the moment. All of my dreams just went down the toilet."

"Yep," he said. "I know the feeling. Want to talk about it over a bologna sandwich made especially by me? That's about all I can afford right now. Last year at this time, I could have flown us on a private plane to Italy for lunch. Knowing me, I probably would have, too." He took out his knapsack and started by handing her a soda.

"Thanks," she said weakly, feeling better after tasting her favorite soda. "Don't sell yourself short. Let me taste what you've got first."

Rob smiled and handed her a sandwich. "I hope you'll appreciate the fact that my mother offered to make us lunch, but I insisted I could do it myself. She did add this salad and the apple for good measure."

"Your mother is about my favorite person in the world," said Tara, pulling the sandwich out of the plastic bag. She took a bite and was pleasantly surprised. "It's good. I'm impressed."

"Well, you know. I usually try to impress people with my culinary prowess. As you can see, there's even a slice of American cheese on there."

"Nice touch," said Tara, taking another bite.

"I'm trying to do as many good deeds as I can in the coming year. How about a pretzel?"

Tara nodded, taking one from the bag he held out to her.

"Do you want to talk about it?" he asked.

Tara looked into his eyes and suddenly felt safe. *He must get it from Libby,* she thought. She felt like she could tell the truth about herself. "I fell for my thesis advisor, but he's married. When I decided not to date him anymore, he became rather angry with me. He's just informed me that my thesis has a serious flaw that can't be fixed."

"Ouch," said Rob. "Sounds like a really good guy. Seriously, I shouldn't be giving anyone advice, but based on what you've just told me, though, it seems like you made the right decision."

"No one ever said that doing the right thing is easy," Tara said, wiping her eyes.

Rob threw back his head and laughed aloud. "You can say that again."

After lunch, Rob took a folder out of his knapsack and said, "If it's not too much trouble, I was hoping that you'd take a look at what I've written so far. Dr. Michaels thinks I have the basis for a good book. I'd like to know what you think."

"Sure, I'd be happy to read what you've done." Tara felt that he was being sincere. "I'm honored that you'd like me to see your writing."

"You need to promise to be honest. I know you don't know me very well, but it's not going to help if you sugarcoat your comments. If you really have a problem with a passage, I want to know what you're thinking. Fair enough?"

"Okay," she replied. "Remember, I've got my master's in art history, not English, but I'll do my best to be helpful." Tara looked down at the folder, pleased to have something to take her mind off her troubles with Peter and her father. Something about Peter's smug expression had seemed reminiscent of the same self-centered look that her father had bestowed on her and Ashley. She felt more disgust than disappointment. Shifting her attention back to Rob, she said, "I'm really touched that you trust me with this new project of yours."

He smiled warmly at her. "I've got a lot of work to do, but I think I've got a really good story to tell. Maybe I should call it *The Prodigal Son*."

"Maybe you should call it *My Way Back*."

He winked at her. "Thanks for understanding. I've been judged more than I care to read about."

"Everyone loves a good comeback story. You can turn this experience around, Rob. Maybe even find a charitable cause and donate a percentage of the profits to helping others in need." Tara went on to tell Rob about her mother's foundation and about how many kids Candice West had kept off the streets and back in school.

"That's a great idea. I never would have thought of that. Your mother sounds terrific."

"Yes, she's done a lot for the community," said Tara with pride.

"Okay, so I've taken up enough of your time. I'm sure you need to get back to studying."

Tara rolled her eyes.

"You can't just give up, Tara. If your paper is really good, you can find another expert on Miró somewhere and ask him or her to make comments.

Then you can tell this professor of yours that you've got proof that his analysis of your work is biased. I mean, this guy isn't omnipotent. Somebody was an expert long before him. Or, even better, what about Miró's descendants? Somebody else must have known him, don't you think?"

"You're absolutely right," said Tara, recalling the list of people she had met over the years. "I think I know just who to call. What a great idea, Rob."

They both stood up. "Thanks," he said.

"Sure," said Tara. "You make a great sandwich. I'll look forward to reading your work."

"Great," he said with a smile.

"Bye," she said reluctantly.

"See you soon, I hope," he promised as he walked away.

That night, Tara took out Rob's paper to read it, wondering if she was going to like his writing style. While she hated to think about Peter, she had admired his work, which had fueled her attraction to him.

Running her hand nervously over Rob's first page, Tara plunged into the text, making notations where she thought additional details were necessary. At one point, she laughed aloud, admiring his self-deprecating humor. There was promise here. She liked how well he could draw the reader into his story. Pleased with what she saw, she wrote him a long, encouraging note.

CHAPTER 17

Ashley

Ashley was struggling to open her back door when Libby flung it open.

"Well, hello there. Did you get what you needed?" asked Libby.

"Almost," she replied, putting down several shopping bags. "I think I'm just about caught up. What have you done?" she exclaimed, observing the spotless countertops and neat desktop. There wasn't even a child's sneaker anywhere in sight.

"Oh, I helped straighten things up a bit while you were gone. That's all."

"It's so quiet. Where is everybody?"

"I just read to Sally and she's resting with Janie upstairs. Tucker and Cameron are playing basketball with their friends down the street."

"This is unbelievable," cried Ashley. "Hey, guys, Mom's home!"

For the next few minutes, Ashley was greeted by squeals of delight as Janie and Sally fought for her attention. She kissed them both firmly. "Did you guys have fun with Mrs. Marshall?"

"Yes," they said in unison. Janie told them that Mrs. Marshall had read her three books and played a word game with her.

"Has anyone ever told you that you're a remarkable person?" she offered.

"You're so kind," said Libby. "But really, I'll babysit for you anytime. I adore young children." She checked her watch. "Now, I need to head home and make up some supper. You know, Rob's staying with us for a few weeks while he figures out what to do next."

"Is everything okay?" asked Ashley.

"Well, it turned out as well as could be expected. He'll be on probation for a year. He's also got to do about a thousand hours of community service, and he can never hold corporate office again. On a bright note, he's been talking with Tara about writing a book about what happened. I think it would be very healing for him to tell his side of the story."

"That's a great idea. Tara's such a brainiac that she's the ideal person to help out. I'm so happy for your family," Ashley said, walking to the refrigerator to get a glass of water.

"He came over earlier for an hour and played basketball with Cameron and Tucker. I hope that was okay."

"Certainly," said Ashley. "Who won?"

"It was pretty close. But I'd say you've got some fine athletes on your hands."

Suddenly, Ashley felt nervous. "Libby, how can I possibly repay you?"

"Honey, I'm happy to help you anytime. The meeting is at my house next Tuesday," she offered.

"I'll try to make it," said Ashley.

In the next few minutes, Ashley thanked Libby profusely as she walked her to the car. She tried to pay her, but Libby wouldn't accept any money. Ashley headed back inside to assess her food supply.

Opening up the refrigerator, she saw a large bowl covered in aluminum foil; it was labeled *Dinner. I can't believe she even made us supper,* thought Ashley, trying to figure out how to repay her friend. The house was awfully quiet. She figured she had about fifteen minutes before the kids came downstairs hungry. Ashley looked around and suddenly wondered what Steve was doing. It was going to be hard, she realized. Though she didn't expect him to care about her, he could take the time to check on his kids.

She contemplated a life alone. It was the first time she had allowed herself to think about the ramifications of a divorce. Unable to control herself, Ashley marched over to the freezer in search of an ice cream bar. She scanned the shelves, spying a package wedged into the back. Taking out several squares, she laid them out on the counter and began devouring them.

A knock sounded at the back door. She was startled by the intrusion, feeling as if she had just been caught doing something completely shameful. Checking to see who was there, she was surprised to find Libby. She quickly wiped her mouth.

"Hi," she said nervously.

"Hi," she said. "I'm sorry to bother you, but I forgot my reading glasses. Have you seen them?"

Ashley looked at the counter, conscious of the empty wrappers. Libby's glasses were sitting right there. She reached for them, completely mortified to have been caught on one of her binges. "Here they are."

She politely took the glasses and scanned Ashley's face. "Are you okay?" Libby asked, her voice showing real concern.

"Not really," she said. "My life's a complete mess."

"Oh dear," she said in a motherly tone. "Let me give you a hug. Everything is going to be all right. Let's sit down here at the kitchen table and talk about it."

Feeling Libby's warm embrace, Ashley felt a huge sense of relief. "I mean, you know my father has lied to my mother for over forty years. Even worse, my husband cheated on me with his secretary, telling me it was my fault because I'm overweight. So now I'm a single mother of four children with no job prospects. I can't figure out how I'm going to support us."

"Ashley, I'm so sorry about all of this. I wish I had some magic words to take your pain away. But I do think things will get better. They always do. Didn't you say your mother was coming to visit?"

"Yes, but I haven't spoken to her in ages. She's

coming in two days so that we can try to resolve things."

"That's wonderful. What a good step forward. Just remember that your mother loves you, no matter what. Maybe you should consider asking her to help you. After all, these are her grand-children."

"She's offered over the years, but I've refused. I mean, she's not warm and caring like you. She's obsessed with her looks and hair and fashion. I just hate it."

"Well, that's what made her successful. You have to admire that there are millions of young girls who dreamed of becoming the famous Marrie one day. She's done well for herself. It's not like she sat at home all day; she's worked hard."

"I never thought about it that way."

"Most important," Libby said wisely, "I don't want you to sell yourself short. You're a beautiful young woman, and you've done a great job raising your children. Be proud of who you are."

"I think that's the nicest thing anyone has said to me in years," said Ashley quietly.

"It's all going to work out, sweetie. I promise."

"Thanks," said Ashley. "Now, you need to get home and take care of your family."

"Call me anytime. I mean it," said Libby, picking her glasses up off the table.

"You're the best," said Ashley, walking her to the door.

Steve called that night to arrange a time to get his things.

"Tomorrow morning will be fine," she said curtly. "What about your children? When are you planning to see them?"

He went on about his current business problems but never committed to a time or date to get together with any of them. Ashley knew she would call a lawyer in the morning and arrange for full custody and spousal support. She was almost certain Steve wouldn't put up much of a fight.

Her mother arrived as planned on Friday morning. Marrie might be over sixty, but Ashley noticed that several people still paused to look at her as they waited at the baggage claim area. Ashley couldn't help being impressed by her mother's meticulous purple traveling suit, crocodile bag, and coordinating three-inch pumps. Comfort was not in her vocabulary.

"I've missed you so much, darling," Marrie said dramatically.

"I've missed you, too," Ashley confessed, wondering how she was going to break the news about her father. "How was your flight?'

"Oh, you remember how it is getting out of the city. We were twenty-ninth in line for takeoff. Anyway, I'm here." She seemed to be evaluating Ashley's appearance. "You're looking well," she said politely.

"Thanks," said Ashley, certain she was lying just to keep the peace for the next forty-eight hours.

"We have so much catching up to do. It's a pity I couldn't get your father to join me. He's off to Africa or something on a story."

"Why doesn't that surprise me?" said Ashley. She reached over to take the handle of her mother's compact wheeled bag.

"I can't wait for you to tell me everything," said her mother.

"I'll bet you can," Ashley muttered under her breath.

"What?" Marrie inquired with one arched eyebrow.

"I don't know where to begin," said Ashley. "Why don't you start?" Ashley looked down at her mother's high heels. It would be an amazing feat if she could make it to the parking lot without tripping.

"I was asked to do a new modeling campaign, so it's been very exciting. You know the New Liberty stores? They wanted to feature older women in their jeans. Imagine me wearing jeans or khaki pants, and dancing to some hip music. It's all very fun."

"That's exciting. When will the ads come out?"

"In about a month. My contract states that I get a substantial discount on their clothes. I'd like to pick up some things for you and the children while I'm here."

"Sounds great," said Ashley politely. *She's trying,* she reminded herself.

They talked the whole way back to the house. Ashley hoped that her mother would like what she had done to the bedroom over the garage. It had been Steve's idea to fix up the space for when they had guests. Since her mother's last visit, Ashley had paid a handyman to fix the small bathroom and repair the cracks in the ceiling.

In the past week, she had spent every waking minute preparing the space: purchasing new linens, vacuuming the rug, hanging a shower curtain. There were even fresh flowers on the chest of drawers. It had given her something productive to do with her evenings instead of eating ice cream bars.

"Here we are," said Ashley as she pulled into the driveway. "I've redone the spare bedroom over the garage. It'll give you some privacy if the kids get too boisterous."

"That was very thoughtful of you, dear. I'm sure I'll love it. When do you pick up Sally?"

"I think we've got about an hour before I have to go and get her," said Ashley, hauling her mother's bag out of the backseat of the car. "You can settle in and I'll make some tea."

A short time later, Ashley swirled some sugar into the bland-tasting lemon tea her mother favored. *No wonder she's so thin,* she thought idly. She noticed that her mother hadn't changed out of her high-heeled pumps.

"How come your feet aren't killing you?" Ashley asked.

"I like them," she replied simply.

"I guess we're different," she said.

"Not as much as you'd like to think," said her mother. "I want you to know that I'm very sorry if I hurt you with my comments. I was only trying to be helpful. I've always found it useful to look good; it makes me feel less vulnerable."

"I'd hardly think of you as vulnerable," said Ashley.

"You'd be surprised. Anyway, it's been a long time since we've done this." She took a sip of her tea. "Thank you for your letter about what happened with Steve. I'm glad that you felt that you could confide in me. I do love you, Ashley, but I'm not perfect."

Ashley looked her in the eye. "Thanks, Mom. I'm glad you came, but I've got something else to tell you and it's tearing me apart." She looked over to see her mother adjust her jacket. "I've found out something about my father."

"What are you talking about?"

"I can't hold this inside any longer. It's a long story, but I think you're not his only wife."

"Ashley," her mother said, her spoon clattering to the countertop. "What did you just say?"

"I have to tell you the truth. Dad's also married to a woman named Candice who lives in Washington, D.C. They have a daughter, Tara, who's a graduate student here. Tara and I met when I became involved in this scrapbooking group. She had an album of pictures of Dad and her mother over the years." Ashley burst into tears. "I'm so sorry. I couldn't keep it from you."

Silence.

"I know," said her mother quietly. "I'm just sorry you had to find out."

"Tara loaned me her album to show you. I know this is simply awful for our family, but I thought you should—" Ashley halted in midsentence. "What?"

"I knew that he was married when we met, but I couldn't help myself. We fell crazy in love like a couple of teenagers. Anyway, there was no way I could ever give him up, so I accepted the situation."

"Why did you get married?" said Ashley incredulously.

"Because I loved him. Because I wanted him and, in my mind, we were meant to be together. We've always adored each other. When I got pregnant, I became worried about being a single parent. I knew my parents would disown me if they thought I was having a child out of wedlock. I did have some wild times in my youth, but my upbringing was very traditional. Your grandparents were deeply religious and I didn't want to disappoint them.

"In the sixties, people looked at life differently than they do today. I wanted you to have a more conservative existence. It was our hope that you would never find out the reality of our arrangement."

"So all those years—" Ashley stopped talking as the pieces fell together. "You placed your name on my school forms and health forms and left out Dad's because you knew you weren't really legally married. Right?" She felt absolutely stupid. Why did she wear blinders in her personal life? The truth had always been there. She recalled that household bills and other documents were rarely addressed to her father. Her mother and Murray, her accountant, took care of all legal and tax forms.

She suddenly recalled questioning Marrie about it once. Her mother had said that she had a successful career in her own right; she didn't want to be controlled by any man. Paying her own bills was for her the highest form of independence. Her answer had seemed perfectly reasonable at the time, especially in the light of the seventies feminist movement. Being a celebrity helped too, of course. Ashley had never thought to ask her about it again.

"I wanted to protect you from families who might not have approved of the relationship between your father and me. Fortunately, I had already established a reputation as a top model, so I never really got too many questions on why I didn't go by Mrs. West. Anyway, it's not as if I was the type to be involved in the PTA or anything." She snorted in amusement, touching Ashley's arm in a show of solidarity.

"But you have no legal rights," argued Ashley, placing her hands in her lap. "You're not entitled to anything of his in the eyes of the law."

"You know, I made enough money on my own not to worry about such things. Your father has always been generous. He bought me my apartment in New York as well as everything else."

Ashley had trouble accepting her mother's calm explanations of an illegal arrangement. "Mother, you do realize that I'd be considered illegitimate in the eyes of the law."

"The world has changed. What difference does it make anymore?" she said with a wave of her hand. "Nowadays, women are having children out of wedlock all of the time. There are all sorts of arrangements that are acceptable now that weren't back when our decision was made."

Ashley wanted to run upstairs and curl up in a ball. Clearly, she was never going to convince her mother that their family life was a complete charade played out by two self-centered, attention-seeking individuals. Perhaps she was right. Her parents were a match made in heaven. "I still don't understand. I hate that I'm getting divorced, and the kids don't have any relationship with their father. But I refuse to allow him to save his good side for other women and then come home and do nothing to help out his real family. I'd rather be alone with my children than maintain a farce of a marriage just to have a warm body in the house.

Why did you settle for half a marriage?" questioned Ashley.

"Your father and I have always gotten along very well. He meets my needs in many ways. I don't have to cater to him all the time; I have the freedom and the financial resources to do as I please. Our arrangement suits us." She took Ashley's hand. "I don't want you to be unhappy about it."

Ashley wanted to exclaim, *You've got to be kidding, Mother!* "What's next? I mean, after all, the marriage is technically not valid." Ashley wanted to snatch her hand from her mother's, but instead she calmly disentangled herself by getting up from her seat.

"It's worked for forty years; I see no reason to change anything. There are these marvelous earrings I've had my eye on. Perhaps I'll let your father treat me to them. After all, he is a very wealthy man."

If only I were more shallow, Ashley thought. *Perhaps I wouldn't feel things so deeply. What about love?* she wondered. She didn't think the real thing actually existed.

The rest of the weekend actually went very well. Marrie managed to play cards with Tucker and Cameron and work on some coloring with the girls. She made a few good suggestions to help Ashley spruce up her home and even helped prepare dinner one night. Most important, Marrie's separate bedroom allowed her a chance to take a break from the chaos of her grandchildren. She would tell everyone that she needed a "rest" and retreat on a regular basis each day. Despite her frequent "rest breaks," Ashley appreciated Marrie's effort to fit into her lifestyle.

On Tuesday, Ashley dragged herself out of bed to take care of the kids. Now that her mother had gone back to New York, it was tough just handling the daily routine. Steve had cleared out his closets and taken his bureau and several other pieces of furniture. There was no tear-filled good-bye. They would talk through their lawyers. Her only goal was to get as much money as possible from a settlement.

That morning's meeting was at Libby's house. Something made her spend more time than usual on her hair, and when she put on a pair of pressed pants, they were too large. At least the divorce proceedings had taken away her appetite. After changing into a simple wrap skirt and a clean white blouse, she checked her appearance in the mirror. She was proud of the fact that she didn't look as bad as she felt inside. After all, as her mother said, one must keep up appearances.

After dropping the kids at school, she decided to head over to Libby's a bit early. She knew if she didn't go there directly, some other errand or task would take away her attention. Pulling a tote bag full of supplies out of the back of her car, she knocked on the back door. Libby greeted her warmly.

"Good morning," she said cheerfully, holding a mug of coffee. "You look gorgeous today."

"Thank you," said Ashley, telling herself not to add some negative comment about herself. *Be positive.*

"Can I get you a cup of coffee?" she offered. "I was just getting everything ready. How are things going?"

"Much better." She asked about each of her children.

Moments later, Rob arrived and Libby made the introductions. Ashley found it hard to accept that this boyishly handsome man had been in such trouble; he didn't look the part.

"It's so nice to meet you. Your mom told me that you're writing a book?"

"I'm just starting the project, but it's about the evils of the corporate world. Who knows what'll happen. I start my community service work next week."

"What will you be doing?" She noticed the strong set to his jawline.

"I don't know yet. I think they want me to help troubled youth in the area. I know that would be good for me."

"I think you'd be great working with kids. They'd look up to you."

"Would they?" he said, looking away. "I'm not sure how much of a role model I am to anyone."

"Listen, my kids think you're great. They were

talking about you this week. You can't let this thing define who you are."

"Thanks," he said.

The front doorbell rang. Libby excused herself to get it.

"That's my cue," said Rob. "I've got a meeting this morning. You ladies have fun."

Ashley said good-bye and reached for her bag. She watched him leave. Tara came to stand beside her. "Was that Rob?" she asked.

"Yes, I think he was going to escape from us. Libby told me that you're going to help him with his book project." Ashley grinned. "More important, he's really cute."

Tara pinked up a little, but said seriously, "I don't know how much help I'm going to be, but I'll try. Hey, you look great today," said Tara, surveying Ashley's neat appearance.

"Thanks," said Ashley. "I really appreciate it."

"There's nothing to appreciate," she said. "When are you going to realize that you're really pretty? You always make it sound like I'm lying to you or something."

"Okay, I hear you," said Ashley, holding up her hands in mock surrender. "You're really starting to sound like a big sister."

Tara smiled. "I like that."

Ashley pondered her words. "You're right, though. I'm going to be more positive about myself."

"That's what I want to hear. Good for you. So, what are we going to work on today?"

"I've got some fun pictures of the kids that I took this week. Want to see them?"

"I'd love to," said Tara.

Margy, Catherine, Tina, Annie, and Megan arrived over the course of the next fifteen minutes. Ashley delighted in showing off her new photographs, probably the first she'd taken in years.

"Okay," she said. "So I used a disposable camera that I bought at the grocery store," she admitted, watching as everyone laughed. "I wouldn't want to mention that there were several rolls that had been sitting at the developer's for about a year or more."

"These are wonderful photos," said Megan.

"Speaking of photographs," remarked Annie. "Our favorite city councilman, Marion Washington, was photographed having coffee with a woman other than his wife."

"They could have been taking care of important city business," said Margy.

"I doubt anyone expects this council member to conduct his staff meetings from the inside of a hotel room."

"Oh, my," said Catherine.

Ashley noticed Tara's fingers tighten around a photograph, but she said nothing.

"Okay," said Tina. "You two can't keep us in suspense much longer. What happened when you confronted your father? I've been dying to call all week, but decided that it was probably none of my business. It still isn't, but . . ."

Libby put her arm around Ashley's shoulder. "Let's not push. I think both Ashley and Tara have had a pretty tough week." Ashley appreciated Libby's emotional support. The rifts were healing between her and Marrie, but she felt comforted by Libby's presence.

"It's all right," said Ashley, glancing at Libby. Taking a deep breath, she turned to Tara. "Do you want to tell them or shall I?"

"You go ahead," Tara offered. Ashley couldn't help but notice Tara's hunched shoulders and short stubby nails as she leaned forward in her chair. *It's probably stress,* she thought, knowing how particular Tara usually was about presenting herself.

"Kent West never flinches under fire; it's what he's known for. We could have been talking about the weather. He seems to think it's okay to love and be married to two women. He tried to launch into a diatribe on how other cultures find this practice acceptable." Ashley hoped she sounded calmly objective, rather than sarcastic.

"Is he familiar with the legal system in this country?" asked Annie with one raised eyebrow. When all the others turned to her, she said, "Relax! I'm not going to tell Tom. It was just a question!"

"I'm not sure what's going to happen next," said Ashley nervously.

Tara got up and left the room. Ashley excused herself to follow her back into the kitchen. She watched Tara as she paced back and forth.

"Are you okay?" asked Ashley, not really knowing what else to say.

"I don't know what to do. This is so difficult. I'm frustrated that I haven't made any decisions about anything yet," said Tara. "Part of me wonders whether it's even necessary anymore. Your mother doesn't have plans to resolve this issue, right?"

"I guess not. But it still doesn't alter the fact that he's a complete liar."

"We should probably join the rest of the group. They'll be wondering about our conversation. I want to keep things light."

Ashley walked back into the room to take a seat. She wanted to do several pages of photographs of the kids in their bathing suits at the beach. As she reached into the bag, she saw an old photograph of herself and Steve posing in front of the house with the children. It struck her again how badly she had wanted a normal family life, and how much her loneliness as an only child had probably led to having four kids. Suppressing the urge to break down in front of the group, she threw the picture back into the pile. She would save her tears for later when she was alone in her empty bed.

"Look at this picture," said Tina, showing it to the others. "We took the kids to India last summer to see their grandparents. At this outdoor dance festival, the kids ate some chicken made with too much curry. Look at Angie's face. Does she look like she's having fun?"

Ashley was too preoccupied to do anything more than smile politely.

That night, as she reached for one of the kids' cupcakes, she recalled the compliments she had received on her appearance. To stop herself from eating junk food, she phoned Tara and made small talk.

"You sound down."

"I guess I just can't believe that Steve is completely gone. I mean, we don't even talk," said Ashley. "We only communicate through our lawyers these days."

"Ashley, Steve's old news. You deserve better. But, honestly, you need to take care of yourself. You're a really special person with great character. Look at your kids and be proud of the choices that you've made." She paused. "You also need to be happy with yourself and heal before you even worry about another relationship. But I do know, when the time is right, something wonderful is going to happen."

"Thanks for the pep talk," she said. She wondered how Tara always knew the right things to say to make her feel better about herself.

"Anytime," said Tara. "That's what big sisters are for."

"I'm really glad I found you," said Ashley. She

didn't know how she would cope with the divorce without her support. It was rather fantastic that Tara had appeared in her life just when she needed her most.

"Me, too," said Tara. "I'm taking you shopping in the morning to celebrate that new figure of yours. You're not Marrie. You can still be a nice person *and* have good clothes."

Ashley laughed. "I'll come by after I drop off the kids."

"I can get you some coffee at the drive-thru."

"No, thanks. I'll bring my own along with something to eat," said Ashley. "I'm really glad you're in my life," she added, suddenly looking forward to the following day.

"I feel the same way," said Tara.

CHAPTER 18

Tara

Tara needed to plan what she was going to say to her mother. The truth was never easy to hear, but Tara felt her mother needed to know. Her mother had tons of admirers on the Hill; she would find a way to bounce back. Tara took a deep breath, hoping that she had made the right decision.

A short time later, Ashley arrived, carrying a

supersized diet soda. She came inside, juggling her own coffee cup and a small white bag.

"Perfect timing," said Tara. "So, I've been thinking about my mother. She should know the truth about her marriage."

"I would wait a while," said Ashley, taking a bite of her muffin. She fidgeted with her napkin.

"What are you talking about?" asked Tara. "What's gotten into you this morning? You were the one who seems to think that honesty in relationships is so important."

"I do, in theory. But sometimes reality doesn't work that way. All I'm asking is whether it's really our responsibility to right the wrongs of our parents."

"Did they put something in your coffee?"

Ashley took a deep breath. "My mother knew about it."

"She what?" exclaimed Tara.

"She knew," said Ashley. "I've been waiting for the right time to tell you."

"You're kidding me," cried Tara.

"It makes sense, you know. My mother was a sixties hippie chick who had dozens of boyfriends before she found our father. Come to think of it, I'm not convinced she was completely faithful over the years, either. Your mother's different. I hate to see anyone get hurt over another's dishonesty."

"Like you?" said Tara.

"Exactly. Sometimes I wish I didn't know that Steve cheated on me. Even with the kids, I'm lonely in the house by myself, though it looks as if I may get to keep it as part of our settlement."

How often we accommodate other people's deceptions, Tara thought. "Well, I still can't believe it," she said, still amazed that Ashley's mother had just accepted the arrangement. "No wonder Daddy was so cavalier when we confronted him. Why should he get off so easily? Men shouldn't be allowed to be liars and cheats!

"But I've been thinking about what to do with Daddy, and I've come up with a plan. I'm not suggesting that we be so direct in making Daddy confess. I think we can outsmart him." Tara thought for a moment, "Mom called the other day saying that she was going to be in New York for a major fund-raiser with the first lady and Senator Wilkins. She wanted to know if I could attend."

"So?"

"I think I'm going to go. Wouldn't it be interesting if you and Marrie had a quiet dinner with us the night *before* the big event?"

Ashley gulped. "What do Candice and Marrie have in common besides Kent West? Anything?"

"Oh come on, I do think that we could keep the conversation going. Candice absolutely loves this program. It wouldn't surprise me if she got Marrie involved in the whole thing. But, most important, it would certainly come as quite a surprise if our father arrived at the restaurant expecting to just see one of his families and found us all seated together! I'd like to see him squirm, even if it's only for a few minutes."

"I don't think I can do it!" said Ashley.

"Why not?" said Tara. "You'll be helping make the point that cheats and liars should get what they deserve."

"I'd like to make the same point to my soon-to-be ex-husband."

"Maybe you can," said Tara. "Let's tackle New York first. I'll make all the arrangements on my side. I'll have to call Roberta to make sure he's available that night. This is an important weekend for Mom, so I'm sure he'll make an effort to be in town." Seeing Ashley's nervous expression, she added, "Don't worry, it's going to be fine. Seriously, he owes her the truth. What he's done is completely wrong."

"I hate to tell you this, but I don't think we're going to see him flinch."

"It's worth a try, isn't it? Besides, it gives us a great excuse to spend the weekend in the city." Tara suspected that Ashley was thinking about Steve's betrayal. She knew that Ashley, like Candice, had been completely duped by someone she loved. It wasn't right. Tara watched Ashley's expression harden. She breathed a sigh of relief, knowing that her sister was going to help her.

"I haven't been back to New York in fifteen years."

"Maybe it's time you reclaim that part of your life. I can't wait to show you some of my favorite places. Wait until that ex of yours sees you when I get done; *regret* is such a lovely word. For starters, I'm throwing away every single pair of sweatpants that you own." Tara relished the idea of helping Ashley feel better about herself. She reminded Ashley that it wasn't a makeover, it was just a return to her old stylish and self-confident self.

"I can't afford to go shopping . . ." pleaded Ashley.

"Yes, you can. I'll bet your mother would be glad to help the cause." Based on Ashley's stories about her mother, shopping was obviously one area where Marrie excelled.

"You're right. Anyway, I really appreciate your help," said Ashley.

"I'm looking forward to it. But, more important, I've only just begun . . ." said Tara with a wicked grin.

"What about you? I mean, Peter and all?"

"It's over," said Tara firmly. "Now I have a bunch of nieces and nephews who'll hang out with Auntie Tara."

"Oh!" said Ashley with a laugh. "I almost forgot. Sally drew you a picture."

Ashley took out her child's picture. Scattered across the page were rainbows, a bird, and a big scribble.

"I knew she was a genius," Tara said, taping it to her refrigerator.

When Rob called and asked her to dinner on Friday night, Tara was excited to see him again. *It isn't a date,* she told herself. He was just a good friend. Just the same, she took some time off from studying to find a cute print halter top to wear. As she'd told Ashley, retail therapy was always a good thing. Not sure where he planned to take her, she used that as an excuse to purchase a new pair of dark denim jeans as well.

She thought about calling Libby all week, but decided to wait. What was she going to say? *Hi, Libby, I think your son is really cute. Do you approve?* No, it made sense to see how things went tonight before she brought the subject up with her. After all, she and Rob had simply shared a bologna sandwich together and exchanged a few e-mails, though they were growing longer and more amusing.

On Friday night, Tara noticed that her palms were sweaty. She wasn't a teenager, she reminded herself. When the doorbell rang, she nearly jumped in anxious anticipation. *Stay calm.*

"Hi there," he said casually when she opened the door.

"Hi," she responded a bit shyly. Tara couldn't help but notice how good Rob looked in his dark sport coat. She remembered a story Libby once told about how Rob had spent a week on some billionaire's yacht. It made her nervous.

"What's the matter?" he asked. "You don't like my jacket? Wrong color?" he joked, turning around.

"No," she laughed. "You just look a bit more polished tonight, and well, it caught me off guard." She reached for her handbag and shut the door.

He looked over at her. "I wasn't expecting to like you either," he said honestly. "I mean, my *mother* arranged for me to call you in the first place. You were definitely not what I expected."

Tara laughed. "So, what did you expect?"

"Well, I kind of thought you'd be pretty boring."

"Boring?" repeated Tara. "Me?"

"You asked," he said as they walked to his parked sedan. He opened the door for her. "And don't tell me you weren't expecting me to show up at your door in a striped suit, if you know what I mean."

"Okay, okay," she said. "Guilty as charged. But the more I read your work, the more I can understand what happened to you. If the whole corporate culture is flawed, then that gray area between right and wrong grows wider. It's amazing what you can talk yourself into," she said, remembering all of her rationalizations about Peter.

He took them to a small and charming Italian restaurant. Tara was pleased with his choice. "I like it here," she said as they headed inside.

"You have no idea what a breath of fresh air you are," he said. Rob greeted the manager by speaking to him in Italian, which prompted a huge smile, a pat on the back, and a place at a cozy table in the corner.

"How many languages do you speak?" asked Tara, placing her napkin in her lap.

"A couple," he said casually. "I've done a lot of traveling. I must say, though, I don't miss it." He ordered them a bottle of wine. When the waiter came to pour it for them, he raised his glass in a toast. "Here's to new beginnings," he said.

"I like that," said Tara, feeling the warmth of the red wine as it eased down her throat.

"I have some news that I think you'll find interesting," he said staring at her. "But, before that, I want to thank you for all of your suggestions on my book proposal. You're very talented."

"Thanks," said Tara modestly. "So what's going on?"

"I've got two New York publishing houses competing for the rights to my story."

"You're kidding!" said Tara. "It happened that fast? You just submitted it last week."

"Dr. Michaels was kind enough to show my work to her agent, who was very enthusiastic. The agent went ahead and called up editors at several publishing houses. I've already got two offers, but I'm waiting for one of them to increase their bid. At the rate I'm going, in a few months, I may even be able to pay off a chunk of my legal bills and rent an apartment."

"Oh Rob, that's fantastic news! I'm so thrilled for you."

He placed his hand over hers. "I couldn't have done it without you."

Much to her surprise, Tara enjoyed the feel of his skin next to hers. She felt happy for the first time in a long time. "I've really enjoyed reading your work," she said. "I think you're going to do great."

"I hope so," he said. "Maybe someday I'll be able to afford to take you to a nicer restaurant."

"I like it here," repeated Tara. "And I like your bologna sandwiches."

"So it's not about the house, the car, or the restaurant, huh? What else is there?" He winked at her.

"Maybe something real," she replied softly.

"I like the way you think," he responded with a big smile.

Tuesday's scrapbooking meeting was at Tina's house and Tara wanted to get there early to talk with Libby. After her usual trip to the drive-thru, she couldn't help but feel nervous about her budding friendship with Rob. Libby knew about her father and well, her family situation was not particularly normal—not even close. Her celebrity father was a bigamist; she and Ashley were planning to trap him into admitting the truth in a public forum. There could be a media frenzy over the story, which was going to be stressful. The Marshall family had already been through enough. Tara's hands tightened on the wheel as she recognized the reality of her situation.

She was the first to arrive at Tina's house, which was decorated in bold shades of rich red and hot pink. The oversized silk pillows on the family room floor provided extra seating.

"Good morning, Tara. I see you've already made your soda run," said Tina with a knowing smile. "I've got muffins and fruit in the kitchen if you'd like some."

"Thanks so much, Tina. Is Libby here yet?" asked Tara.

"I think she's in the kitchen."

Tara felt a bit awkward as she made her way to the back of the house, carrying her scrapbook supplies. When she saw Libby, she said nervously, "Hi, I was hoping to talk to you."

"I hope it's not about Rob," she replied seriously.

"And if it is?" Tara swallowed hard.

"I promised myself that I wouldn't interfere. I'm far too excited about the two of you to say a word. Thanks to you, Rob is back on track." She came over to give Tara a hug.

"Oh Libby, I'm so relieved, but my father . . ."

"Now, listen to me. You're not responsible for the actions of your father. It wasn't your fault. You're a beautiful and brilliant young woman and I couldn't be happier that my son's eyes light up every time he hears your name."

"Really?" said Tara.

"I told you I wasn't going to get involved," she admonished.

"Involved in what?" said Ashley as she walked into the room.

"My personal life," said Tara.

"How's that possible? It's going to be all over the news," said Ashley.

When both women stared at her as if she'd lost her mind, Ashley held up her hands. "Okay, sorry. It was a joke."

Tara gave Ashley a warning look.

Ashley shrugged and walked over to the kitchen table, serving herself a bowl of fruit. "You'll appreciate the fact that I passed over those delicious-looking muffins."

"Don't make me the food police," said Tara wisely.

"It's good to see that you both are acting exactly like sisters."

Moments later, Margy, Megan, Annie, and Catherine joined them in the family room. As everyone unpacked their supplies, Ashley whispered to Tara, "What were you talking to Libby about?"

"If you must know, Rob," said Tara, removing a package of colored pencils from her case.

"What about Rob?" she said curiously.

"Lower your voice," said Tara.

"How's Rob doing anyway?" asked Megan, taking out some patterned border stickers for her page.

"Thanks to Tara, he's working hard on a book about his experiences at Amvale," said Libby. "He's also doing community service work every week and looking for a new apartment. Ed and I couldn't be happier."

"I wish you'd fix *my* life," said Ashley with a raised eyebrow. "I'm all yours."

"I'll see what I can do," Tara promised. "Other people's problems are easy."

"Good, I could use some help," said Tina. "I'd like to work on this upcoming exhibit that the museum is doing on Andy Warhol. It would be a nice change. My proposal is due next week. Would you have time to take a look?"

"Sure thing," said Tara cropping a new picture of herself and Ashley. "Sounds like a great idea to work on something different like that. I love Warhol's work, especially his portrait of Marilyn Monroe."

"So, how's your doctorate going?" asked Megan.

"A few weeks ago, my thesis advisor told me that my analysis had a major flaw, so I've worked hard to correct the problem. It's been extremely stressful." Tara didn't want to look up from pasting the picture on the page.

"That's odd. Didn't you have to present an outline and show your theory before you started writing?" said Megan, putting down her pictures. "A major flaw doesn't magically appear. . . ."

Tara shrugged, refusing to look Megan in the eye.

"I'm trying to find an outside expert who'd be willing to take a look at my paper before my advisor cuts it to shreds during my defense."

"That's just not right that your advisor would turn on you like that," said Annie, leaning forward. "Unless he had a vested interest in seeing you fail. That still doesn't make sense, you've been working together for more than a year."

"My advisor changed his mind about my work when I refused to have a personal relationship with him."

"So he's going to punish you by ruining your future?" said Megan, incredulous. "That's terrible!"

"Absolutely not!" said Annie, visibly angry. "We'll see about that! This is the kind of thing that gets me all fired up. I'll have Tom make a call to his old friend, Blake Tarkenton, on your behalf."

"You know Blake Tarkenton?" said Tara excitedly. "I've been trying to reach him for weeks, but my calls and letters haven't been returned."

"Who's he?" asked Ashley.

"The world's leading expert on Miró; he lives in London."

"But he spends most of his time in sunny California. He was a friend of Tom's family. I have his number at home. I feel quite certain he'd take a look at your analysis and give his opinion. Whatever happens, he'll be honest. Your work should be reviewed in a fair and unbiased manner."

"Oh Annie, I'd really appreciate any help you could give me," said Tara, relieved.

"I'll make the call this afternoon. Consider it done," said Annie with an affirmative nod.

Tara could have cried. "Thank you so much, Annie. You have no idea what this means to me, all my years of work."

"No problem, dear. You know I can't stand it when anyone abuses the power they've been given. It's one of my pet peeves. But more important, I want to show you guys this new paper I found. It's just beautiful."

CHAPTER 19

Libby

"We've got a great day to play," said Ed, reaching for his golf bag. "When does Sarah arrive?" he asked as he checked his clubs to make sure they were in order.

"Caroline's dropping her here after lunch. We're going to make cookies, have dinner, and watch a movie. I can't wait. She's a wonderful child." Libby took another sip of her coffee.

"She sure is," he replied. "Sorry to miss the fun! You sure you don't need me to do anything?"

"Absolutely not. Go and enjoy yourself!" Libby

smiled at her husband, whose eyes sparkled with delight at the thought of having a twenty-four-hour golf date with his buddies. Ed planned to drive to Atlanta to play an exclusive men-only course, eat a full-scale cholesterol-filled steak dinner, and stay the night in the fancy clubhouse with three of his friends. It was his idea of paradise.

"I'll call you tonight after dinner," he said, coming over to give her a kiss on the cheek. "Love you, Lib. Tell Sarah that I'll miss her!" He practically skipped out the door.

Things are normal again, she thought, trying to keep the tears from misting her eyes. Just a few months ago, she'd thought that her family would never recover from the scandal. But, little by little, they all seemed to be healing. Even as Libby cleaned up their breakfast dishes, she realized that she'd never appreciated the joy in living each day as much as she did now. Checking the coffeepot, Libby left it on for Robby, who'd probably stayed up late working on his book.

Libby was itching to get some pages done in her scrapbook before Sarah arrived. Stepping into her bright, sunny family room, she headed to the cabinet to take out several pages of paper, a brown ink pad, some pink ribbon, and a few journal pads that Annie had dropped off. Thanks to Caroline, there was a stack of photographs of her grandchildren. Annie had told her she could try taking the ink pad along the edges of the paper to give the page an aged look. Filled with excitement, Libby placed all of her supplies in front of her and imagined how this distressed look would turn out.

Libby stamped the brown ink around the edges of the page to create the faded-looking effect. Pleased with the result, she made a mental note to call Annie and thank her for the tip. As she flipped through her pile of photographs, a picture of Sarah wearing a flowered halter dress caught her attention. To think, Sarah had turned ten this past year! Or, as Caroline jokingly said, "She entered the dreaded double digits." Libby wasn't going to beat herself up about the fact that parts of this year were a complete blur.

She grabbed a piece of paper to jot down some words to describe Sarah: *joyful, creative, carefree, fashionable.* Her mind searched for the right phrase to describe Sarah's search for the right party dress. *That's it,* thought Libby excitedly. Libby would call this page *A Passion for Fashion.* She could then figure out how to put some snippets of a cheetah print, maybe a picture of some high heels. Searching through the pile again, Libby wanted to find the picture of Sarah in a pink top. She'd call that page, *Pretty in Pink.*

When her stomach began to growl, Libby got up, stretched, and realized that she'd been consumed by her project for nearly three hours. There was a note from Rob on the kitchen counter, saying that he'd be back this afternoon. She hadn't even heard him come downstairs. Libby made herself a turkey sandwich and sat down to savor every bite.

A short while later, Caroline arrived with Sarah, who brought her overnight bag, a giant stuffed dog, and a bag full of seashells.

"Oh, I've missed having you for the night," said Libby, enfolding her in a big hug. "We're going to have a great time. I can't wait to hear about all the things you did on your trip to the beach." She looked over at Caroline. "We'll talk in the morning about what time works for you to pick her up. Make sure Alexandra knows that it's her turn next."

"Sure thing, Mom," said Caroline. She turned to give Sarah a kiss good-bye.

"Grandma, look at these shells we got at the beach last weekend. They're beautiful. I'll bet you could use some of the smaller ones in one of your albums."

"What a great idea! Come into the family room. I want to show you what I did this morning," said Libby excitedly. She was so pleased with how her pages of Sarah had turned out.

"Wow!" said Sarah. "That's sooo cool! I do have a passion for fashion!" She pointed to her metallic wedge sandals. "So, I guess this means that Uncle Rob isn't the total center of attention anymore," she added, placing her hand on her hip. "Mom says he's not going to jail and everything's going to be all right."

"Your mom's right. Your uncle learned a valuable lesson, and now he's going to tell his side of the story in a book. In the meantime, let's go make some chocolate chip cookies."

"Awesome," she said, racing for the kitchen to get started.

Libby followed close behind and took out the mixer, eggs, sugar, flour, and the rest of the ingredients. Placing everything they needed on the kitchen counter, she put on her red checkered apron and washed her hands. It had been months since she'd spent a worry-free afternoon.

"Grandma, how many eggs?" asked Sarah as she cracked one egg on the side of the mixing bowl.

"Two, dear," replied Libby. She found two baking sheets and turned on her double oven. She went over to the counter and helped Sarah with the handheld mixer. "Why don't you see if you can measure out two cups of brown sugar?"

"I can do it," she said earnestly, reaching for the measuring cup. Libby helped her mix in the sugar and they added the chocolate chips. "I like cooking!" Sarah said.

She's so adorable, Libby thought, admiring Sarah's enthusiasm. Libby wanted to tell her that this wasn't exactly cooking, but she didn't want to spoil her fun. Sarah was a near-exact replica of Caroline when she was ten years old. The clothes may have changed, but those blond pigtails and pert little nose were identical. Libby made a mental note to find one of her scrapbooks to show Sarah a picture of her mother at her age.

"Hey, Sarah," said Rob, coming into the kitchen. Tara followed him into the room. "What's cookin'?"

"Hi, Uncle Rob," she said, quickly wiping some flour from her sleeve. "Grandma and I are making chocolate chip cookies."

"I'll bet you knew that they're my favorite," he said, giving her a big bear hug. "This is my friend, Tara," he said.

"Hi there," said Tara.

"I know you! You're Grandma's friend," she announced proudly. "Uncle Rob, you're not scrap-booking now, are you?"

"No way!" he replied quickly.

"I know Tara and Grandma make those pretty albums together. What are you going to do the whole time?"

"Ah, that's a good point," said Rob patiently. "I'm really busy working on a novel and Tara's helping me edit my book," he said easily.

"I like to write, too. I'll help you," said Sarah with a firm nod. She stuck her finger in the mixing bowl and pulled out a wad of chocolate chip cookie dough.

"Hold on a second there, sweet thing," said Libby, trying to stop Sarah's assault on the dough. "We need to make sure we've got enough to actually make the cookies." Just as she stood up, Libby watched as Rob stuck his finger in the dough and took a mouthful.

"This is great stuff!" he replied, smiling mischievously.

Sarah burst out laughing.

Rob adopted a serious tone. "We've got to do a taste test around here. What do you think?" He stuck a spoon into the dough and handed it to Tara.

Tara tasted the dough. "I'm not so sure, guys. I think I need another bite to really give my opinion." She handed the spoon back to Rob for another bite.

"Just wait one minute! I'll be the judge of this contest!" exclaimed Libby. She took out a huge serving spoon and put it into the dough to grab the biggest bite of all.

Sarah's eyes grew enormous. "Grandma!"

"Hey, Mom, I think you won this round," said Rob, patting her on the back.

Libby ate the spoonful of cookie dough with relish, not feeling the slightest bit guilty. "This is really good," she said happily. "But I do think we need to get this dough in the oven before it's all gone."

"Uncle Rob, are you and Tara going to watch the movie with Grandma and me tonight? It's going to be really fun." Sarah implored as she looked up at both of them.

"As much as we'd love to stay, we've got plans. Tara is going apartment hunting with me this afternoon. I think I've got a couple of great leads!"

"Are you moving back to Atlanta?" asked Sarah anxiously.

"Nope," he said. "I think I'm going to stick around Belloix for a while while I finish my book. After that, who knows?"

He looked at his watch, then over at Tara. "I think we should get going. I told the real estate agent I'd meet him around two o'clock."

"Sure thing," said Tara. "Thanks for letting me taste your marvelous cookie dough!" she said. She turned to Libby. "I've got to show you this new paper I found downtown. The patterns are really unusual."

"I'd love to see it," said Libby. "We'll talk later. Good luck on the apartment search!"

When they left, Sarah seemed to ponder this new piece of information. "Tara's really pretty and smart. Uncle Rob kept staring at her when she wasn't looking. I think he really likes her."

Libby laughed as she put the cookie dough on the baking sheet. "I do, too. They're good for each other."

"Do you think she's going to be his girlfriend?"

"It wouldn't surprise me one bit," said Libby wisely. "I think your uncle Rob has finally found the right path."

CHAPTER 20

Ashley

Two weeks later, Ashley was seated on a plane bound for New York City. She bit her nails, worried about leaving her kids for the weekend with Libby, again; confronting her father, again; and becoming an official single mother once the divorce was final in a few weeks.

Tara looked over at her. "Are you doing okay?"

"Splendid," said Ashley. "Once I finish with my nails, I was thinking of moving to my fingertips." Tara handed her a fashion magazine with the cover story "Ten Ways to Get Happy."

"I just read this. They suggested that people cut out caffeine and sugar from their diets." She pointed to her soda with a dramatic sigh. "Oh well."

"Doesn't that stuff make you have to go to the bathroom all the time?"

"My system's used to it," said Tara, taking another sip. Her hands could barely fit around the huge cup with the familiar red logo on the side.

"I need to find something special for Libby. She probably knows my children better than their own grandparents do."

Tara thought for a moment. "I remember her talking about this expensive French perfume that she likes. Something like that would be a nice thank-you gift. You know, I think she not only likes you, but also empathizes with your status as a young mother."

"I love it when you use those SAT vocabulary words in everyday conversation," said Ashley. "So, you've been apartment hunting with Rob?"

Tara raised one eyebrow at her, then pointed at a picture in a magazine. "I think that jacket would look good on you," she said. "Wait a minute," she cried, pointing to the advertisement on the next page. "Isn't that your mother?"

Ashley peered at the woman in the khaki pants. "It's her! On her last visit, she told me that she was modeling for some store like Liberty Jeans or something."

"And you forgot about that?" said Tara, sitting forward in her seat to peer at the famous Marrie. "She's stunning," she said. "I can see why Daddy fell for her."

"That's very mature of you," said Ashley. "I'm not there yet."

"Neither am I, really. But it doesn't do me any good to dislike her. This is so weird."

"I agree. I'm so nervous about this weekend; I may have to start chewing my toenails."

"That would be quite the acrobatic move," Tara said.

On the cab ride into the city, Ashley was grateful for Tara's calm presence. Tara had an old friend who lived in a one-bedroom apartment on the Upper East Side. She was away on business, so she had offered them the use of her place for the weekend. Ashley had insisted on taking the pull-out sofa, grateful that she didn't have to pay the price of a hotel. With Tara in the lead, they dropped their bags at the apartment and headed straight out.

As they walked along Madison Avenue, a tall man dressed in a feathered headdress passed by. The sights and sounds of the city were a refreshing change, Ashley thought. She suddenly smiled, wondering what people would do if that gentleman walked down the main street in Belloix. Traffic would probably come to a halt.

"Look at that woman over there," said Tara, pointing to a blond woman in a chic tailored suit. "Her heels must be about five inches high. It's pretty amazing that she can even walk, let alone do it gracefully. She looks so glamorous. People-watching is one of the things that I miss most about living in a major city," said Tara, turning around to face her. "That and the food. Speaking of lunch, there's a great little sandwich shop not far from here where we can get a quick bite to eat."

"I'm so nervous about tonight that I'm not sure I'm going to be able to eat much of anything." Ashley didn't want to mention the fact that her feet were starting to ache thanks to her new stylish flats; she knew better than to complain. Tara would simply tell her that she looked great and not to confuse practicality with fashion. Ashley thought she might need to pop a few aspirin if she was going to wear heels again tonight. Trying not to long for her jeans and sneakers, Ashley reminded herself that her new look was worth a little pain.

"Remember, I'll do all the talking. You simply have to show up. I just want to fluster him a bit. He deserves it."

They made their way to the sandwich shop. It was crammed with people. Tara pushed through the crowd, spotting a tiny round table in the corner. "Let's grab it!" she said.

Ashley saw a frazzled-looking woman with young children at the table next to her. One kid spilled his drink and the other little girl was whining to get out of her seat. Feeling the need to do something, she stopped to help mop up the mess.

"Thanks," said the mother.

"I have four of them at home," said Ashley. "Believe me, I understand. Here you go, sweetie," she said, handing the girl a crayon. Ashley immediately thought of Sally; she couldn't believe how much she missed her little troublemaker even though it had been only a few hours.

The woman seemed to appreciate her effort, and they chatted for several minutes. When Ashley looked up to find Tara, she could tell by her expression that she was annoyed. Ashley immediately excused herself and made her way to the table. "Sorry," she mumbled. "I just couldn't help myself."

"Why don't you try being a little selfish for once?" said Tara, ordering up sparkling water and chicken salad.

Ashley had the same. While they waited for lunch, they mapped out their plans for the afternoon, which included shopping at several high-end stores. Ashley knew better than to protest.

"What are you wearing tonight?"

"You're not going to believe this, but Anna St. Clair gave me a beautiful black dress as a going-away present. I'm still shocked that the lady at the dry cleaner was able to alter it in the hips to fit me."

"I can't wait to see it. I'm sure you'll look fabulous. Has anyone ever told you that you have the most amazing bone structure?"

"No," replied Ashley. "I've just thought of myself as having really big bones—kind of like a brontosaurus." Ashley laughed, taking a sip of water.

"Stop trying to be funny."

"Okay, I'll be serious for a moment. Libby caught me wolfing down ice cream bars and didn't judge me like Steve did, or even look at me in disgust. She just gave me a hug. You have no idea how much that meant to me. I'll always appreciate how she handled that moment." Ashley was ashamed of her binges. She knew Steve had been repulsed by her eating, which had only made her feel worse about herself. Unconsciously touching her stomach, she was grateful that she could now confide in Tara. "Now enough about me, let's move on to lighter topics. So, have you kissed Rob yet?"

"I can't believe you just asked me that!" Tara recalled the feel of Rob's lips on hers; it made her smile with pleasure.

"You didn't answer my question."

"Yes, I have," said Tara looking down at her salad.

"And?" said Ashley, leaning forward.

"He's pretty hot! I'm not saying another word about my personal life."

Ashley grinned in triumph. "I knew it!" she said. "How hot?"

Tara threw her napkin at her; it landed on top of Ashley's plate, nearly knocking over her water glass.

Ashley felt as if the afternoon had passed by in a matter of seconds. They hit several shops on Madison and Fifth Avenue. Tara seemed to be a walking dictionary of designer clothing and how to find the perfect knockoff.

Tara looked at her watch. "I made a dinner reservation for seven thirty at Del Posto downtown. We need to be on time. I told Roberta to tell Daddy Dearest that our dinner reservation was for eight. What about Marrie?"

"She'll be there. She can't wait. A chic restaurant where she can be seen is perfect."

"I meant, what did you say to her about my mother and me?"

"Oh," gulped Ashley. "I said that you and I had become close friends and it was important for her to get to know you. As for her rival, she's actually always wanted to meet Candice."

"What?"

"Curiosity, I suppose. Maybe she just wants to check out the competition."

"Rather progressive, don't you think?"

"I've told you that she's very liberal. Marrie doesn't think like you and me. She'll probably have a great time even if Dad arrives. She only gets upset if there's a problem in the fashion industry. Other than that, life is good."

"I always thought you were kidding when you talked about her hair and makeup obsession," said Tara.

Ashley raised one eyebrow. "I wish it weren't true. But, unfortunately, she's the exact opposite of Candice."

"This is going to be quite an evening," said Tara. "Now, what's up with your shopping? You've only bought two outfits and a jacket. That's not enough."

Ashley eyed Tara's load of shopping bags. "Are you sure you're a doctoral candidate?"

"I like to buy in bulk. You can't find any of this cool stuff in Belloix. I should really live here."

Me, too, thought Ashley with a dreamlike sigh. She hadn't had this much fun in so long. As much as she loved her kids, time off was a good thing. Unfortunately, her joy was about to come crashing down: it was almost time to face her father. She had a nasty feeling in the pit of her stomach.

It didn't take her long to get ready. The expensive dress felt really good, thought Ashley, looking at herself in the mirror. It reminded her of when she did live in New York, and she and Steve were young and in love. She removed a pair of diamond earrings from her makeup bag, staring at them for a moment. Steve had given them to her for Christmas one year. *How did things go so wrong?* she wondered.

Tara walked into the room, looking simply elegant in white wide-leg pants and a fitted black silk top.

"You look fantastic!" said Ashley.

"Thanks," said Tara. "So do you. What's that in your hand?"

"Some diamond earrings Steve gave me."

"They're too small," announced Tara. "You can wear a pair of mine. Save those for Sally."

Ashley put the earrings away, waiting for Tara to return. When she did, she realized that the ones in her hand were enormous. "Where did you get those?"

"An old boyfriend," remarked Tara. "They have absolutely no sentimental value whatsoever."

"Great," said Ashley, putting the large diamond and gold hoops in her ears. "Thank whatever-his-name-was for the loan."

Ashley jumped as the buzzer rang. "Who's that?"

"I ordered a car service to pick us up. I thought it would make things easier tonight."

Ashley gulped, trying to settle her stomach. They took the tiny elevator downstairs and headed down to the lobby to find their car waiting. It was a black four-door sedan that looked brand-new; the driver greeted them and held open the door as they slid into the plush interior. Ashley felt incredibly indulged; the last time a professional driver had taken her anywhere was her senior prom.

It seemed to take forever to get to the fancy restaurant downtown. Ashley tried to think of something witty to say to break the tension, but no remarks came to mind. Instead, she quietly bit down one of her freshly polished nails. She studied Tara's profile. There was a determined set to her chin. Her fingers were clenched around her black satin evening bag.

"It's right over there," announced Tara cheerfully. "I told Mother I'd meet her at the bar area. I've been here before, so I think I know where we're going."

Ashley's curiosity about Tara's mother was aroused. She was contemplating meeting the brainy, intellectual woman who sounded like the antithesis of her own mother.

"There she is," said Tara, pointing to an immaculately groomed woman in black silk pants and ruffled pink blouse. Her salon-styled hair was pulled up in a chignon. A large pearl choker emphasized her slender neck.

Candice seemed extremely elegant and self-confident as she walked up to embrace Tara and greet her. Ashley was shocked. She had pictured some frumpy, overweight lady with big glasses and no personality. That the woman was so attractive made her father's dual relationship dilemma completely baffling.

After all, she thought, Steve claimed he had cheated on her because he'd found her body unappealing. Certainly, Candice appeared every bit as glamorous as Marrie and completely comfortable in his world. Perhaps her father simply found it thrilling to lead a double life; after all, he loved adventure in his professional life. His need must have seeped into his personal relationships as well.

"Tara, darling," she said. "I'm so glad you made it. You must be Ashley. Tara's told me so much about you. I can't wait to hear about your day."

"It's been fantastic," said Ashley, observing her brown eyes. "Tara's been wonderful in helping me become reacquainted with the city. It's been a long time since I've visited here."

"How lovely," Candice said.

"Hey, look over there," said Tara. "That's Paige Henry. I love her work. She recently did a documentary on Rupert Madden, this gifted pianist who can only play with his left hand. It was brilliant." Tara turned around again, pointing out another celebrity who was arriving. Suddenly, she nudged Ashley.

"Where's Marrie?" she whispered.

"She'll be here. She's always fashionably late."

They ordered three glasses of white wine from the bartender and sat down at a nearby table to have a drink before dinner.

"So what did you girls do today? Don't tell me, you checked out the latest exhibit at the Whitney?" Candice leaned forward in her chair, giving them her full attention.

"Well, we'll save the intellectual pursuits for next visit. Since Ashley hasn't been here in a while, we decided to help the New York economy a bit."

"I'd forgotten what really beautiful storefront windows looked like, or fashionable clothes for that matter. Tara's helping me find my way back from looking like a fashion emergency." Ashley looked up and watched the very glamorous Marrie enter the restaurant. She noticed the subtle stares sent her mother's way. "Speaking of fashion, my mother has just arrived."

Ashley saw the look of surprise on Tara's face. As usual, her mother looked like she'd just stepped off the runway. Marrie was wearing a gold sparkle halter top and a pencil skirt. Five-inch black patent stilettos finished off the look.

Candice broke the silence that had descended over the table. "Isn't that Marrie?"

"You *know* her?" asked Tara, incredulous that Candice had recognized her rival.

"I've always been a big fan of hers."

You won't be after this evening, Ashley thought.

She managed to blurt out, "Really? Why?" Realizing what she had just said, Ashley quickly amended her remark. "I mean, I can see why she's inspired millions of women."

"She was kind of an icon for women of my generation. Everybody wanted to look like Marrie—except me, of course. Too much trouble. I'm happy with who I am."

Ashley couldn't believe what she had just heard. It was the first time in her life a woman didn't envy her mother's looks. *Now that's self-confidence,* she thought. *No wonder Tara has such a good head on her shoulders.*

"Hello, everyone. Sorry I'm late," Marrie said breezily as she kissed Ashley on both cheeks. "I've just been in London and I do so love the way they greet people over there. It's so civilized."

When Ashley watched her mother kiss both cheeks of Candice and Tara, she thought she might be physically ill. The kisses combined with that hint of a fake English accent were enough to make her lose her appetite.

"What are you girls drinking?" she asked, peering at their glasses. Ashley watched as her mother lured the bartender over to the table so that he would recite every possible white wine option. This swarthy Italian kid flirted with her mother as if she were actually his age. Needless to say, Marrie basked in the attention. Ashley would have liked to tell the group that Marrie was going to take two sips of whatever she ordered anyway, so this ritual seemed a rather waste of time.

"Marrie," said Candice. "I'm so delighted to meet you. I'll never forget that ad campaign you did in the early seventies that brought the world's attention to the war in Vietnam."

Ashley was so shocked that she was rendered speechless for a moment. She turned to face her mother. "You did what?"

Marrie smiled brightly and winked at Ashley. "Oh, you're so lovely to remember that about me."

Ashley was certain that her mother hadn't paid a bit of attention to the political ramifications of an ad campaign she'd done. At least she was smart enough not to take credit.

The waiter came to announce that their table was ready. Ashley looked at Tara as they got up to move to a table in the right-hand corner of the restaurant. As their mothers chatted amiably, Ashley said, "He'll be here in fifteen minutes, and then what?"

"The curtain opens on our family drama. Seriously, I just want to see his face when he walks in and finds us all together."

"I need another drink," said Ashley dryly.

"I think things are going really well," Tara added with a wicked gleam in her eye. "I'm going to sit right where he can see me."

"Why am I the only one who thinks this is a really bad idea?" said Ashley.

"He deserves it," said Tara as she swept over to sit

between Candice and Marrie. "This is perfect," she added, as she allowed the waiter to pull her chair in for her.

Ashley ordered another glass of wine. She listened as her mother talked about her work. "But I really do hate working with live animals. That was the thing for a while, you know. They'd always want to put lions in the background of a shoot. I never knew what was going to happen next. I remember the time these two monkeys got loose and landed in an extra's wig."

"I'll take monkeys over a group of filibustering Washington politicians any day," Candice quipped.

While the group was immersed in conversation, Ashley looked up and saw Kent West enter the restaurant. She had to admit, he was a dashing figure in his navy suit and silk tie. She saw the look of surprise cross his face when he spotted them.

"There's Daddy," said Tara gamely. "I'll run and say hello. I haven't seen him in ages."

"Um, I've got to run to the restroom," said Ashley, quickly getting up from her seat and following Tara.

Kent West glared at Tara. "Just what the hell do you think you're doing?" he said, his nostrils flaring.

"I think Mother should know about all of my friends," insisted Tara. "It's not right for her to be made the fool."

"You're the one who's being foolish," he snapped.

339

"You have no right to interfere. I should disinherit you for pulling a stunt like this."

"Mom deserves to know the truth."

"I've never interfered in your personal affairs," he said.

"Personal affairs! You were never even involved in our lives, Daddy. The only time I could count on seeing you was the news. Other than that, you were off to Africa or Asia or wherever. We were pen pals. Isn't that ridiculous? Mom deserved better and so did we."

"And your grandchildren only know you from the television. By the way, I think they're getting along beautifully."

Kent looked over at the table. His nostrils flared. He spat out, "This was a very stupid thing to do. I'm not going to let anyone get hurt."

"You're a little late to worry about that. Tell her the truth," demanded Tara.

Kent West looked flushed and uncomfortable. "You know what, ladies, I just realized that I've got to meet my producer back at the station. Breaking news . . . Sorry to miss dinner," he said formally.

"You've missed out on our lives, Daddy," said Tara angrily.

"When are you going to get it through your thick head that I *belong* to millions of viewers in thirty-six countries?" he shot back. "Now, be a good girl and tell your mother that duty calls."

When the door had closed behind him, as if on

cue, a man in a tan jacket came up to them and said, "Wasn't that Kent West? I can't believe he was just here. He's the greatest. I wish I'd gotten his autograph."

Ashley didn't know whether to laugh or cry. "You didn't miss a thing," she replied.

The man eyed her strangely and walked away.

"Hungry?" Ashley asked Tara.

"Sure," said Tara. "I'm surprised Daddy's head fit through that door," she said.

They returned to the table and Candice said, "Wasn't that your father? What happened?"

"You know Daddy. There's an international crisis somewhere. He got some call and had to rush out to the station."

"That's strange," she said. "Why didn't he come over and at least say hello?" She seemed to ponder things for a minute. "Ah well, I'm sorry, I was looking forward to having him join us," she said, picking up the menu.

"I got angry at him for leaving, again," Tara said firmly as the waiter came to take their order.

"Something always comes up," Ashley said, looking over at Tara.

"His work is very important, dear," Marrie said quickly.

Candice looked confused. She turned to Marrie. "How do *you* know about Kent's work?"

Ashley's heart started pounding at the silence that had descended over the table.

"I'm one of his biggest fans. Seeing him on television every night makes me feel like I know him," Marrie lied smoothly.

Candice seemed satisfied with her response. "I'll have the chicken. It's just divine. You should try it."

Ashley watched Candice carefully. Though she didn't let on that she suspected anything, Ashley knew she wasn't stupid. "That sounds wonderful," she said. "I think I'll have the same."

Their dinner ended with a round of chocolate mousse. Ashley noticed that her mother did her fake eating thing by dabbing her spoon into the dish and swirling the mousse around so it looked like she had actually enjoyed a few bites. Looking over, she saw Candice taking a sip of her coffee, completely engaged in a conversation with Tara. Marrie was the first to look at her watch and announce that she needed to get her beauty rest. She did the same European kissing thing on both cheeks as she departed. Ashley politely decided to walk her to the front door of the restaurant so she could have the manager get her a cab.

"What a lovely evening," Marrie said. "I'm off to Milan tomorrow for another shoot. I think your father is going to meet me there."

Ashley wanted to say so many things about honesty, greed, or just plain shallowness, but it wasn't going to make a difference. "How lovely for you," she replied politely.

"Oh," said Marrie. "I've been meaning to tell you all night. You look absolutely amazing in that dress. Keep it up, darling. Oh, my cab's here. Gotta go." She leaned in to kiss Ashley on both cheeks. "I mean it, that dress is just fabulous on you."

"Thanks, Mom," she said.

Seated on the return flight home, Ashley could barely keep her eyes open. The past forty-eight hours had been a whirlwind of emotion.

"I'm so tired I could sleep for a week," said Ashley, stifling a yawn.

"Me, too. It's been a productive weekend," said Tara. "I have to admit, I really love what I bought. And the look on Daddy's face when he saw us was priceless. I do think we caught him off guard. I thought he'd have at least had the nerve to come to the table, but I guess not."

"What do you think he'll tell her?"

"I'm sure he'll concoct some series of half truths; he's an expert at that."

"I think she knows more than she lets on," said Ashley. "I watched her throughout dinner. She's a pretty smart, self-confident lady. You're lucky."

"My mom's great," said Tara. "You really think she suspects something?"

"I definitely do, but she's not the type to discuss her feelings with anyone, including you."

"I guess you're right." Tara fell silent for a moment. "Imagine if our story was leaked to the press. I can see it now. The venerable Kent West and his family. I'm sure he'd get really high ratings. His male viewer approval ratings would probably skyrocket. I can imagine the talk shows now: 'The Resilient Kent West—From the Front Lines to Family Drama . . .'" Tara pretended to give a drumroll. "What a story, and he'd be right in the center of it. He'd probably thrive on all the attention."

"I'd say our trip was a success in the shopping department," said Ashley, shaking her hand. "As for righting the wrongs of our parents, I'm not sure it's up to us anyway."

"At least we *tried* to do something rather than pretend it didn't happen. I can live with that," said Tara. "He's not going to change, but it was good to see him caught off guard."

"What am I going to do with all these clothes?" exclaimed Ashley.

"Enjoy them," said Tara. "I must say, your mother steered us to all the coolest places. You might as well take advantage of it."

"You're right. Everyone has their strengths. I guess she's the one to call if I'm having a bad hair day. She certainly couldn't handle anything more complicated than that."

Tara laughed. "Don't worry, you can call me with the bigger problems."

"I plan on it; it's nice to finally have a family member I can count on."

Ashley pushed open the back door of her house. It was so quiet. She looked around the kitchen to find everything neat and clean. "Looks like Libby's straightened things up a bit!" she called. "Can I get you a soda or something?"

"Sure. Where are the kids?" said Tara, wielding several shopping bags.

"Tucker! Cameron! Hey, guys, I'm home." Ashley thought she heard some muffled sounds coming from another room. Putting down her overnight case, she walked into the family room to see if the kids were hiding. What she saw made her stop cold. The room was a different color; it had been painted celery green. There were slipcovers on all of the furniture. The shelves had all been rearranged.

She felt disoriented. She made her way to the living room. It was painted a soothing chocolate brown. All of the children's toys had been removed and the furniture was arranged neatly. The dark curtains were gone, revealing attractive window frames that had been painted a crisp white. Ashley walked in a circle confused by the change.

"Surprise!" a chorus of voices shouted.

Ashley couldn't believe it. Margy was standing there in overalls with her husband and daughter Erin beside her. Tina, Catherine, Annie, Megan, and Rob Marshall were also holding paintbrushes.

"Oh, my God," said Ashley. "What have you done? Where are the kids?" Ashley was so shocked that she needed to sit down. Someone handed her a glass of water. "Look at my house. Actually, it doesn't even look like my house! Am I dreaming?"

"It was Tara's idea," said Tina.

"Mine, too," cried Megan.

"Actually, we all wanted to help," said Catherine. "You deserve a fresh new start!"

"Where are the kids?"

"At Libby's house having dinner. All of them helped. We were up late last night."

Ashley couldn't believe her eyes. There were curtains on the dining room windows, accessories everywhere, and everything had a place. "This is just amazing. No one has ever done anything this nice for me in my entire life!" said Ashley, starting to cry. Each member of the group came over to embrace her.

"We need to get a picture!" said Tara, getting out her camera and handing it to Margy's daughter.

"I don't know what to say," announced Ashley.

"Just smile," said Tara. "We could call this page *Ashley Gets Her Style Back*."

"I like that," she said with a huge smile. "This is just the beginning!"

Center Point Publishing
600 Brooks Road ● PO Box 1
Thorndike ME 04986-0001 USA

(207) 568-3717

**US & Canada:
1 800 929-9108**
www.centerpointlargeprint.com